P9-DEB-376

CITY OF PEARL

Recent titles by Alys Clare from Severn House

A World's End Bureau mystery

THE WOMAN WHO SPOKE TO SPIRITS

The Gabriel Taverner series

A RUSTLE OF SILK
THE ANGEL IN THE GLASS

The Aelf Fen series

OUT OF THE DAWN LIGHT
MIST OVER THE WATER
MUSIC OF THE DISTANT STARS
THE WAY BETWEEN THE WORLDS
LAND OF THE SILVER DRAGON
BLOOD OF THE SOUTH
THE NIGHT WANDERER
THE RUFUS SPY
CITY OF PEARL

The Hawkenlye series

THE PATHS OF THE AIR
THE JOYS OF MY LIFE
THE ROSE OF THE WORLD
THE SONG OF THE NIGHTINGALE
THE WINTER KING
A SHADOWED EVIL
THE DEVIL'S CUP

CITY OF PEARL

Alys Clare

This first world edition published 2019
in Great Britain and the USA by
SEVERN HOUSE PUBLISHERS LTD of
Eardley House, 4 Uxbridge Street, London W8 7SY.
Trade paperback edition first published
in Great Britain and the USA 2020 by
SEVERN HOUSE PUBLISHERS LTD.

British Library Cataloguing in Publication Data
A CIP catalogue record for this title is available from the British Library.

ISBN-13: 978-0-7278-8898-3 (cased)
ISBN-13: 978-1-78029-635-7 (trade paper)
ISBN-13: 978-1-4483-0334-2 (e-book)

All Severn House titles are printed on acid-free paper.

Severn House Publishers support the Forest Stewardship Council™ [FSC™],
the leading international forest certification organisation.
All our titles that are printed on FSC certified paper carry the FSC logo.

Typeset by Palimpsest Book Production Ltd.,
Falkirk, Stirlingshire, Scotland.
Printed and bound in Great Britain by
TJ International, Padstow, Cornwall.

For my mother,
who loved to travel and who lived
life with courage and elegance;
with love, always.

ONE

When Gurdyman said he had an idea for a new venture he and I might undertake together, I'd imagined some task or experiment – exciting, undoubtedly, and very likely dangerous – on which the two of us would embark down in the crypt beneath his twisty-turny house. I was his pupil, and he was teaching me the ways of the mystic world beyond the veil. Some call it magic, and refer to my teacher as a wizard, although Gurdyman uses neither term. On the rare occasions when I ask him wide-eyed exactly what we *are* doing, he says that we are *exploring possibilities*.

When I push him, he adds reprovingly that there's nothing special about it, and that we are simply following certain paths somewhat further into the mist than is the norm.

So, when I reminded him one morning as the late October days began to shorten that he had mentioned the two of us embarking on a new task, and suggested that the moment might have arrived for him to tell me what it was, I had in mind that he might begin to instruct me in the properties and the use of some volatile and alarmingly unpredictable substance, or describe to me in the secret darkness of the crypt some method for the stretching of consciousness.

In no way whatsoever was I prepared for what he actually said.

He didn't answer immediately. He was pouring a purple-coloured liquid that steamed slightly from a small glass vessel to a larger one, and it was taking all his concentration.

I waited.

The last drop landed with a tiny *plop* and Gurdyman put down the little bottle with a smile of satisfaction. Then, turning to me, he said, 'We're going to Spain.'

I thought he was joking.

In the weeks since my life changed, he'd often tried to cheer me up with a little trick or a joke, and I always pretended to smile or even laugh. I was rotten company, I knew, and I didn't blame him for wanting to lighten the mood. So now I grinned weakly and said, 'Oh, good. When shall we leave?'

He said promptly, 'With all speed, as soon as possible. The weather will be cold and still for the next week or so. The sea crossing is long, child, and the journey has hardships enough without adding seasickness.'

'But—'

'You will need warm clothes, a change of linen and a blanket or two,' he went on. Briefly his bright blue eyes met mine. 'And the shining stone,' he added softly. 'You must not leave that behind.'

And I realized he wasn't joking at all.

I became caught up in the urgency. Which was odd, really, because Gurdyman wasn't in fact displaying any urgency; it must have stemmed solely from me.

'You will wish to inform your kin back in your village,' Gurdyman said that evening, 'for, although they are used to your absence since you spend so much of your time here in Cambridge with me, you have led them to expect occasional visits, and these will not be forthcoming for some time.' When I didn't immediately reply, he frowned and went on, 'Lassair, you *must* tell them. Not to do so would undoubtedly lead to great anxiety, for your parents and siblings love you dearly.'

'Of course I'll go and explain!' I said hurriedly. I'd had to drag my mind back to the present, for I was reeling from what he'd just said and wondering desperately just how long he meant by *some time*. 'I'll set out at first light tomorrow.'

As I rode out of Cambridge and set off north-eastwards for Aelf Fen, it seemed to me that for the first time in days I had nothing to occupy my mind.

And so, inevitably, my thoughts returned to what had happened earlier in October.[1]

In short, I had lost the two men I loved.

[1] See *The Rufus Spy*.

One of them was called Rollo Guiscard, and he died in my arms. He and I had been lovers, briefly, some time ago. He had absented himself for months that turned into years, and I hadn't heard a word. He returned, in fear for his life and desperate for my help, and I had gladly given it. He'd been right to be afraid.

I gave him a wonderful funeral pyre; a fire so fierce and all-consuming that, if ever I gathered my courage to return to the place, I didn't think there would be the smallest remnant of him or his possessions to remember him by.

But he *had* left a legacy for me: by one means or another, it seemed he'd bequeathed to me a large proportion of his wealth. In addition, in preparation for what was to be our last journey together, he had purchased a horse for me. She was a bay mare with a large star on her brow, and her name was Starlight. After the terrible events that led to Rollo's death, she and Rollo's gelding had fled before the fire, and I'd thought them lost. But they had found their way back to the stables in Cambridge from which they had been purchased, and in time news of their presence had come to me. Having no need of two horses – and barely need of one, or so I'd thought – I sold Bruno, Rollo's gelding, and used the proceeds to pay for my mare's stabling and care.

I'd found her presence in my life to be a great comfort.

It was foolish, perhaps, to tell myself that something of Rollo remained with her; that she shared my memories of him on our last venture; that she too grieved for him. I didn't care if it was. Just then I was in need of every scrap of consolation I could find.

The other big advantage of having a horse was that, on days like today when I had a journey ahead of me that once I'd have had to make on foot, I rode. In style, too, for Starlight was a stately and beautiful horse.

Rollo was the first of my two loves to be lost to me.

The second was Jack Chevestrier. After Rollo's death I'd gone to his house and sought him out, expecting, I think (although in truth I wasn't really capable of reasoning just then), that we would resume the fragile, tentative relationship which had only recently begun.

But Jack turned me away.

He did it with chilly politeness and utter finality.

'You're grieving, and you need somebody to comfort you, to look after you,' he said. 'I'm afraid that somebody won't be me.'

Then – and I could still hear the words falling like stones inside my head – 'I'm going out now. When I get back, I'd like you not to be here.'

So I had gone back to Gurdyman.

Who told me, as he gave me the comfort that Jack had quite rightly detected I so desperately needed, that he had something in mind for us to do . . .

'Stop thinking about that day,' I said aloud, angry with myself for allowing the trip back into the recent past and the ensuing flood of self-pity that always rushed up when I did.

I was going home to my village, albeit only for a short visit, and I forced my thoughts ahead to that.

I left Starlight in the small enclosure behind my parents' house. I took off her saddle and bridle and put them under cover in the place where my mother keeps the hens' food, then rubbed down my mare with handfuls of straw and made sure there was water in the trough. I'd brought feed for her, which I put in a pail. She looked at it and then at me, her large dark eyes seeming to say, 'I'm to stay here? With *chickens*?'

I went and stood close to her, my arms round her neck, and she nuzzled against me. 'I know it's not what you're used to, but then you've been spoiled, haven't you?' I reached up and fondled her ears. 'You must learn not to be so fussy,' I added sternly, 'and anyway it'll only be for one night at most.'

I left her, hurrying round to the front of the house and the door to the living quarters. My mother stood on the threshold. 'You came on a *horse*,' she said. There was a faint note of accusation in her voice, and I wondered if she thought I'd stolen my mare. Either that, I reflected ruefully, or she was admonishing me for growing too grand.

'Yes, Mother, she's my horse, her name's Starlight, and

today I made the journey from Cambridge more swiftly and comfortably than ever before,' I said briskly. 'Nevertheless I'm ready for something to eat and a warm fire.'

She was still eyeing me. But now, smiling, she stood aside and said, 'You'd better come in, then.'

I sat down in my usual spot beside the hearth, and she built up the fire and set a pan of stew to heat, tearing off a chunk of bread from a large loaf. The stew, I guessed, had been the midday meal. The room, as always, was neat and tidy, everything clean and in its place, bedding rolled up and stowed away in corners, lamps set ready for nightfall.

'Your father will be back presently,' my mother said. I'd been looking at the place where he always sat, and she must have noticed. 'He's leaving the lads to work on their own for the last part of the day, to encourage them to be more responsible.'

My father is an eel-catcher, and a very experienced and skilful one. He is teaching my younger brothers Squeak and Leir to follow in his footsteps. It was good to know that they were now taking on more of the load. It was a hard life, and my father deserved a little respite.

'Good,' I said through a mouthful of stew and bread.

'So how's life in the big city?'

'It's all right.' There was no point in telling her about the forthcoming trip as I'd only have to repeat it all when my father arrived, so I devoted myself to the food.

Presently the door opened and my father came in. I leapt up and he opened his arms to envelop me in a hug.

He alone of my family knew what had happened to me. Knew about Rollo dying, knew about Jack. Knew *all* about Jack, for in my grief and my despair I had blurted out rather more than I should have, and told my father that Jack and I had very briefly been lovers, and that I'd conceived his child and then very soon lost it.

Far from reproving me, my father had simply held me very close, called me his dearest child and said, *I am so very sorry for all your pain.*

Now, as I stood once again in his arms, I remembered every moment of that scene, which wasn't surprising as it had happened so very recently. I was quite sure he did, too.

After a moment, he broke away, giving my hand a small, private squeeze, and said in his normal voice, 'Nice to see you, Lassair. Is all well with you?'

'Yes thank you, Father. And with you?' I turned to my mother, including her in the question, and for some time we spoke of family matters; of the younger brothers, of my shy elder brother Haward, his wife Zarina and the two little ones.

Then, when a brief silence fell, I said, 'And what of Grandfather?'

My paternal grandfather had only recently been introduced to the family. I had met him some time ago,[2] and learned that he, and not my Grannie Cordeilla's husband, was my father's true father. His name was Thorfinn, he was a very large white-haired, white-bearded Icelander whose nickname was the Silver Dragon, and he had given me a powerful heirloom known as the shining stone. Ever since I had learned who he was, I'd been badgering him to tell my father. It simply wasn't fair, I'd shouted at him once, for me to know when my father didn't; to be forced to keep such a secret from someone I loved so much. In the end, and, again, very recently, Thorfinn had sought out my father and revealed the truth. The family, I suspected, were still reeling . . .

'I thought I might have found him here?' I added when neither of my parents spoke.

With a grimace in which there was a perfect mixture of amusement and frustration, my father said, 'If you wish to see him, as I'm sure you do, you will find him on his boat, which is moored on the inlet which he habitually uses.'

'Why not in the house with all of you?' I demanded.

My father gave a brief chuckle. 'I think your use of the words *all of you* provides the answer,' he said. 'It is a little crowded in our house, as you well know, and he professes to require long spells of solitude after spending any amount of time with us.'

'The family is quite extensive,' I said. 'It's rather a lot of new people for him to get used to.'

My mother gave a sort of harrumph. 'Quite a lot for the

[2] See *Land of the Silver Dragon.*

people to get used to too, suddenly being told that he's their true grandfather and they've got to welcome him to our hearth!'

My father reached out and took her hand, and his gesture seemed to comfort and calm her, as he always managed to do. He turned to her, and said softly, 'It's not been easy, I'll grant you that.' Still looking at her, he went on, 'Your mother's been magnificent, Lassair. Took the news in her stride and set about preparing a feast for him.'

Typical of my practical, down-to-earth mother, I thought. I wondered, as I often did, where we'd have been all my life without her.

'You had a feast?' They nodded in unison. 'With everyone here?' They nodded again. 'How did it go?'

My father chuckled. 'After one or two initial difficulties, such as your eldest sister refusing flatly to believe it and trying to order him out of the house, quite well, considering.'

'She did *what*?'

I have to admit that I don't really like my sister Goda. She is married to a man who seems to put up with her bullying, self-dramatizing personality, and in fairness she has learned to be a thrifty and efficient wife and mother. But she's not a loving person.

'She planted herself before Thorfinn, hands on her hips and a scowl on her face,' my mother said, grinning, 'and told him that her grandfather was her grandmother's husband and he'd been called Haward, same as her brother, and she didn't need another one, so he'd better be on his way and stop upsetting good folk with his lies and his false claims.'

'What did Thorfinn do?'

'Oh, he just stood there, holding his ground, smiling gently, and when she paused for breath he said, "My dear granddaughter, I appreciate your distress and I admire your spirit, but I fear you must open your eyes and look at what is before you." Then he pulled Father to his side, and what with the pair of them looking so alike, even Goda had to see he was telling the truth, so she lifted her chin, looked him straight in the eye and told him he should have announced himself years ago.'

She had his sort of courage, I reflected. She was, after all, his grandchild. 'How did he respond?'

My father laughed again. 'He said she was quite right, apologized and tried to put his arms round her, but she wouldn't let him.'

'She stayed for the feast, though,' my mother said with a touch of malice. 'Ate as much as the rest of her lot put together, just as she always does. It takes more than a long-lost grandfather popping up to put Goda off her food.'

'You must have been quite a crowd,' I remarked, trying not to sound wistful.

'Oh, we were, and then a day or so later some of the cousins turned up, word having spread, and we had to do it all again.' Her smile widened. 'The old man began to look quite furtive by the end of it, as if he was looking for somewhere to go and hide where he could get away from us all.'

I thought back to my grandfather's home in Iceland. There, too, his living space was shared with many other people – relatives, servants, general hangers-on – but it was a great deal more spacious than our small house, and, in addition, I seemed to recall that as the head of the household, he had reserved a sacrosanct corner just for himself.

No wonder he needed to spend time alone on his boat.

'Did you have some special reason for wanting to see him?' my mother now asked. I noticed that she was looking at me shrewdly, as if she had already half-guessed that I hadn't come merely for a social visit.

'Oh, no, I—' I began. But then I thought, why not tell them? It was rare to find the two of them at home during the day with nobody else present, and it seemed as if fate had generously provided me with this opportunity to tell them my news without half a dozen other people exclaiming, butting in and giving their opinion.

'Well, actually Gurdyman has asked me to go on a journey with him,' I said.

They were both looking at me expectantly, as if to say, *Yes? Go on then, tell us all about it!*

'You're his pupil,' my father said after a moment when I didn't speak. 'I suppose travelling to other places is all part of your instruction?' He turned it into a question, and I didn't really have an answer.

'I've gone to local places with him, of course,' I said eventually; my mother was beginning to look concerned at my hesitation, as if she had already made up her mind that I was trying to break some terrible tidings to them and didn't know how, which in fact wasn't far from the truth, and I knew I had to explain. 'But this is a little different, because we'll be travelling to Spain.'

Both of them repeated the last word, in very different ways: my father said it with excitement and even a tinge of envy; my mother with horror, as if I'd announced I was going to be dragged down to hell.

'Before you ask, I don't know *why* we're going, at least, not yet, because Gurdyman hasn't told me. But it's no cause for worry,' I hurried on, for my mother was still looking aghast, 'because Gurdyman lived there when he was younger, first in some village on the pilgrimage trail where his parents ran an inn, and later further south, where he was taught by very wise men who—' I stopped abruptly, for I didn't think it was the moment to mention the arcane skills that Gurdyman had learned in Muslim Spain – 'er, who taught him a lot about everything.'

My father's eyes upon mine told me that he knew perfectly well what I'd been about to say, and also that he wasn't going to tell my mother either.

'*Spain!*' my mother said again after a moment, this time in a hushed whisper. Then, nervously, 'I suppose he knows his way about, and how to look after himself?' *And you*, hung unsaid in the air.

'Yes, Mother,' I said confidently. 'He's been everywhere, and long journeys hold no fears for him.'

I hoped, even as I spoke, that my confidence was not misplaced.

I set out to see Thorfinn.

I found his boat just where I'd expected to, and, just as he always did, he had rigged up a cover over the narrow deck and made a camp on the bank, where a fire smouldered gently in a ring of stones. I called out as I hurried along the last stretch of the high bank towards his mooring, and he drew aside the heavy awning and climbed ashore. Just as my father had done, he took me in a wordless embrace.

When he let me go, he held me at arm's length and stared into my face. He frowned. 'Ah,' he breathed. Then, very kindly, 'You must give it time, child.'

He too had witnessed my grief.

'Can we go onto the boat?' I asked, trying to sound bright. 'There is something I must tell you.'

He nodded, holding aside the awning for me to step aboard. When he too was seated, I told him my news.

But, strangely, I had the impression that he already knew I was going away, and where I was going.

'It is a land full of marvels and magic,' he said distantly.

I was very surprised. 'You know it? You've been there?'

He smiled. 'I have been everywhere,' he murmured. Then he said in a more normal tone, 'Like many of my countrymen, I ventured inland up its great waterways, always exploring, always pushing on.' Abruptly he stopped.

But I could have continued for him, for I remembered what he had told me of his past: how, after the shining stone had come into his possession, he had believed himself invincible. Speaking of himself as he once was, he had said, *The gods observe those who are brash and overconfident, and, in time, remind them forcefully and painfully that they are but human.*

Thorfinn had drawn back from the gravest peril, saving both his crew and, eventually, himself, although the latter had been my grandmother Cordeilla's work. Perceiving that the shining stone would otherwise tear him asunder, he had left it in her keeping, and in time it had passed to me.

I felt a darkness in the close confines of the boat that was nothing to do with the absence of light. And I was beset with the strange thought that I was standing on the very fringe of something very important; something others knew of but that was outside my ken. So far . . .

I shuddered.

My grandfather noticed, or, more likely, he too sensed the strange, unsettling mood. He pushed back the awning, the low, golden sunlight poured in and he said brightly, 'You'll be wanting to get back to the village before sunset. I'll walk some of the way with you.'

One other strange thing happened before he left me on the path. We said our farewells with a hug, and then, stepping back, he said, just as Gurdyman did, 'When you set out, you must not leave the shining stone behind.'

'Why?' I whispered.

He was about to tell me something – I could see it in every inch of him – but he stopped himself. Instead he said, with a slight tone of reproof, 'Because it is a part of you now, child, as of course you know very well, and you will do better when it is with you.'

Before I went back to the village I went out to the island where some of the family ancestors lie buried. I waded across the narrow stretch of water, climbed onto the grassy shore and made my way to Granny Cordeilla's grave. I knelt down and spoke to her.

'I left something with you last time I came to see you,' I reminded her. 'It was given to me to take care of, and to hide away in a place where nobody would find it. He's gone now, the man who gave it to me, and so it's mine.'

For as Rollo lay dying in my arms he said, *I have gold. Some you already have, for you hid it for me.* He had also left a great deal more with a woman in Cambridge who was one of his local agents, and he had spoken of that too. He said I was to seek her out, and he told me where to find her. *Tell her who you are. Tell her I said you're to have it all.*

I remembered the woman's name: Eleanor de Lacey. And that she lived beside the river. I didn't think she would be hard to find, and I was sure there would be no difficulty over getting her to obey Rollo's last instruction. But I hadn't sought her out. I was afraid of doing so, for telling her what had happened to him, breaking the news of his death, was something I didn't believe I could face. Not yet. Apart from anything else, telling outsiders meant it became a generally-known fact and there would no longer be anywhere to hide from it.

I felt tears on my cheeks.

Then I thought I heard Granny Cordeilla's voice. *You're in pain, child, and it will be that way for a long time.*

'I know!' I sobbed. 'I don't know how to bear it!'

But you are *bearing it*, she replied.

I bent forward over the cold earth and the stone beneath which she lay, folded my arms and dropped my head onto them, and for some time I simply sobbed. After a while I felt a bit better.

I moved the stone aside and reached down into my grandmother's tomb for the large leather bag that Rollo had entrusted to me. I dragged it out, not without difficulty for it was weighty. I pulled at the drawstrings that held it closed until I had made a space big enough for my hand and reached down inside. I felt the hard round shapes of a huge hoard of coins and, closing my fist around a handful, drew them out.

The late sunlight caught answering flashes from the shiny metal. Many of the coins were of gold and looked new-minted, their images sharp and unworn. I had no idea of their value; I wondered, however, whether attempting to use them as currency for everyday transactions might arouse suspicion, since I knew I didn't look like a wealthy woman. There was also a large number of silver pennies, some of them clipped, some of them, like the gold coins, bright and new. I had no idea what was a reasonable sum to take upon a long journey to a far country. I was ignorant in such matters.

So I extracted a dozen gold coins and some fifty pennies, as well as some other coins of varying sizes that I was unable to identify, and put them into the linen bag I'd brought for the purpose. I was going to fashion a body belt to wear beneath my clothes, and keep only a small amount of cash in the purse that hung from my belt. I might be ignorant about money but I knew all about human greed, and it seemed folly to put temptation in the way of my future travelling companions and the many people I would be meeting along the way.

I closed the leather bag and replaced it in Granny Cordeilla's grave. I pushed the stone back into place, then bent to bestow a final kiss upon it.

'Goodbye for now,' I whispered. 'Wish me good luck.'

God's speed, child, she replied. *May the ancestors protect you.*

Then there was silence.

As I had expected, it was too late now to return to Cambridge that day, even mounted on a fine horse. As I made my way back to my parents' house, I made a small detour and tapped softly on my aunt Edild's door. She is a healer and had been my first teacher, and during the years I worked with her I lived beneath her roof. But now she was married to the man who had long been her lover, although barely a soul had known about it. I was very wary of Hrype. To begin with he had clearly been fond of me, and it had been he who introduced me to Gurdyman . . .

As I recalled that fact, I felt a brief resurgence of that strange sensation I'd felt on Thorfinn's boat. Just for a moment, I heard a fragment of sound: at first it was the drone of a thousand invisible insects in a summer woodland, but then I thought I heard human voices mingled in it and there was a sudden *plink*, as of metal striking stone, deep, echoing and resonant.

Then it was gone and I was back in the present.

Since I had been Gurdyman's pupil – I picked up on the thought – my relationship with Hrype had undergone a drastic change, and now I sensed hostility from him every time we met. Since this was more than enough reason to avoid him, I preferred to stay in my parents' busy little house whenever I spent the night in Aelf Fen.

As I stood waiting for Edild's response to my knock, I prayed that she would be alone.

She opened the door and the familiar smells of herbs and sweet incense surrounded me in a cloud, and warmth like an embrace poured out from the lively fire in the hearth. Her face lit up and she stepped forward to greet me with a hug. She was indeed alone, and I suppressed the unkind thought that Hrype's presence might have tempered her welcome.

'Come in,' she said, taking my hand and leading me inside. 'Are you staying? Hrype is away,' she added, and, again, I wondered if the invitation was issued only because he wasn't there.

Stop it, I ordered myself. She loves you, she probably misses you, and she's asked you to stay for no other reasons than those.

'I'd love to have done,' I said honestly, 'but my parents are expecting me back.' I hesitated. 'I didn't know you'd be alone.'

She met my eyes. I knew she understood. She nodded, turning away. 'Then at least come and sit by the fire a while, and let me make you a refreshing drink,' she said. I thought her voice sounded falsely bright, but it was probably just my imagination.

I studied her as she set about selecting herbs for my drink, which she sweetened with a big dollop of honey. She was humming as her busy hands worked, and a sweet expression softened her features. There was no need to ask if she was happy. She was probably only *un*happy, I thought, when her niece and her husband were both under her roof and she had to put up with – and try to diffuse – the antipathy between them.

'I came to tell you all that Gurdyman's taking me on a journey,' I said when we were both settled by the hearth. I told her the details, such as they were, again explaining that as yet he'd revealed very little about our purpose.

'You say he spent his young life there?' she asked.

'Yes.'

She nodded thoughtfully. Then she said, 'He grows old, Lassair.'

I was going to ask her how she knew that, since to the best of my knowledge she and Gurdyman hadn't met, but then I remembered that Gurdyman and Hrype had known each other a long time and saw each other regularly. No doubt Hrype talked to her about his old friend. 'Yes,' I agreed.

'Then perhaps this mission is no more than an elderly man's wish to revisit the places of his youth.'

'Perhaps.' I hesitated, for I very much wanted to share my thoughts – my apprehension, if I'm honest – with someone close to me. She was looking at me, with such concern in her eyes that I knew I could speak. 'Please don't tell anyone this, Edild, especially not Mother or Father, but I think there's more to it than that.' I paused, then plunged on. 'I think we're going to the place where he began to be what he now is.' I was watching her closely and her swift nod told me she understood. 'I think he wants me to—'

To learn from those who taught him, was what I'd been about to say, but I stopped myself. It sounded so arrogant, as if an outstanding practitioner such as Gurdyman was no longer sufficient for me.

She nodded again. Then she said calmly, 'Well, you are his pupil, Lassair. It is a part of his duty to ensure that you encounter others who are so much further advanced in the arts.' That put me in my place. 'It is, after all, what I did,' she added more gently. 'You were my pupil first, and then, when it began to appear that you had aptitude in areas in which I could not instruct you, another teacher was found.'

I reached out for her hand. 'I've never forgotten our days here together,' I said quietly.

She lifted our joined hands and put a soft kiss onto mine. 'Neither have I.'

I spent a happy evening with my family. Haward, Zarina and their children joined us for supper and the gathering became cheerful, full of laughter and deep affection.

And at last, my mind so full with the daily doings, the preoccupations, the worries and the joys of my family and my home village that there was barely any room for apprehension about the coming journey, I settled down in my usual corner, wrapped myself in my shawl and my mother's soft wool blanket and went to sleep.

TWO

I was back in Cambridge by noon on the following day. I delivered Starlight back to her stable, grateful all over again for the gift of her that had saved me a long walk on what had turned out to be a chilly morning. She nuzzled into my chest as I patted her and stroked her graceful neck up under her thick mane, muttering my thanks. 'I'm going away for a while,' I whispered to her – she flicked her ears at the sound of my voice – 'but I will come back.'

I'll swear she knew what I was saying and that her gentle exhalation of breath was her response. I thought of Rollo, giving her to me. He'd had the two horses with him, Starlight and his gelding. *I thought you'd like the mare*, he said, *as she's slightly smaller.* The words were not profound, not romantic or remotely loving: purely practical. But still the memory of them was undermining me.

Such is the nature of grief.

I had recovered myself by the time I was back at Gurdyman's house. I had just deposited my leather satchel up the ladder in my little attic room when I heard him in the corridor below.

'I need you to go out again straight away, Lassair,' he called out, 'so keep your shawl about you.'

I went down to him. 'Where am I to go?'

'To the quay, where you are to find us a craft that will transport us by the fenland waterways up to the coast – to Lynn, I think would be best – so that we may pick up a sea-going ship.' He held out a small purse. 'Here is some money, if you need to pay in advance to ensure our passage.'

'And' – I needed to make sure I understood – 'I'm to ask about that, too? The sea-going ship?'

'No,' he said firmly. 'I wouldn't mention that.'

'Why?'

He gave me a strange look, half admonishing, half furtive.

Guilty, even. 'Oh, no particular reason,' he said, smiling broadly and not entirely convincingly. 'Simply that it's probably best not to advertise the details of our comings and goings where there is no need for it.'

Then, before I could pursue the matter – for surely we were advertising our movements already by taking a boat up through the fens to the coast? – he muttered something about an experiment to watch and hurried away down the passage and back to his crypt.

And I knew he had just told me a lie, because he'd said only a couple of days ago that he was packing away all his equipment prior to our departure and improving on the moment by having a good sort out.

There *was* no experiment to watch.

I left the house and strode off through the maze of narrow passages, emerging onto the main road that runs south-east to north-west beside the centre of the town and that leads up to the Great Bridge. I turned off to the right just before the bridge, leaping down onto the quayside. Ahead of me, up on its artificial mound to the right of the road, was the castle, and I was very glad my errand hadn't sent me there. Jack lived in the deserted settlement beyond the castle where the workmen who built it had dwelled. Had he seen me nearby, he might have thought that I was lurking around in the hope of meeting him. That I was going to beg him again to let me go back to him.

I wasn't.

There were several river craft tied up along the quay and among them was one that I recognized. Her name was *The Maid of the Marsh*, and I had met her master when I'd tried to help a distressed noblewoman who had arrived in the town alone and troubled.[3] At least, so I had believed when I'd met her. *The Maid of the Marsh* was the vessel on which she had arrived; a long, narrow craft, not large, with oars down her sides and a mast amidships. There was a big open space on her foredeck for cargo, already filling up. Any passengers she carried had to make shift as best they could on the deck, with

[3] See *Blood of the South.*

no shelter other than what they could contrive for themselves.

As I approached, a short, sturdy man with a cheerful expression and a face creased with laughter lines called out. 'Looking for me?' he said.

'Yes, I believe I am,' I replied. 'May I come aboard?'

'Indeed you may.' He waved his arm in an expansive gesture towards the narrow plank that provided access to the boat. 'Watch your step, mind.'

I felt his eyes on me as I negotiated the plank and walked up the deck to where he perched, in the stern. 'I know you,' he said. 'You came to seek me out before, with that big lawman.'

I'd been with Jack but I was trying very hard to forget the fact. 'Yes. My name's Lassair.'

'Lassair!' he repeated. 'Yes, I remember. And I'm Alun.'

I grinned. 'I remember that, too.'

'What can I do for you?'

'I need passage up to Lynn, and soon, if possible. Could you take me?'

'Gladly. I'll be leaving tonight. That soon enough for you?'

'Yes,' I said. Gurdyman had said we needed to depart with all speed, so if tonight was too soon for him that was just too bad.

'Just yourself, is it?' There was a definite twinkle of interest in the master's eyes, and I recalled now that he was a bit of a flirt.

'No, there will be two of us,' I replied repressively.

'You and that big lawman?' I'd swear he winked at me.

'Me and an elderly man,' I said.

He muttered something that sounded like, 'Shame!' Then he said, 'We leave at sunset. Be here in good time, then you can settle in the most sheltered spot, which is there.' He pointed.

'Thank you. Do I pay you now?'

He eyed the purse I was holding out. 'No need,' he said. 'When you come aboard will do fine.'

I thanked him, made my careful way back across the plank and onto the quay and walked away.

So that was the first part of our journey arranged. *The Maid of the Marsh* would take us to Lynn, and after that some larger craft – a knarr? a cog? – would take us on the next stage. All the way to wherever we were bound, or would we have to change ships again? I recalled what little I knew about sea voyages, wishing it were more.

Why was Gurdyman being secretive? It alarmed me. But another aspect of his behaviour was providing greater cause for unease; I had noticed something about him, something I tried to tell myself was only in my imagination. But I didn't believe my own denials.

Gurdyman was afraid.

Back in the passage outside the twisty-turny house, Hrype watched as Lassair hurried off. Then he let himself in and went down to the crypt.

He knew without a doubt that he would find Gurdyman there.

'I imagine you've just dispatched her to find you a boat,' he said. He looked around, taking in the very tidy shelves, the absence of any ongoing experiments or note-making on the long workbench, the books and scrolls packed away neatly in their chest and the large leather bag standing open on the floor. There was a thick woollen blanket taking up quite a lot of space in its base, on top of which were some items of personal linen and a soft suede purse. Gurdyman was in the act of folding an undershirt, tucking a small muslin bag of dried lavender between the folds. 'I judge by all this activity that you really are going?'

'Yes,' Gurdyman confirmed without looking up from his task, 'and as soon as we can.' He glanced up. 'As you rightly surmise, Lassair has indeed gone to arrange our passage up to the coast.'

'You'll take the sea route all the way?'

'Oh, yes,' Gurdyman replied on a sigh, 'for we shall have to travel by road once we make landfall, and that will be quite sufficient. The longer walk is too much for me now. Also, we must travel by the fastest means.'

Hrype frowned thoughtfully. 'You will sail to Corunna? You told me, as I recall, that it was the preferred port.'

'You remember accurately. There are other ports closer but they are small and far less used, and we might find ourselves waiting too long for a ship to take us to them.'

Silence fell, interrupted only by the sound of Gurdyman's soft leather slippers on the stone floor as he moved about the crypt, collecting various small items and stowing them in the leather bag. After some time, Hrype said, 'You haven't told her, have you?'

'No.'

Hrype waited, but it seemed Gurdyman was not going to elaborate. 'Don't you think you should?'

'It is nothing but the vaguest of suspicions!' Gurdyman said tersely. 'There are any number of perfectly sound and reasonable explanations.'

'None of which you find the least convincing,' Hrype said.

Gurdyman put down the pair of small phials he was holding and turned to stare at him. 'You cannot know,' he said. His tone was cold.

'But I do,' Hrype countered. 'I know, old friend, because you are packing away your life's work and preparing to set off on a journey to a far country at entirely the wrong time of the year, during which all the usual perils of travel await you, not to mention the particular one you so clearly fear.'

'I don't—' Gurdyman began hotly.

'You do.' Hrype's firm voice overrode him. 'Even if you take the less strenuous sea route rather than going overland on foot, what you are undertaking is taxing for a man of your age.' He paused. 'And once you reach Corunna,' he added quietly, 'you will, as you just pointed out, have no choice but to walk, because the destinations for which you are bound lie inland; one of them by hundreds of miles.'

'Less than three hundred,' Gurdyman muttered.

'Will you not think again?' Hrype asked.

Gurdyman walked over to him, coming to a halt a pace or two away. 'I have no choice,' he said.

'But to take her with you is surely—'

'I have no choice over that, either,' Gurdyman interrupted. 'For one thing, I require her presence. As our experiences with

Mercure demonstrated,[4] a man such as he – as I – needs his anima.'

'But she—'

Once again Gurdyman didn't let him finish. 'For another thing, Lassair needs to get right away. She is not herself, Hrype. She has suffered two devastating losses, three if you consider the child that was miscarried. Her spirit is gravely diminished and her powers are at present negligible.'

'So why, then, do you insist on taking her if she will be no use to you?' Hrype demanded angrily.

'Because she will recover once she is away from here!' Gurdyman shouted. 'Don't you see? It is being in this town, upon which is centred all the drama and the tragedy of recent events in her life, that is the problem! She is in a fugue, and it is as if she views the world and its potential through a dark and suppressing veil, and can no longer see it for what it is.'

'And going on this journey with you, with all its inherent perils, will shock her out of this fugue?'

Gurdyman didn't answer for a moment. Then he said, with utter conviction, '*Yes.*'

Hrype bowed his head. 'So be it,' he murmured. 'I cannot after all stop you.' He looked up again. 'But I still think you should tell her about the dead vagrant.'

Gurdyman gave a groan of frustration. 'Tell her what, precisely? That while she was away on her mission with her Norman a beggar died in the alley outside and was found propped against the wall beside my door? Finding dead beggars in the back alleys is a common occurrence, Hrype, as we all well know.'

'But this one was different, wasn't he?' Hrype said silkily. 'This one disturbed and scared you, so that when I visited you later that same day, you had taken to your bed over there' – he indicated the mattress on its simple frame in the corner, its blankets folded at its foot, its pillows plumped and stacked – 'and you were deathly pale, struggling for breath, and complained that your heart was leaping and jumping.' He leaned closer. 'You asked me to prepare a potion of belladonna,

[4] See *The Night Wanderer.*

and even after you had taken it, still you felt weak and trembling.'

'I had been overworking,' Gurdyman said.

'You had been working no harder than you usually do,' Hrype replied. 'Admit it, Gurdyman: the instant you inspected that dead man and saw what he clutched in his hand, you were struck with dread.'

'He was a thief!' Gurdyman protested. 'He was probably a pickpocket, and had but recently robbed some rich townsman of the contents of his purse.'

'He wasn't much of a thief,' Hrype observed. 'He was searched, and he had but the one item on him,' he went on relentlessly. Gurdyman made no reply. 'One large, perfect pearl,' Hrype added softly. 'Held tight in the hand of a dead man, whose corpse was left outside the door of perhaps the one man in the town for whom such a jewel held significance.'

'Coincidence,' Gurdyman said.

'A jewel that you took from him and hid away, so you told me, as if you could not bear to look at it,' Hrype said very softly, as if Gurdyman hadn't spoken. 'And the dread is still here. It is present right now, in the crypt with the two of us like an extra presence, only this one is dark and filled with dangerous power.'

Gurdyman turned sharply to face him, but before Hrype had more than a glimpse of his expression he relaxed it into blandness.

Hrype went on looking at him, staring right into the bright blue eyes, and eventually Gurdyman looked away.

Hrype walked towards the steps leading up out of the crypt. 'You are a stubborn old man,' he said, 'and you will not listen to the voice of reason.'

'Reason, is it!' Gurdyman cried.

'It is. Moreover, you insist upon taking Lassair with you, and you tell me it is for her own good.'

'I would have thought you, of all people, would be pleased to see the back of her!' Gurdyman exclaimed. 'She is hardly your favourite person, Hrype.'

Hrype stopped dead. He said nothing for a few moments, as if pausing to judge his reaction. Then in a cold voice he said, 'You are right, and there have been times when I have resented her for over-confidence; for demonstrating far too clearly that she can do easily and without apparent effort what it took me years of endeavour to achieve. But if you think that means I'm glad to see her taken into peril by an old man who is putting his own need above hers, then you are mistaken.'

Then he ran lightly up the steps and off along the passage, and presently Gurdyman heard the bang of the street door as he slammed it behind him.

When I got back to the twisty-turny house, Gurdyman was putting the last few items in his capacious leather bag. I thought he looked a little pale; perhaps, now it came to the point, packing up his work and abandoning the crypt where he had lived and worked for so long was proving more stressful than he had anticipated.

If that was the case, then the sooner I broke the news about our imminent departure, the better. 'I've arranged passage up to Lynn for us on a boat called *The Maid of the Marsh*,' I said brightly, 'and we'll be setting out at sunset. Her master says we need to get there in good time so we can settle ourselves in a sheltered place.'

I wondered if he would protest; if he would say that this evening was far too soon and order me to go back and try again. But he merely nodded, smiled briefly and said, 'Then you had better go out to the market square and forage for some food for us. I suggest we partake of a substantial meal now, and that we pack up provisions to take with us, for I doubt that we shall be able to purchase more until we reach Lynn.' I turned to go. 'And after that,' he called after me, 'you must pack your satchel, remembering to include the most frequently required remedies. Yes, I know you always carry a few supplies with you,' he went on, before I could protest, 'but on this occasion I think you should take as much as you have available.' He indicated his own bag. 'I have space to spare, and can probably pack anything you cannot fit in.'

I nodded. Suppressing the disturbing thought that this

journey was all at once becoming far too real and immediate, I hurried on up the steps and went to do his bidding.

Gurdyman might have obeyed his own command and partaken of a hearty meal, but I had little appetite and only ate the small amount I did to please him. My mind had already turned to packing my satchel; to deciding which, among my meagre sum of personal possessions, I couldn't bear to leave behind. My shawl – a long-ago gift from my sister Elfritha before she went to Chatteris to be a nun – went everywhere with me, usually wrapped round me or bundled up on the top of my satchel. It is of fine wool, soft even from the time of its making at my sister's hands but now, after years of wear, even more so. It is in shades of green, which she knew were my favourites. I would also take the shining stone in the leather pouch I made for it when I became its guardian. Then there was the collection of small bottles and jars that I always carry, and that contain the most frequently required remedies. A collection of pieces of old linen, worn with age, laundered and neatly folded, for bandages. A pewter spoon that my little brother Leir found and solemnly presented to me. A horn comb made by my brother Haward. A clean cap and a change of underlinen. The thick, warm cloak that Jack had given me. *Don't think about Jack.*

And that was more or less all.

I glanced round my little attic and my eyes fell on the bed. Blanket! I really should not set off without a blanket, and a good, warm one at that. I folded the best one into a strip and then rolled it, tying the roll with several lengths of strong twine (another useful item to take on a journey). I ought to be able to carry it across the top of my satchel or, if we encountered cold weather, wrapped around my body.

When I had finished – and tidied and swept out the room for good measure so as to leave all in good order – I sat down on the floor and wondered what to do next. Looking out through the little window, I judged that it was still an hour or two before sunset. I tried to think of something to occupy my thoughts but for once I couldn't. All I could see in my mind's eye were the faces of the people I loved and who I would be leaving behind. For an undefined length of time.

For a while I let the images come. Better to do it now, I thought, and to shed my cowardly tears where there was no witness. Then I dried my eyes, picked up my satchel and my cloak and went down the ladder to seek out Gurdyman.

We left the twisty-turny house as the sun was falling down the western sky. Like me, Gurdyman had been determined to leave everything neat and tidy, and the old house shone with cleanliness and order. He locked the door, tucking the big iron key away in his bag.

I hated to think of the house, left all by itself during our absence. 'Will nobody go in while we're away?'

He turned to me with a smile. 'Oh, yes,' he said gently, and I sensed that he understood my question perfectly well because he felt the same way himself. 'There is another key,' he added, 'left in the hands of someone I trust.'

He didn't say who, and I didn't ask.

We walked at a steady pace through the alleyways, out onto the road and towards the bridge. I couldn't bear to look towards the castle, and Jack. I kept my eyes down, watching my boots fall one by one onto the track, sending up little puffs of dust with every step. And then we were going down the steps to the quay and, on the deck of *The Maid of the Marsh*, Alun was waiting for us. He traversed the gangplank with the casual ease of someone who did it several times a day and took our bags, depositing them on board before returning to offer Gurdyman his hand. Too sensible to be proud, Gurdyman took it. I followed him.

'If you want my advice,' Alun said as he put the coins Gurdyman had just given him away in his purse, 'I'd settle yourselves over there.' He pointed to a place beneath the boat's high side a little forward of where the mast rose up, immediately behind a pair of barrels and a large stack of bulging sacks. 'The piles of cargo will provide you with some shelter, and if it rains, as it well might, you can rig up a shelter over the angle formed between the sacks and the side of the boat.' He indicated. 'You'll be clear of the oars there and you won't have to keep leaping out of the way.'

Gurdyman was nodding, clearly seeing the sense of the

suggestion, and swiftly we claimed our spot and settled down. The early evening was mild, with only a light breeze blowing off the water. I folded up my blanket and sat on it, keeping my cloak handy for when the temperature dropped. Gurdyman didn't speak, and I could think of nothing to say.

A few more passengers came aboard. A man and his wife, the man with an angry, resentful expression, as if the prospect of the journey was not to his liking; a woman with a small child; two men in the dark garb and cowled robes of monks. There was a steady increase in activity as the crew prepared for our departure. An air of busy efficiency crept over the boat. Then, as the bright oranges and pinks of the sunset splashed brilliantly across the deep blue sky, men on the shore let go the fore and aft mooring ropes, others on the boat pushed us away from the quay with long poles, the oarsmen bent over their oars and, slowly at first but gaining pace with surprising speed, *The Maid of the Marsh* set off for the coast.

THREE

We went on for hours, until long after it was fully dark. I slipped into a doze, and would have gone into deep sleep had it not been for the woman with the child, who came over to our sheltered corner and asked if she and the infant could share it because the child was cold. I moved over and made room for her, and we put the infant – a little boy – between us to keep him safe and warm. Lying on my blanket, with our two cloaks and her blanket over us, we were snug and as comfortable as it's possible to be on a hard wooden deck. Some time later I was woken again and I stayed awake long enough to register that we had stopped, and that the crew were settling for what was left of the night.

I woke to sunlight and a creaking sound: above my head, tilted at an angle, the sail was filled with the wind blowing steadily out of the west. At some point while I slept we had emerged from the narrow, twisting waterways into one of the many places where several of them combine to make areas of relatively open water, and the oarsmen were taking a well-earned rest.

Gurdyman was standing in the stern talking to Alun and the woman with the infant was sitting beside me, trying to get the child to eat bread dipped in milk. I got up, folded my blanket and cloak, then went along the deck to use the boat's rudimentary hygiene provisions, which consisted of a bucket behind a flimsy screen for bodily waste and another one of river water for washing. Not that many of the passengers and crew would have utilized the latter, I thought, although I did. My early training with my aunt had drummed it into me that nobody should start the day's work without clean hands but particularly not a healer.

When I returned to our place, the little boy was grizzling. 'What's the matter with him?' I asked his mother.

'He had a fever, but it's gone now.' She frowned down at

her son, one hand gently stroking his soft brown hair. 'He's hungry but he won't eat.'

The little boy was peering shyly up at me from the safety of his mother's arms. 'Is that right?' I said to him. He nodded. 'You don't want the milk sops your mother has for you?' He shook his head violently. 'Hmm,' I said, putting on a pretend frown. 'I wonder if a honey cake might tempt you?'

His big hazel eyes lit up. I reached into the food bag that Gurdyman and I had brought with us and extracted a small round cake. I could see that the little boy wanted to grab it and stuff it whole into his mouth, but he had been well taught, and he took it from me between finger and thumb and whispered something that was probably his version of 'Thank you.'

Then he stuffed it whole into his mouth.

He became my friend after that, and I shared with him a sample of the delicacies we'd packed. Appetite comes with eating, they say, and it was true in his case. By mid-morning, he was wolfing down the milk sops and asking for more.

He wasn't my only patient. One of the monks had a sore foot; I'd noticed him limping when he came aboard, and it was clear this morning that he was in pain. I went over to him.

'Would you like me to have a look?' I asked him.

He was old, with an almost bald head and a thin face that told of a hard life and years with not enough to eat. Although his companion – a man with dark eyes in a pale face and an unsmiling demeanour – was younger, he was clearly senior, for the old man looked at him before answering. The dark-eyed man gave a curt nod, then turned away as if he didn't want to witness his companion's self-indulgence. Kneeling before the old monk, I drew off the worn sandal.

His feet were in a dreadful state, with cracked crusts of hard skin around the heels and long, yellowish toenails. I could see straight away what pained him: on the big toe of his right foot he had a huge whitlow. The tip of his toe was a hard scarlet ball, the skin swollen and hot to the touch, and the side of the nail was full of pus. I reached for my satchel, took out my little pouch of tools and extracted a thin, sharp blade, which I wiped with lavender oil. Then, before the old monk properly understood what I was going to do, swiftly I lanced the swelling and, as gently as I could, pushed out the pus.

It must have hurt like the very devil, but he didn't cry out. Glancing up at him, I saw he was biting his lips, his face twisted in pain. One of the crew had provided a bowl of hot water, and I bathed the toe and wrapped it in a clean dressing. 'You'll need to change the dressing regularly,' I said. 'Will someone be able to do that for you?'

From behind me the younger monk said, 'Naturally,' in a dismissive tone that suggested I'd been foolish even to ask. Then, tiring of the whole business, he strode away towards the bows.

To my surprise, the old monk leaned down and winked at me. 'I'm grateful to you, lass, but even more so to this toe of mine, for all it's pained me, for it's got me out of a long walk!' He chuckled, nodding towards the stiff back of the younger monk. 'Even he realized I couldn't stumble and limp all the way from Cambridge to the coast!'

The younger monk was still up in the bows, clearly intent on disassociating himself from the rest of us. I reached into Gurdyman's and my food bag again and gave the old monk a honey cake. His expression of wonder at the taste – perhaps something he hadn't experienced for decades – was something to behold.

My last patient was the woman who had come on board with her husband. She was in her middle years and complained of a blinding headache; it was, she admitted, a regular occurrence. I gave her some of the willow powder I keep in my satchel, with instructions on how to take it, and squeezed out a cloth in cold water for her to put over her forehead. Some time later, she gave the cloth back to me, saying she was feeling much better. 'I can't pay you,' she muttered right in my ear, 'seeing as how *he* holds the purse strings' – she shot a glance at her husband – 'but I'd like you to have this.' She pressed something small and round into my hand. 'Don't look at it now!' she hissed. 'He might see!'

I waited until she had moved away and the husband wasn't looking, then opened my hand. In it lay a pale little bead, a pearl, threaded onto a piece of finely plaited wool. For the briefest of moments, I heard that summertime drone of insects again, and had the weird and disorienting sensation that I was somewhere else. But then it went away, and I stared down at the pearl.

It was beautiful, its lustre reflecting the soft light. I wondered where the woman had obtained it: it looked as if it had come from a rosary. I felt sad to think she had given away what must surely have been one of her few treasures, and, catching her eye, held it out to her, offering it back. She shook her head, smiling. 'It's for you,' she mouthed.

I was about to tuck it away in the belt around my waist, where I'd hidden Rollo's gold and coins, when I saw Gurdyman staring at me. His face was ashen, his expression one of dread. I went to get up, thinking I should hurry over to him and ask what ailed him, but then he managed a smile – it looked more than a little forced – and turned away.

Once again, I was struck by the unsettling realization that he was afraid.

We reached Lynn very early the following morning, catching the last of the outgoing tide and sweeping along at a good pace. *The Maid of the Marsh* was skilfully steered to a free berth halfway along a quay lined with similar craft, and Gurdyman and I said our goodbyes to Alun and his crew and went ashore. Gurdyman led us to a quiet spot beneath a sturdy harbour wall, out of the path of the busy crowds, and there he stood, quite still, looking across at the larger, sea-going ships along the next quay. Guessing he was searching for a likely vessel for us, I left him to his contemplation, amusing myself by watching our fellow passengers disperse. The angry man and his wife passed quite close by. He ignored us so totally that our two nights and a day aboard a small river boat together might never have happened, but she turned and gave me a quick smile and mouthed *Thank you.* The woman and her little boy were running towards a slim, handsome man who was flying down the quayside to meet them, and their reunion, the man picking up his son and holding him high in the air, the child laughing wildly and the man's face alight, while the woman looked on, tears of joy in her eyes, was a pleasure to witness. The two monks were the last to leave the boat, the younger one helping his companion and carrying both their small packs. The older monk, catching sight of me, turned and gave me a wink, and, from the roguish smile on his face, I surmised that his foot no longer pained him and that he would have been perfectly capable of carrying his own pack.

After some time, Gurdyman came out of his reverie. 'We shall seek our breakfast,' he announced, 'which I believe will be readily available, for wherever there is an assurance of many mouths to feed, somebody will be there making their living by fulfilling the need. And then' – he turned and smiled at me – 'we shall do the rounds of the ships over there' – he pointed – 'and find the one whose destination best suits our purpose.'

We found a stall where a woman in a clean apron, her sleeves rolled up over strong, muscly arms, was doling out porridge from a big, bubbling vat into wooden bowls, and ate our portions standing on the quay. The porridge was delicious, and Gurdyman had a refill. Then we picked up our bags – the food bag felt light, for I had been too generous in sharing out its contents, and I mentioned to Gurdyman that we should replenish our stores before we set off again – and ventured out along the further quay.

So many ships! Some were bound northwards, along the eastern coast of England to Scotland and beyond, to the cold, distant lands across the pale green seas. I had sailed that way, on a long, slender ship called *Malice-striker* which had taken me all the way to Iceland. Now, however, Gurdyman and I would be setting out in the opposite direction, and with reluctance I tore my gaze away from a beautiful craft that looked so similar to *Malice-striker* that, just for an instant, I thought I had been transported back into my own past.

Gurdyman was leading us towards a line of perhaps half a dozen cargo ships, tied up nose to tail at the far end of the long quay. They were large, sturdy vessels with a mast and a square sail, as well as oars, with wide, open decks for cargo and, in some cases, small structures erected over the steerage oar so as to provide rudimentary shelter for the ship master and, perhaps, for passengers. Whichever would be our means of transport, I thought, we were not going to find any comforts other than those we provided for ourselves.

I'd been feeling quite excited and almost cheerful as we came into Lynn. Now, with the uncomfortable realities of the next stage of our journey staring me in the face, my heart sank and my spirits drooped. I wanted to go home. But then I thought, where is home? My village, where my life of hard but satisfying work with my beloved aunt in her clean, cosy little cottage went for ever when she married Hrype? My parents' home, where I knew I was always welcome but which I left behind me when first I moved out? In Cambridge, with Gurdyman? But he wasn't in Cambridge any more, he was *here*, setting out on this voyage that seemed like something out of a fantasy, a dream, except that it wasn't.

With Jack?

But Jack didn't want me.

I bowed my head, fighting a sudden desire to weep.

Then Gurdyman said cheerfully, 'I think we shall try our luck there, with the vessel at the end of the line – her name is the *Amethyst* – for I believe I recognize her master, and I know him to be a good man.'

I looked up, sensing his abrupt movement away from me, and, shouldering my satchel, hurried after him.

I stood and watched the conversation between Gurdyman and the ship's master. He was a lean, rangy man, dark-haired, light-eyed, and he had an air of steadiness about him that immediately appealed. But as I leaned closer to hear what the two of them were saying, I noticed that he was shaking his head. 'It's late in the season for such a voyage, but you wouldn't get passage all the way to Corunna at any time, not with one of us,' he said. 'Nobody from these parts ventures so far. Me, I rarely go further south than Bordeaux, and then only if there's very good money in it.' He grinned briefly.

Gurdyman nodded, appearing undismayed. 'How far can you take us?' he asked.

'I'm sailing for the French coast as soon as we've finished loading,' he said, 'and our ultimate destination is St Malo. I'll take you there, and gladly, for I know your coin is good.'

Gurdyman smiled. 'Thank you. We have indeed had many dealings with each other, and you have worked hard for me, often bringing home goods from faraway places that I had despaired of finding.'

'I like a challenge,' the master observed.

'You think we will be able to find ships prepared to take us on south?' Gurdyman asked.

'Probably,' the master replied. 'Far more ships take on passengers these days, what with the pilgrimage route to Santiago, although, as I said, we're too near winter now and few are making the journey. You'll have to take it in stages, mind, but at least a spell in port while you find your next ship will give you a chance to recover from the time at sea.'

I had begun to feel optimistic again as he spoke, but at his last words my misery threatened to return.

'We are good sailors,' Gurdyman said stoutly. 'Lassair here' – he turned to include me – 'has sailed into the north and returned to tell the tale, and this is far from being my first sea voyage.'

The master grinned. 'It's not so much your own seasickness, it's witnessing and dealing with everyone else's,' he said. 'Plus the crowded quarters, the lack of anything to do to pass the long hours, the cold, the wet, the general discomfort, and the scorn of a crew of busy, overworked sailors who tend to despise those with the time, the leisure and the money to sit on their backsides and be taken by others' hard work on pilgrimages. Not my crew,' he added, 'I wouldn't let them be so discourteous to paying passengers.'

'We are not going on pilgrimage,' Gurdyman said mildly.

The master looked at him in amazement. 'Then why in the name of sweet Jesus are you putting yourselves through so much hardship and peril?'

'My mother and father are buried in Galicia, and I have not yet visited their graves,' Gurdyman replied.

I managed not to show my surprise, for this was the first time he had mentioned this fact as the reason for our journey, and I didn't for a moment believe it was the true one. Was it merely a convenient excuse, designed to satisfy the curious?

If so, it worked, for the scorn and disbelief on the master's face turned to respect and even, perhaps, admiration. 'I understand,' he said quietly. 'I shall do what I can to assist you, and you are welcome on board my ship.'

We had time for some hurried provisioning, and a stallholder took pity on us and helped us carry our purchases – cheese, dried meat, some apples, bread, a little barrel of small beer – to the ship. Gurdyman went on aboard the *Amethyst*, but I darted back to another stall and purchased ginger and cloves; if there was to be seasickness among the passengers, then I knew ginger to be a good remedy, and cloves were good for easing the pain of toothache, such a common ailment and one which, out at sea where there would be no hope of immediate access to relief unless someone like me could provide it, would instantly become ten times worse.

I looked around. Was there anything else I should buy? I couldn't think; all this was new and strange, and I was lost.

But just then, when despair threatened to flood over me, Gurdyman's bald-topped, silver-encircled head appeared over the ship's side and he said cheerfully, 'Hurry up, child, I've found a splendid place for us and I want you to see it!'

I looked up and found myself responding to his smile. 'I'm coming!' I called back.

The plank that linked the *Amethyst* to the quay was a good deal more sturdy and substantial than that of *The Maid of the Marsh*, with a handrail on one side, and I ran up it confidently and easily. Hoping that my sure-footedness was a good omen, I crossed the broad deck and went to join Gurdyman.

A little over a fortnight after Gurdyman and Lassair's departure, Hrype was honouring his undertaking to his old friend. Cautiously, not wanting to be observed, he negotiated the maze of lanes leading off the market square and paused in the shadowy alleyway outside Gurdyman's house. Presently he would go inside and, he decided, spend the night in the house.

It was late in the day, and the gathering darkness exacerbated the sense of something being not quite right. He stood quite still for a moment, trying to analyse what was amiss. There was a presence, quite unmistakable to a man such as he; the same dark, powerful presence he'd felt down in the crypt with Gurdyman.

He recognized it and then, not without effort, put it aside.

He held the big iron key ready in his hand. But just then he heard footfalls somewhere nearby, and quickly slipped into the deeply shaded angle formed by the protruding porch of a house a little further up the alley. He waited until the footfalls started to fade away and he could be certain not to be observed. Although he knew Gurdyman would welcome his presence in the house – why else, indeed, had he provided the key? – something was warning Hrype not to let anyone else know he was there.

Despite the fact that whoever had made the footsteps was moving off, still he sensed a presence.

That dark, potent presence.

He leaned forward, watching without being seen, but there was nobody there. He had observed before the strange behaviour of sounds in this maze of little alleys and passageways off the market square, so that sometimes you would have sworn sounds came from very close at hand whereas in reality they were merely an echo of something further off.

The footfalls had stopped.

Just for a moment, Hrype had a brilliantly clear image of someone else stopping and listening, just as he was. This other someone was waiting to see what he would do next.

But surely that was mere fancy, for nobody knew he was here.

He stood, still and silent.

The distant hum of noise from the market square faded and died, and he imagined the last of the stallholders packing up and heading for home, some cheerful after a successful day, some disgruntled and hoping for better things tomorrow.

At last, all was quiet.

Hrype walked on soft feet up to the door, unlocked it, opened it a crack and slipped inside, closing and bolting it behind him.

And wondering, all the time he did so, why he felt so apprehensive.

A lamp hung from a hook just inside the door. Hrype struck

a spark and lit the wick, and in the utter darkness of the closed house, the light was a warm, comforting glow. He walked on down the passage that led straight through the house, looking into the small, enclosed room where there was a hearth, shelves for pots, platters, spoons and knives and a space for food, now empty and swept clean. He went up the first few rungs of the ladder that led into the attic room where Lassair slept. His head above the level of the floor, he held up the lamp and looked round. The space was clean and neat. Descending, he went out into the open court with its high walls at the rear of the house. Again, all was as it should be. He stood in the middle of the court, listening. He thought for an instant that he heard whispering, but, holding his breath and keeping absolutely still, the tiny sound was no longer there.

But, just as before, once again he had that sudden bright image of someone else's awareness of him: now that unknown person was trying to tell him something, but speaking so quietly that the words were nothing but a soft sibilance that made no sense. As if – he was struck by the thought – they were in another language.

He looked around. There was nobody there. Of course there wasn't. Not a sound to indicate the presence of someone on the other side of the high wall.

With an abrupt movement, irritated with himself, he went back along the passage and, just before the door onto the street, turned to his left, down a short flight of steps, then turned left again and, at the end of that passage, down more steps into the crypt.

As in the rooms above, all was orderly. Nowhere else, Hrype reflected with a smile, was Gurdyman's absence more evident than here, in the room where he spent the majority of his time. The crypt was impersonal now, and might have been anybody's cellar. Hrype wondered fleetingly if Gurdyman had performed some sort of ceremony prior to departure; if he had drawn on his vast experience and selected the words that would pull forward an imaginary veil and conceal from the curious every trace of what the crypt had witnessed and experienced in the long decades of Gurdyman's occupation.

How long *had* he been there? Hrype now asked himself. And, instantly following upon that: *How old is he?*

The realization that he had no idea how to answer either question made him feel uneasy.

And then the various disturbing elements that had troubled him since he stood in the alley outside, and that subconsciously he must have been struggling to suppress, suddenly seemed to gather themselves together and attack simultaneously.

He spun round and hurried up the first flight of steps, along the passage, up the second flight and out into the dark space inside the door. Fumbling now, trying to hold the light in the right position to see the bolt, he felt the hook on the top of the lamp slip through his fingers. The lamp fell to the hard stone floor and shattered, and the light went out.

The after-image of its glow was like a large and very beautiful pearl.

Shaking his head to drive it away, he felt all around the edge of the door until he found the bolt. He drove it back and flung the door open. The alley outside was shadowy and deserted but after the sudden darkness inside, the light was sufficient for him to get the key in the keyhole and lock the door. Then, already ashamed of his fear and his panic, Hrype jumped down the steps, wanting only to get away.

He missed his footing and turned an ankle. Stumbling, a hand on the wall to keep him steady, he made his way back to the porch where he had concealed himself earlier. There, leaning into the angle of the two walls, he waited until his heartbeat began to slow.

After a while, he recalled that he had planned to spend the night in Gurdyman's house.

He grimaced, his mouth turning down in a bitter twist.

He knew there was no possibility of that now.

There was something that lurked there, watching, waiting, its intention not clear but almost certainly malign and—

He closed his mind on that thought. Standing there, still so close to the house, was not the place to dwell on it.

He waited a little longer, then tried his weight on the damaged ankle. It held him, although the stabs of pain it was sending out told him he would be unwise to walk far tonight.

He frowned, thinking. Not far away there was an ancient well, beyond which stood a deserted house where a friend of Gurdyman's had lived and died, together with a companion.[5] Nobody went anywhere near it now, for it was said to be haunted. Hrype could reach it, he was sure. He would rest his ankle, eat his provisions, drink water from the sacred well. He had his warm cloak and he would sleep within the house's old walls. He was quite sure its spirits would not harm him, for he had met them in life and did not fear them in death.

They would not have harmed anybody who ventured there in friendship, he thought as he limped away, for they had been a force for the good.

He slept soundly, undisturbed by bad dreams or even, as far as he could recall, any dreams at all. He was aware of a – a *kindness*, was the best word to describe it, within the abandoned little house. As he ate the last of his bread, watching the waxing light outside, he reflected that a fanciful man might say it was fate that had led to his turned ankle, leading to his spending the night under this particular roof, for the healing spirit within had not only taken the pain of the sprain away but also the fear he had felt in Gurdyman's house.

He seemed to hear a soft voice say, *There is a threat but it is no threat to you.*

A threat.

Yes, he had felt it.

The reassurance that it was not he who was in danger comforted him. He made sure the house showed no sign of his presence, thanked the resident shades for their welcome and their help, then wrapped his cloak round him, put up his hood and headed back into the town.

He moved with caution along the alley that led to Gurdyman's house, searching with all his senses for any hint of what he had felt the previous day. There was nothing.

But it was cheerful, sunny morning now, and the market square, as he had slipped across its corner, had been loud with

[5] See *The Night Wanderer.*

the everyday sounds of the town going about its business. There were people hurrying along the alley too: Hrype stood back for two fat women with baskets on their arms, and then for a man and a lad, the lad carrying a tray of fresh-baked bread. All four nodded to Hrype, and the man wished him good day.

Normal.

Hrype repeated the word once or twice as he drew level with Gurdyman's house. He looked for a few moments at the spot where Gurdyman said he had found the dead beggar with the pearl in his hand. Gurdyman had tried so hard to deny how much the incident had disturbed him, but Hrype hadn't been convinced. 'You were afraid, old friend,' he whispered now. 'You saw a significance, either in the dead man himself or what he held in his hand, and whatever it was you saw, it changed you.'

He sighed, for Gurdyman was far away now and out of his reach.

He made his way to his place of concealment beside the porch, drawing his cloak close around him and his hood forward to conceal his face. He would watch a while, he decided, and wait to see if any of last night's sensations returned. Then he would—

Someone was coming up the alley. Heavy steps beat on the ground, and it seemed to Hrype that a shadow preceded the sounds, moving inexorably closer . . .

A figure appeared at the bend in the alleyway: big, broad-shouldered, tall, dressed in a scarred leather jerkin and with a knife in a sheath on his belt.

Jack Chevestrier.

Hrype drew further back into his hiding place.

He watched.

Just as he had done, Jack looked up and down the alley to make sure he was unobserved. Then he went up the steps to Gurdyman's house, raised the heavy iron ring that lifted the latch and tried to open the door. It was locked – Hrype clearly recalled locking it last night – and, after trying once or twice more, Jack stopped. It seemed to Hrype that his shoulders dropped a little. Then, leaning in closer to the door, he tapped on it and Hrype heard him call out, 'Gurdyman? Gurdyman? Are you within?'

Standing absolutely still, Hrype watched.

After quite some time, Jack jumped down the steps and strode away. He passed Hrype's hiding place, and Hrype saw his face.

So you miss her, do you? he thought as the sound of Jack's footsteps faded away. *You believed you wanted her gone, and now you find out your mistake.*

He knew it was petty, but he did not want to be the one to tell Jack that Lassair had left. And, since he was probably the only soul in the town who knew where she was heading, and how long she was likely to be away, that meant Jack was never likely to find out.

He left his hiding place and set out up the alley, in the opposite direction to that which Jack had taken. He would take the walk in easy stages, out of consideration for his ankle, but still he reckoned he would be back in Aelf Fen by late afternoon.

As he strode off he realized he was smiling, but whether it was at the thought of home or of Jack's sorrow – in Hrype's view, largely brought upon himself – he didn't bother to work out.

FOUR

The best part of a month into our journey, at last Gurdyman and I were nearing the end of the sea voyage. Corunna was not far now, and the master said confidently that we would arrive early in the morning. One more night on board, I thought as I tried to get comfortable. I could manage that without complaint, couldn't I?

The voyage had not been too bad. The *Amethyst* had transported us across the Channel to St Malo largely without incident, and there we had quickly found a coastal vessel that took us on to a small port on the southern coast of Brittany where the ship was to collect a cargo of salt. We had to wait a couple of days for onward passage to Bordeaux, but, as Gurdyman and I remarked reassuringly to one another, it gave us the chance to purchase more supplies, wash out some of our garments (stained with salt water, other people's vomit and, in my case, loose stools from a sick baby I had nursed while her mother had a much-needed sleep) and spend two nights in the blessed comfort of a bed, with blankets, sheets and a pillow and set on a surface that didn't move around underneath us.

Some time ago I had found, to my great relief, that I was a good sailor. Well, I told myself as this present voyage had reinforced the fact, I am the granddaughter of an Icelander who has sailed the known world, and it was on his ship that my body had learned how to deal with the sea's movement. Gurdyman, too, seemed so far to have been unaffected: it was true that he had quite often shut himself off from me, sitting for long spells with his eyes closed in silent meditation (I was sure, although I couldn't have said why, that he wasn't asleep) and at times had looked pale. But something told me that these signs of a disturbance in his equilibrium had nothing whatsoever to do with being on a ship on a restless sea.

In Bordeaux we were delayed for over a week by a violent storm. No ships sailed in all that time, and the small group waiting with various degrees of impatience for onward transit to Corunna (and, in almost everyone else's case, the shrine at Santiago de Compostela) just had to put up with it. Gurdyman and I found an adequate inn, where the food was abundant if monotonous, the wine was good and the sleeping accommodation dry and vermin-free. All in all, we considered ourselves fortunate.

At last the skies had cleared and the sea had begun to calm down. The master of the ship on which we had booked our passage announced he would leave on the evening's tide, Gurdyman and I hurried on board and, old hands at this sailing by now, found a good position aft, in the lee of the solid structure built over the steering oar. Gurdyman had purchased a couple of good feather pillows in Bordeaux, which did a lot to improve our comfort.

For some time our progress was slow and laborious. As I leaned on the rail and watched the land on our larboard side slide so slowly past, I sometimes thought we'd never get to Corunna. But then the wind changed. The oars were drawn in and stowed away, the huge square sail was hastily raised and, even as it made its jerky way up the mast, already it was filling with wind. Soon we were flying over the water; a sensation so exhilarating that I wanted to laugh out loud.

But laughter was not appropriate, for the strong wind blowing from the north-east was ruffling up the sea and several of the pilgrims were suffering badly. There were enough buckets and bowls to go round – the master was clearly used to seasickness in his passengers – but people become selfish when they feel so ill, too preoccupied with their own distress to be careful where their bodily outpourings land. Tempted to think unkind thoughts, I made myself remember my first day on a ship, how sick I had been and how kindly I had been treated. Then, ashamed of myself, I reminded myself that I was a healer, and set about doing what I could to help the sufferers. Besides making them drink water between bouts of vomiting, sponging them off and shielding them from the worst of the crew's derision, this didn't amount to very much.

The days flew by, time speeding up because I was so busy. I slept soundly, vaguely aware of Gurdyman close by but usually too tired to give him much thought.

So it happened that it was only when the distant smudge of the Galician coast came in sight that I took a good look at him. Had I not known without a doubt that it was him, I wouldn't have recognized my teacher and friend. He was even paler than before and he looked as if weight had fallen from him, his plump cheeks saggy and his eyes dull, sunk in his head. And it wasn't just his physical appearance that had changed; it was also his attitude. Towards me, in particular, for he had always been friendly, affectionate and, unless he was deep in concentration or had shut himself away to perform some risky new experiment, open and approachable.

Now it was as if I was travelling with a stranger.

He saw me looking at him and must have read my anxious expression for, before I could say a word, he put up a hand to forestall me and said brusquely, 'I need firm ground beneath my feet, child, and a bed that is not made of harsh planks.'

'But you—' I had been going to say, *But you haven't shown any sign of being affected by our long sea voyage!* Or, even, *That is not what ails you, Gurdyman, but something is clearly causing you deep distress, so won't you share it with me?*

He was staring fixedly at me, however, his eyes narrowed, as if daring me to continue.

I shut my mouth.

We tied up at Corunna and went ashore. Like everyone else, we picked up the road south to Santiago de Compostela: I'd heard people saying what a relief it was that it was safe now here in Galicia for pilgrims wanting to visit the Shrine of Saint James, for in the preceding years the Christian armies had gathered themselves for an all-out, combined effort and had expelled the Muslims from the north. Not knowing how much of a threat this Muslim presence would have been, I had no idea if the dangers were being exaggerated.

I was told by a man I fell into step with as we left Corunna that the Christians, wanting to stamp themselves and their faith on the land, had immediately set about a building programme, and the magnificent new cathedral at Santiago was among the results. The aim, or so my companion would have it, was to show how well the people of the north could build, and how their edifices to their religion would rival and surpass the palaces and the mosques of Moorish Spain.

I decided to reserve my judgement.

We joined up with another small band of pilgrims, all in a mood of high excitement so that there was a holiday atmosphere on the road. For two nights we bunked down in large dormitories where there was almost as little space and privacy as there had been on board ship.

'Do not expect to rest for long in Santiago,' Gurdyman said to me on the third day as the city became visible up ahead, 'for very soon we shall set out again and join the pilgrim route returning eastwards along the endless miles to the Pyrenees, and the gathering place of St Jean that lies at their foot.'

'But surely *we're* not going back!' We had only just arrived . . .

'Of course not,' he said crushingly. 'We shall travel that road only for some fifty miles, whereupon we shall leave our companions and seek out our first destination.'

I was about to ask what this destination was, but up ahead a lad had just sighted the outline of the new cathedral. 'Santiago!' the lad shouted, and the cry, taken up by everyone else, rapidly became so deafening that it drove out thought, never mind conversation.

We were to have one brief night in the town. I left Gurdyman resting and, determined to make the most of the few hours of daylight remaining, went out to look around.

Despite the fact that we were now in late autumn and pilgrims preferred to travel in spring and summer, Santiago was seething with people. It was an exciting place and its inhabitants shared a powerful sense of reverent awe at being in the vicinity of the saint's bones. There was also – and for me this was the dominant emotion – the lively cheeriness of people making the very most of this unique time away from their everyday lives, their work, the endless repetition of routine. As well as the pilgrims, there were gangs of carpenters, masons and labourers engaged on building the new cathedral. Staring up at its soaring granite walls, I thought that, although far from finished, already it was the most enormous structure I had ever seen.

I joined on to the rear of a short queue of pilgrims and waited my turn to go inside the chapel.

A very fat man in a vaguely monkish habit stood before the altar, relating the story of St James in a loud voice and repeating the tale in two different languages. He told us that after James had been beheaded in Judea, the two parts of his corpse were collected and brought back to Galicia (although I noticed that he didn't say why this faraway and surely unlikely spot had been selected). His tomb had to be abandoned when the Christians were driven out of the north by the Moors, and it was many years later that a hermit called Pelagius saw brilliant lights in the sky and, upon investigating, found the burial place. The king, whose name was Alphonse, then claimed James as the patron saint of his dynasty and his kingdom and commanded a chapel to be built over the tomb. This first structure was destroyed by a Moorish army a little later – the monk was vague on details, I noticed – but then in the year 1060, work began on the new cathedral beside which we were standing.

The monk's voice dropped to a whisper and, as we strained forward to hear, he announced that before we heard mass we would be allowed to go down into the crypt of the original chapel and stand in the presence of the saint.

Filing down with my companions, I was pushed, shoved and elbowed, my nostrils filling with the smell of sweat and garlic. There were too many people around for me to see ahead, and it was therefore a surprise to find myself suddenly before an open space in which were three stone sarcophagi.

'The saint and his two disciples,' breathed the monk behind me. 'They stay with him out of loyalty and love, even in death.'

Being dead, they didn't have much choice, I reflected. But I kept the thought to myself.

I stared at the central sarcophagus. Was there truly a saint's decapitated body inside? My companions clearly believed it was so, for most of them had kneeled to pray and many were in tears. I wondered why I felt so unmoved. Perhaps it had something to do with the fact that I wasn't really here as a pilgrim.

Although I was only beginning to realize how much was being kept from me, I knew already that Gurdyman and I were on a very different mission.

As I walked beside Gurdyman on the second morning out of Santiago, at last I plucked up my courage and said, 'Where are we going?' I bit back the other question: *And what in heaven's name are we doing here?*

He didn't answer at first, and I had the sense that he was having to bring himself back from somewhere deep within his own thoughts. Then, with a smile, he turned to me and said, 'I am sorry, Lassair, that I have been such a poor companion. I have dragged you from your home and from all that you know, all those you love, with scant explanation.'

With *no* explanation, I could have said.

'But now that we have achieved the first part of our journey without mishap, it is time for me to enlighten you.'

I could have laughed with relief.

There was a pause while he gathered his thoughts and then he said, 'Now, let me see, what have I told you of my youth?'

'You were born to elderly parents who were so pleased to have a child that they wanted to go on a pilgrimage to give thanks,' I said. 'You—'

But he was chuckling. 'Elderly!' he exclaimed. 'Yes, I suppose I did say that.' He looked at me. 'I think, Lassair, that, just in case I misled you in any way, or you have forgotten pertinent details, I had better begin at the beginning.'

Cheered at the thought of how well a story would help pass the miles, I said happily, 'Please, go ahead!'

And this is the tale he told me, as we walked the roads of Galicia on a day of early winter sunshine and the mountains, already white at their summits, rose up ahead of us and to our right, and the soft chatter of our small group of fellow travellers filled the air with a steady, gentle murmuring.

'Well. Now,' he began. 'I was born many years before the

Conquest, in a village inland from Hastings on the track leading towards London. My father brewed ale, and considered himself the luckiest man alive because he loved his work and, even more, he loved the woman to whom he was married, who had a beautiful spirit and the kindest smile. The pair of them were beloved in their small community but, despite their close and happy marriage, they had not been blessed with children, and this was an enduring sorrow. My father watched as his beloved wife slowly and steadily became increasingly sad, and even a little strange.'

She was probably entering the years when a woman ceases to be fertile, I thought, and, longing for a child, beginning to realize that her time was running out.

'Then, to my father's dismay,' Gurdyman went on, 'she began to speak of visions. She always saw the same image: an angel dressed in pink. My father, loving her as he did, tried everything he could think of to help her, which I suspect was not very much, for, generous and kind though he was, he had little imagination and, like the majority of men, not a great deal of insight into what it is to be a woman. He attempted to curb her wild talk of her pink angel, for he feared that if her odd behaviour came to the notice of the wrong people, trouble might ensue. He believed, I imagine, that it would be assumed she had lost her mind, and he was terrified that somebody would come and take her away.'

Not an unreasonable fear, I thought. People were very frightened of madness.

'Then my father had a new and far worse anxiety, for his wife began to suffer from bouts of sickness. Beside himself, terrified that he was going to lose her, he watched her more closely than ever before. And, far from growing thin, losing her teeth and her hair and beginning the long decline to death, she began to grow plump. The sickness stopped, her hair shone, her skin was luminous . . . she was pregnant.'

So thoroughly had he drawn me into the story that, although I already knew the outcome, for wasn't her son walking there right beside me, nevertheless I was flooded with delight.

'It was a miracle,' Gurdyman said softly, 'for she was advanced in years and had imagined her chance of motherhood had gone for ever. In the privacy of their bedchamber, she whispered to my father that her angel in pink had brought this wonderful, unlooked-for gift, but he hushed her, for such talk – which others might interpret as his wife placing herself in the company of the blessed Virgin – must surely be blasphemous.

'People, of course, began to notice her condition and, fond of her as they were, they rejoiced for her. They began to call her Elizabeth and my father Zachary, remembering the story of John the Baptist in St Luke's gospel.' He turned to me. 'You are of course familiar with it?'

'Tell me again,' I replied.

'Elizabeth was the cousin of Mary and married to Zachary, who was a priest. They were childless and elderly, and Elizabeth was well beyond childbearing age. Zachary was selected to offer incense at the Golden Altar, and there the Angel Gabriel appeared to him, telling him his wife would bear a son, who was to be called John. Zachary was astonished and utterly refused to believe this unlikely prediction, whereupon he was struck dumb, remaining so until his wife gave birth. Relatives urged the couple to name the child Zachary, after his father, but Zachary wrote, "His name is John," and straight away speech was restored to him.'

'But your father didn't doubt that *his* wife was pregnant?'

Gurdyman smiled. 'Oh, no. But then he had the physical evidence before his eyes rather than the mere word of an angel.'

I glanced round swiftly to check nobody had heard, for speaking so frivolously of an angel didn't seem wise in the company of devout men and women on their way home from a pilgrimage.

'The pregnancy proceeded uneventfully,' Gurdyman was saying, 'and in due course a baby son was born.'

'You!' I exclaimed.

'Indeed. The baby thrived, his parents' joy increased and continued to do so as their sturdy little son grew into a happy, smiling and bright-eyed toddler, interested in everything, speaking with sense and meaning far sooner than he had any right to, and badgering his parents constantly with his incessant *why?*' He smiled gently. 'My mother, who had never forgotten her angel in pink and attributed my presence entirely to his intervention, developed a strong desire to give thanks, for such was her happiness that she grew more devout, her heart full of love for the God who had brought it about. Living as she and my father did, in the inn by the track to Hastings, they knew about pilgrimages; and Rome, even Jerusalem, were spoken of, but my mother had a hankering to go to Santiago de Compostela. So, when the infant – I – was three years old, they packed their bags, collected their pilgrims' scrips and staves and set off.'

'Did they travel as we did?' I demanded.

'No. They crossed the sea quite close to its narrowest part, landing in Dieppe and picking up the pilgrim route through Chartres, Tours and Bordeaux, then down into the Pyrenees and over the Roncesvalles Pass, where Charlemagne fought back the massed ranks of the enemy on his borders and saved his land. They travelled the width of northern Spain and finally reached journey's end in Santiago.'

How long ago were they there? I wondered. Long before the new cathedral, of course, and the town would have been simpler, less grand, less crowded then.

'They gave their thanks, for that was my mother's only thought and she would not rest until she had done so, and then settled down to rest and recuperate before beginning the long journey home. But my father was worried, for walking so far had tired my mother greatly, and she did not seem to have the energy or, he feared, the heart, for the return. They had not gone far when she became unwell, and the sickness grew rapidly worse. My father sought out a place for them to stay until she was fit enough to continue; an easy task since the pilgrimage trail, as you have no doubt already noticed, has many simple hostels along its length. My father chose well, for the tavern-keeper and his family were kindly people and made the little family welcome. Time passed, however, and my mother still did not recover her strength, and so my father, very worried at his rapidly dwindling supply of coins, sought employment. There is always work for a man who knows his ale, and very soon he, his wife and the child settled down to what was obviously going to be a long stay. My mother grew strong again, and soon she too joined my father working in the tavern. A winter passed, and, although it grew very cold up there in the foothills of the coastal mountains, the air was clean and fresh, and, as spring came, my parents realized that for the first time in memory, my mother had passed through the cold months without her usual debilitating cough.'

'And so they decided to stay?' I said.

'They did,' he agreed. 'They worked hard and spent little, happy in their new life, and in time they were able to move into their own small inn, in a pretty village on the pilgrim route. It did not take long for word to spread that there was a certain hostel where the innkeeper brewed ale as good as in any English tavern, and my parents never lacked for guests in their taproom and in the overnight accommodation.'

'So when did you start to be taught by the Arabs?' I said. 'The north – Galicia – isn't under Moorish control, is it?'

'Not now, although it was for a short time,' he replied. 'But I wasn't taught in the north; or, I should say, I wasn't taught all that I know here.' He paused, assembling his thoughts, then said, 'There was always much contact with the Moorish lands to the south. Travellers would entertain us with their tales of life in what sounded like a different world. Fascinating, extraordinary ideas wove through the talk, and I used to listen avidly, my *why?* coming as persistently as when I was three years old.' He smiled. 'My parents, having little intellectual curiosity, would stare at me open-mouthed, as if wondering where my strange mind came from. My mother, I suspect, believed until the day she died that it was a gift from her pink angel.'

'So they taught you? These travellers who had come up from the south?'

'I learned from them, yes, but only sporadically and in random bits and pieces, and many of the visitors were far too interested in my father's good ale and my mother's excellent cooking to spare any time for an inquisitive child. My teacher in my early years was a wise and learned village man named Raymond, who saw my hunger for knowledge and was glad to feed it.' His expression softened. 'Raymond,' he repeated quietly. 'I owe him so much, for he taught me what he referred to as grammar, which embraces also logic and rhetoric.'

I wasn't entirely sure what any of those terms meant but I

didn't want to interrupt, so I just said, 'Mm,' knowingly, and nodded.

Gurdyman smiled to himself.

'Our priest came to hear of my lessons with Raymond,' he continued, 'and raised with him the possibility of my going south to al-Andalus, where the men of learning were far more advanced in virtually any area you might name than the sages of the Christian north.'

Once again I looked round to see if anyone's ears were flapping, and if somebody was about to take issue with this slur on the faith and the learning of the world of our fellow travellers. But nobody was paying us any mind.

'Between them Raymond and Father Rodrigo persuaded my parents that it would be a sin not to utilize what they referred to as my God-given talent for learning, and, since this accorded with my mother's private belief that I was as I was because of her pink angel, in the end, although it grieved them to contemplate losing me, they agreed. And so, as I approached my fifteenth year, I said farewell to them and, in the company of a local merchant who was a good friend of Raymond and Father Rodrigo, I set off south for Muslim lands.'

'And that's where we're going to—' I began excitedly.

But he held up his hand, silencing the tumble of words. 'For now, Lassair, we shall concentrate on our immediate destination, which is the village where my parents ran their inn.'

I didn't want to stay in a little village in Galicia. I'd been in the region for several days. It was very beautiful – wild and mountainous, with unexpected villages and hamlets appearing behind folds in the land where people cheered our little band of pilgrims on their way – and the air of constant elation engendered by the joyful company was exhilarating, but already I was hungry for something new: for the mystery of the south.

There was no point in saying so, however, so I meekly nodded and said, 'As you wish.'

He shot me a swift look, his mouth turning down in a wry smile, and I knew my attempt at mild obedience hadn't fooled him for a moment.

* * *

It took us the best part of four long days of walking to reach Gurdyman's parents' village, and I worked out from other people's talk that this was a brief distance in comparison with the full length of the pilgrim routes that traversed the mighty mass of Spain. And I noticed, with a sinking heart, that Gurdyman and I walked more slowly than almost everybody else, to judge from the steady stream of people overtaking us. I didn't yet know how far it was to our ultimate goal, but it was clear I would have to find us a more efficient and effort-saving means of transport.

Almost without exception, the pilgrims walked. But we were not pilgrims: we were merely sharing their well-worn and well-frequented trails. There was other traffic on the road, and I had observed several examples of what seemed to be a local type of cart. These were simply built and consisted of four sturdy wooden wheels on a pair of axles, over which was a very basic cube-shaped frame made from wooden planks. Some of the carts had a narrow bench along the front edge, a few were even provided with padded cushions for comfort. The little carts were drawn by mules or stout ponies and transported everything from piglets and bundles of hay to elderly people too old to walk.

I had money, I reminded myself. While Gurdyman rested and recovered in whatever hostel we put up at, I would go out and purchase a cart and a pony to pull it. Looking surreptitiously at Gurdyman, I realized it was the only option. He looked all in, and we'd only walked about fifty miles.

As, late in the afternoon, we approached the village, I knew exactly why Gurdyman's father had chosen to settle there. For sound commercial reasons, for one thing: the little settlement slowly coming into view on its slope above us was the first we had come to for quite a long time, and people all around us were greeting its appearance with sighs and cries of relief. It seemed to be divided into two halves, sitting either side of a stream that came flying down from the heights in a roar and a flurry of white spray. Behind me, I heard a man say cheerfully that he couldn't wait to bathe his sore feet in that lovely cold water. The buildings were low, built of stone and roofed in thatch; here and there tubs of bright flowers stood out in brilliant contrast.

The climb up to the village was hard, and we were all panting as we reached the first houses. There were hostels right there at the entrance to the village square, but I guessed that these would all be already full. Seeing me glance at them, Gurdyman shook his head and, taking my arm – he was far too breathless to speak – led me on into the village. We passed several more hostels, outside which men stood with expansive gestures of welcome, inviting us in, but still Gurdyman struggled on, now leaning heavily on his staff. He paused for a moment, staring round and frowning, then his expression cleared and he set off down a sloping track that led to the stream bisecting the village. And there, on a low rise above the rushing water, stood a stone building with a beautifully curving thatched roof, its double wooden doors standing open. There was a woman standing at a bench in a flag-floored room within, kneading dough with her sleeves rolled up over thick arms. She raised her eyebrows and Gurdyman nodded, muttering something. She beckoned us inside by jerking her head. She yelled out what sounded like someone's name, and presently a wiry old man appeared from further down the passage that disappeared into the dark depths of the hostel.

He looked at us expectantly, and Gurdyman said the words I already knew meant *We would like accommodation*, adding that we'd be staying for a couple of nights.

At first the man's face only registered the sort of dutiful politeness he probably displayed to every guest. But then I noticed he was staring intently at Gurdyman. He put up a hand and brushed it over his eyes. Then his expression changed. Opening his arms, he rushed forward. '*Juan!*' he cried, his voice high and as excited as a child's. 'Oh, *Juan*!'

He was sobbing.

Juan?

Then I understood. Gurdyman's elderly parents had been nicknamed Elizabeth and Zachary, in honour of the Baptist's parents. It was hardly surprising that they should have called their son John.

I shot a glance at my mentor. How on earth, then, had he acquired the name Gurdyman?

Gurdyman, returning the old man's hug, was speaking softly to him, and his sobs turned to laughter. Then he broke out in a swift stream of words that I couldn't follow, including me in his fulsome welcome. But then, seeing that I hadn't understood, he said in my own tongue, 'I am Iago. I am young when Juan is young, I work for his mama and his papa here in this very inn, they are like my own mama and papa and they teach me good talk.'

I smiled. 'Very good talk!' I assured him.

But he can barely have heard, for he had turned back to Gurdyman, shaking his head, his round black eyes full of wonder. 'You are here!' he whispered. 'I do not believe, yet here you are, and I know you, I see it is you, for you have the bright blue eyes of your mama, who I loved.' Then abruptly he burst into a storm of tears.

The woman had come to stand close by, and comprehension had slowly cleared the puzzlement on her face. Now, a comforting hand on the old man's thin shoulder, she looked at Gurdyman. 'You are welcome here,' she said cautiously. 'My grandfather teach me your speech,' she added. 'Many *peregrinos* come who speak like you, and it is – it is—'

'Good for business to be able to talk to them?' I suggested, and she gave me a swift grin.

'Yes.' Her smile faded. She looked again at Gurdyman, her expression uneasy. 'You do not – you cannot think to see your mama and papa?'

'No,' he said gravely, 'for they were advanced into old age when last I saw them, and that is many years ago.'

She nodded. 'You know they are dead, then, but perhaps not how?'

But he said – and his tone sent a chill of dread through me – 'I do know how.' He glanced at me, and I thought I saw an apology in his eyes. 'And that is why I am here.'

FIVE

In Cambridge, winter was closing in.

A cold wind blew off the fens in a blast that seemed to carry splinters of ice. Frost covered the ground in the mornings and at times snow flurries turned everything briefly to white. The townspeople stayed indoors, venturing out only when they couldn't avoid it. A self-imposed curfew fell at dusk, as men and women trudged home from their day's work and thankfully slammed their doors on the chill outside.

And Jack, religiously performing his ritual pass by Gurdyman's house each day, realized he had not seen either of the occupants for weeks. The house stood empty, it was now December and no weather for being abroad, and he had no idea where they were.

He had wondered early on whether Lassair had returned to her village. It was possible, but it didn't explain Gurdyman's absence, for why would he go there with her? Why would he condemn himself to the dull routine of a small village out in the middle of nowhere and banish himself to life in a tiny and overcrowded cottage when he had a fine house and a good life here in town? He might go for a few days if there were a good enough reason, but for all this time? Apart from the lack of privacy and the stultifying boredom for a man such as he, what of his studies? For Gurdyman to abandon his life's work for so long was about as likely as him abandoning breathing.

Jack had resisted going to Aelf Fen. If she was there and saw that he had gone to look for her, it would make her think that he—

That he what?

He really didn't know how to answer that question.

He chose a morning of bright sunshine when, for once, the wind had dropped. The air was still and very cold. He called in at the castle to inform his deputies that he would be absent for a few hours – he wouldn't be missed since they were hardly being kept busy just now – and stopped in the market square to buy food. There were few stalls open and they didn't seem to be doing much business, the stallholders standing miserable and cross, bundled up in so many layers that they looked like fat sheep.

Jack fetched his horse, and the animal looked at him out of wary eyes as if to say, 'You plan to ride out? In this chill?' Tacking him up, Jack muttered encouragingly to him, telling him they both needed exercise and a day out in the fens would do them good.

He set out for Aelf Fen. It came as no surprise that he remembered the way so faithfully, for all that he had only been there a few times. The roads and the tracks were deserted. The land appeared to be deeply asleep.

He neared the village, and saw trails of smoke from household hearths rising straight up into the blue sky. There was still no wind. Recalling the layout of the little settlement, he turned his horse to the right just before he passed the path to the lord's dwelling, leaving the main track and climbing up to the higher ground behind the village. In the middle of an open space there stood an ancient and solitary oak tree, and he headed for it. It was bare of leaves now but its broad trunk offered concealment. He slipped off the gelding's back, loosening the girths and looping the reins over a branch. They had stopped half a mile or so back for the horse to drink, and now he began to graze, pulling at the sparse grass with a rasping sound.

Jack stood beneath the tree gazing down on the village.

He stood watching for some time. He had no idea how long, but when he came back to himself he realized he was very cold. There had been comings and goings, but no sign of her.

The day wore on. He ate his food, which, combined with pacing up and down the high ground for a spell, warmed him up a little. He didn't think anybody had noticed him but concluded it didn't matter much if they did.

Presently he saw someone he recognized: the young pale-haired man who he knew to be Lassair's friend, and whom he had once seen in conversation with her; beneath the same tree where he now stood, in fact. He hurried down the long slope and caught up with the man just as he reached the huddle of dwellings.

'You know Lassair,' he said, panting. He raked through his memory for the young man's name, and after a moment said, 'You're Sibert.'

The pale-haired man eyed him suspiciously but did not speak.

'I'm a friend of hers. I live in Cambridge, and I know her and Gurdyman.'

'Oh,' said the young man.

'I mean her no harm,' Jack pressed on. 'But she's not at Gurdyman's house, and neither is he, and they've been away for weeks. I wondered if she – they – had come here?'

'No.' Just the one word, without elaboration.

'But this was her home,' Jack persisted. He could hear the note of desperation in his voice. 'Her parents and her kin live here, don't they?'

'Yes.'

The young man's eyes were fixed on him, and his unease was palpable. It was very plain that he was wary of strangers, especially those asking after people he cared about.

'I want to know if you—' Jack began.

The young man straightened his shoulders, gathered his courage and said belligerently, 'It's no use pressing me or threatening me' – Jack realized he was standing too close and that the young man was in fact afraid, and hastily he stepped back – 'because for one thing she's my friend, and I don't go sharing her private affairs with outsiders, and for another, I don't know where she is either, so I couldn't tell you even if I wanted to!'

'But you must have some idea!'

The young man had already turned away, and was running fast towards the houses. As Jack watched, he reached one that stood a little apart, to the rear of the group, opened the door and banged it shut behind him.

Jack wandered back to the oak tree, leaning against the warm flank of his gelding. The horse raised his head from his grazing and gave a soft whinny. 'I know,' Jack muttered, 'what are we doing here? Why don't I take us both home?'

But something was stopping him.

Presently he saw a figure approaching the village from the north. Tall, lean, wrapped in a thick cloak with a deep hood, the man – it was clearly a man – hurried up to the cottage which Jack knew belonged to Lassair's aunt. He opened the door and a slim woman appeared from the gloom to stand beside him. They spoke for some moments, kissed, then the man strode off again.

Jack drew back behind the vast trunk of the oak tree, nudging his horse sideways so that he too was hidden. Peering out, he watched to see which direction the man took.

For he was almost certain the man was Hrype. Married to Lassair's aunt, father of Lassair's friend Sibert, who Jack had just frightened away. He was a friend of Gurdyman's, and—

A friend of Gurdyman's.

Jack smiled. Then swiftly he tightened the girths, mounted up and, keeping back and out of sight, set off to follow Hrype.

Who just might, he thought with a lift of the heart, lead him to Gurdyman.

And to Lassair.

It was no easy task to trail a man who knew the fens as well as Hrype did. Sometimes he walked through thin veils of marsh mist and his tall figure became indistinct. Sometimes Jack lost sight of him altogether. He knew he must avoid drawing too close, for undoubtedly Hrype would be far more aware of somebody following him than most men. Once or twice Jack was forced to dismount and try to make out footprints, which ought to have been easy since they had been freshly made but in fact proved impossible. *Does the man fly?* Jack wondered grimly. *Does he hover above the ground like some fenland spirit?*

Just then, out in the wilds alone and anxious, he could almost have believed it.

He would have been forced to give up the pursuit had it not been for the fact that, after quite a long time, Hrype began to follow a path. Not much of a path, more a vague animal track, and one of four leading out of a patch of open ground. Jack told himself that it was the most likely one for Hrype to have taken. The alternatives were a path that seemed to double back on itself, another that plunged right down to the water and a third that was even less distinct and meandered off among the brambles and hazel. Jack memorized the location in case he had to return and try these others, then set off along the animal track. Very soon it became too difficult to negotiate on horseback, particularly for a man trying not to advertise his presence, so Jack dismounted, tied his gelding's reins to the branch of an alder beside the narrow path and proceeded on foot.

The undergrowth became steadily more dense, and now Jack was bending double to creep beneath the tangle of bare branches above his head. Brambles had sent out long, thick shoots that twined themselves into the mass, and their sharp prickles, dry and brown now, slashed the skin of his hands and wrists and sometimes his face. He forged on, impatiently thrusting the encroaching branches aside and widening the path. Then all at once the light grew stronger, the vegetation began to thin and, some ten yards ahead, the path, all but undetectable now, emerged onto a sort of beach, beyond which was the dark, still water of a fenland pool. He crept right up to the edge of the undergrowth, crouched down and peered out.

The figure in the dark cloak stood on the land's edge, looking out at a small island out in the water. He had thrown back his hood. He was standing in profile, the late sun shining on light hair shot through with silver. There was a look of Sibert about him, and Jack no longer had any doubt that this was indeed Hrype.

He watched, keeping very still.

After some time Hrype was no longer there.

Jack pressed his palms to his eyes and looked again. The little stretch of beach was empty. *But he was there*, Jack thought, *I was staring right at him!*

He burst out of the undergrowth and ran over to the water. He saw now that there was a narrow causeway leading from the shore to the island, submerged a foot or so beneath the surface. But the water was glassily still: nobody had disturbed it recently. Besides, if Hrype had gone across to the island, surely Jack would have heard the splashing?

He looked to his right, then to his left. No paths led off to the left except the animal track on which he had just been crouching, and besides, even Hrype couldn't have gone back past him without his noticing. But a path led off in the other direction: Jack went to look.

The ground was muddy here. Quite clearly he saw the marks of recent bootprints.

'So he doesn't fly,' Jack said softly aloud.

Memories had been stirring since he first saw this place and now the voice inside his head would not be hushed. He thrust his way back down the animal track, fetched his reluctant horse and urged him to follow, shoving back the encroaching undergrowth to clear the way. He tethered the gelding at the end of the beach and then went to stand looking out at the island, exactly where Hrype had stood.

And he listened once more to Lassair's distress as she told her terrible tale.

I took Rollo out into the wilds of the fens, and we hid in the house that belonged to Gurdyman's friend Mercure. Then Rollo said we should lure the man to us so that he could kill him. I led him back to where Rollo was waiting. The man sent a bolt into the roof, and this one was on fire. I had to get out and I couldn't move Rollo so I left him there. Then I realized the man wanted to kill me too so I got away, along the hidden ways across the water.

She seemed so close. He felt he could have put out his hand and touched her.

A house in the wilds of the fens. Yes, there ahead of him were the stubby remains of walls. *Away along the hidden ways across the water.* Yes, this place was an island, so escape would have to be over water. *This one was on fire.* Yes, there was abundant evidence of a huge fire.

This, then, was Mercure's island, and the place that Lassair had chosen when she – and the man she was with – had desperate need of a safe hiding place. Only in the end it hadn't been safe, for the plan had gone awry.

Without really thinking whether there was any point – for it was very apparent there was nobody on the island – Jack walked out onto the submerged causeway and waded across it.

He climbed up the low slope on the far side.

Slowly he studied the pattern of the stubs of posts and the stumps of walls. The dwelling had consisted of a single room and a short passage of some sort leading to a second room; perhaps a workroom. He wandered through the ruins. He looked up at the thick canopy of alder and willow that grew overhead. The trunks and branches of the trees circling the site of the dwelling were badly damaged.

In the middle of the floor of the larger room there were signs of an intense conflagration. There was a wide circle of black ground, and everything within it had been burned away to nothing. The devastating fire had gone on to destroy the covered way and the workroom; there was another area of total annihilation in the workroom, as if here some spectacularly inflammable materials had fuelled the blaze.

Jack thought about the story Lassair had told him. How, on Rollo's instructions, she had lured the man who was bent on killing him to the island where Rollo was concealed, well-armed and ready. But the killer had struck first, and Rollo had died in her arms. Then had come the second arrow, this one alight, and it had set fire to the building where Lassair sat with her dead lover. Had she tried to drag his body away from the flames? She had said she couldn't move him, so it sounded as if she had tried. He had a sudden flash of insight into how it must have felt to realize she had to leave his body where it lay and flee.

So then had she run along the covered way to the workroom? That had burned, too, although the fire had begun in the main room . . .

And then he thought he understood.

He could almost make her out. She was a faint shape, seen through smoke, and her eyes raced along the shelves and across the workbenches, searching, desperate to find what she was looking for before the flames spread and that room too had to be abandoned.

Now the image was clear and bright and he could see her

feeding the fire, sending her lover into the afterlife like a Viking on his burning longship.

Did she weep? Did she howl out loud with the agony of loss?

Yes, he thought. Of course she did.

He walked slowly back to the main room. There on the floor, in the epicentre of the blaze, Rollo had died, his body consumed by the furious flames that Lassair had encouraged until they were white-hot.

This great conflagration was Rollo's funeral pyre.

Jack circled the ruins one last time. He didn't think anyone had been there since the fire, for there was a darkness about the place and a sense of dread. It was hardly surprising, he reflected, for before the isolated island had burned it had been a magician's retreat. People tended to avoid places that were the haunts of wise men, especially when they had been destroyed in such spectacular fashion.

He knew that his journey here had been for nothing, for both his sense and his heart told him Lassair had not returned.

Just before he headed back across the water he stopped for a last look at the site of the pyre, standing over it with his head bowed. And, staring down at the blackened earth, he saw some small splinters of charred bone.

He shrank away in horror.

But almost immediately he found his courage. He went outside, hunting for an implement, and the best he could find was a narrow length of wood, about the width of his hand. He went back to the pyre and, a pace or two away from its centre, began to scrape the black earth away. As he dug deeper and through the hard crust on the surface, the soil became less resilient and quite soon he had formed a small pit. Then, on hands and knees, he raked to and fro across the patch of burned earth with his fingertips until he had found every fragment of bone. He put them carefully and reverently in the pit, then backfilled the hole and patted the earth smooth.

He went outside to the water's edge and washed his hands. Then, standing over the grave, he said a prayer for Rollo's soul.

He hoped very much that somewhere, some day, he and

Lassair would meet again. He thought she would like to know what he had done.

Hrype watched from the shelter of a hazel grove as the big lawman paced repeatedly across the island. He observed him standing quite still from time to time, clearly deep in thought and probably trying to work out the sequence of events. He saw him spot something on the ground, then set about digging. Then, head bowed, he said some words aloud. Hrype was too far away to make them out but he knew what they were.

He will leave now, Hrype thought. He would wait, he decided, until the man was on his way.

He had realized that someone was on his trail about halfway between Aelf Fen and Mercure's island. He had a fair idea who it was and, when he managed to have a proper look, knew he had guessed right.

Jack Chevestrier.

And he was looking for Lassair and Gurdyman.

Good, Hrype thought as Jack came back across the submerged causeway, mounted up and set off along the narrow trail. He would not find them anywhere hereabouts, for they were far away. But the thought of someone else being concerned was heartening. The quiet voice deep inside Hrype told him that Jack was an ally worth having.

But Jack's concern surely could not stem from the same place as his own, for Hrype's fear for Lassair stemmed from a source that he didn't believe anyone else shared; one that disturbed him more with each passing day of her absence.

He hoped he was wrong. He hoped he had misjudged his old friend, but he couldn't convince himself.

And if he was right, then Gurdyman was not only showing an irresponsible lack of care for his own safety.

He was taking Lassair into the same peril.

SIX

It became clear to the three of us standing with Gurdyman in the entrance to the tavern that he was swaying with exhaustion. Judging by his expression, the talk of his parents' death had affected him deeply. He knew, of course, that they were dead – how could they not be? – but it was as if being back here in the place where they had gone about their daily lives had belatedly sparked off his grief.

The woman muttered something to the old man, who nodded and took Gurdyman by the arm, leading him away down a low, dark passage. I followed, carrying our bags, and we emerged into what was clearly the communal sleeping room. There were some rudimentary beds, some larger wooden frames on which there were a number of thin straw mattresses, and more straw heaped at the side of the large room. There was nobody there. Iago led Gurdyman over to a little bed in the corner furthest from the door and fetched a couple of blankets. Gurdyman protested, but it was only a token resistance. Even as I stood there watching, he lay down with a long sigh, pulled up the blankets and closed his eyes.

Iago walked on light feet to join me in the doorway. We waited, and presently heard the sound of Gurdyman's soft snores. Iago smiled. 'Sleep!' he whispered.

'Yes, he's sleeping,' I agreed.

'He old man now,' Iago went on, lowering his voice still further as if he didn't want Gurdyman to hear and be hurt. 'Long journey, old man, not good.' He frowned at me as if somehow it was my fault that Gurdyman had worn himself out.

'It was all his idea to come here!' I protested.

But Iago put a hand on my arm. 'To honour Mama and Papa, yes, I understand,' he muttered. He gave me a gap-toothed but kindly smile. We turned away from the sleeping room and went back to the woman. She raised her eyebrows in query and Iago spoke briefly, presumably telling her Gurdyman was asleep. She looked at me. 'I am Maria,' she said.

'Lassair,' I replied. I had to repeat my name several times before they had it, and even then the pronunciation was one I'd never heard before.

'I am going to explore,' I said. 'Look round the village.'

They both nodded. 'But not long,' Maria said. 'Food serve soon.'

I had already smelt wafts of appetizing smells coming from somewhere at the rear of the inn, and the thought of a good, hot meal was almost enough to make me stay right there and make sure I had a place at the supper table. As if Maria read my mind, she said with a smile, 'There is plenty.'

Just then a group of three pilgrims arrived at the door and she turned her attention to their needs.

The village was even more attractive in the fading light. Lamps were lit in windows, people began to emerge to discuss the day's events with their friends and neighbours, and from everywhere came the smell of cooking. I returned to the village square and went across it towards the road by which we had arrived, finding a rock to perch on to observe the last few pilgrims still toiling up the slope. With dismay, I noticed that none of them was as old as Gurdyman.

Then, at the rear of a trio of men in monks' habits, I saw a pair of the little carts I had observed earlier. One was carrying supplies: a couple of barrels, a basket of apples, another which, by the smell, held fish. But the other one was driven by a middle-aged man and behind him sat a very old woman.

I envisaged myself at the reins and Gurdyman seated in the body of the cart. I knew I had to find one for us.

I followed the second cart into the village and, when it drew to a stop outside one of the hostels, tried to ask the man if it was his, where he had acquired it, if I could buy one. But I couldn't make him understand and in the end, appreciating he was impatient to see to the old woman – now hollering at him and clearly increasingly irritated by the delay – I muttered an apology and hurried away.

I searched the streets around the square, looking for inn yards with stabling, or for anywhere else that I could spot similar carts. There were plenty of them in evidence, but I was hampered by not being able to explain what I wanted. I gave up and returned to the inn.

Iago was standing outside, clearly looking out for me. Berating myself for not having thought to ask him first, I hurried up to him and said, 'Please, can you help me? I need to find one of those little carts, because I don't think Gurd— er, Juan, will be able to walk all the way.'

He began nodding even as I spoke. 'It is what we say, Maria and me!' he exclaimed. 'I will seek.' He thumped himself on his narrow chest. 'I will find.'

'I have money.' I reached inside the purse at my belt and took out a handful of coins, which I held out to him.

With a sharp frown he closed his hand around mine, his eyes darting from side to side. 'Not show!' he hissed. 'Many people, not all good!'

He was right, and in the urgency of my need I had forgotten the law of travellers, which is not to show conspicuous wealth. 'Sorry,' I muttered. 'But I can pay for a cart and a good horse. Yes? It is enough?'

'Yes!' His shocked expression suggested it was more than enough, and that he was wondering how on earth I came to have so much money. I wondered what he would say if he knew about the remainder of my coins, not to mention the gold, hidden away in the belt beneath my clothes.

Thank you, Rollo, I said silently.

Iago ushered me inside the inn, where he indicated my hand, still clenched on the silver, and made a gesture for me to show him again. I did so. He took several of the coins, then hurried away.

I suppressed the unkind thought that it would be the last I would see of him or my money.

Gurdyman was revived by his sleep, and he and I joined the company for the evening meal. The long table was only about a third full, and Maria explained that the inn was much busier during the spring and summer. With a shake of the head she said, as so many people kept saying, that it was late in the year to be on the roads.

And, yet again, I wondered why Gurdyman had chosen this moment to come.

We sat over a last mug of ale with Maria and Iago, and in the main, out of courtesy to me, they spoke my language. But Maria kept lapsing into her own, and already I was picking up words and phrases. I was thinking about some of these, trying to commit them to memory, when I noticed that the conversation had turned to the past. Iago was laughing, clearly repeating some cheerful anecdote about Gurdyman's father, for I kept hearing the word *papa*. Maria joined in – she too seemed to have known Gurdyman's parents personally – and I understood enough to realize that the two of them had been much-loved members of the community.

Iago was in full flow now, talking very rapidly in a mixture of tongues of the days when Gurdyman's parents first came to the village, of how they set up in their own hostel – 'Yes, yes, this place where we now are!' – and of his and Gurdyman's youthful friendship. 'But he was smart' – Iago leaned across as if to confide in me, tapping Gurdyman's hand as he did so – 'he have lessons with clever man, he learn many things, soon he too fine to work with other boys.' Was there the shadow of an old resentment there? I wasn't sure. 'And then' – Iago gave a dramatic sigh – 'he go away, to the south and the wise Moorish men, for here not *large* enough for him any more.'

A silence fell, and not a very comfortable one. I waited for Gurdyman to break it; to say modestly, perhaps, that he had been young, arrogant and eager to learn, or even that he had been persuaded by those older and wiser than himself that he had no choice but to utilize his God-given intellect. But he didn't.

In the end it was Maria who spoke. She stood up, gathering the empty mugs and the ale jug, and said, 'Ah, we all follow our own path, and it is not easy when we are young to see where it may lead.'

Gurdyman too stood up, muttering something about seeking his bed, and I followed. Like him, I too had earlier claimed a bed in a far corner of the communal dormitory, and I was glad now that I had done so, for almost everyone who had eaten with us had already turned in and the only spaces remaining free were on the big, shared beds.

At the door I turned back to wish Iago and Maria a final good night. Maria nodded in reply, but Iago didn't appear to see.

He was staring at Gurdyman's retreating back, and the expression on his lean face was very different from the delighted smile he had shown when first he set eyes on us.

I didn't like this new expression at all.

My bed was adequately comfortable and I was glad I had selected a place by one of the few small windows, for the other bodies sleeping nearby had evidently not seen a wash cloth or clean clothes for some time. The cool little breeze blowing across my face was very welcome, and I had enough covers not to feel its chill.

For it was a cold night: I thought as I woke briefly in the deepest of the darkness that I could smell snow in the air.

But we were high in the foothills of the coastal mountains here, I tried to reassure myself. When we left to go on with our journey, whenever that may be – I resolved to extract some details of our itinerary from Gurdyman as soon as he was awake – our general direction would be south, and down onto the lowlands.

Wouldn't it?

I realized with a prickle of alarm that I didn't really know.

I slept again, warm and comfortable, and the solidity of the granite walls around me made me feel safe.

But then, as the first silvery signs of dawn were beginning to lighten the sky, something woke me. For some reason I felt afraid, and all at once the inn was no longer the secure refuge it had been. What had disturbed me? One of the other occupants of the room stirring in their sleep? Getting up, perhaps, to use the latrine outside in the back yard? I glanced around, but could spot no empty spaces among the occupied beds. Over in the far corner I made out the hump of Gurdyman, wrapped up in his blankets and unmoving.

What, then?

I lay very still and strained my ears. And after a moment I heard a very clear, quiet whisper that appeared to come from just outside the window. Just the one word. *Brujo*. Then, even more softly, the voice muttered something else. I couldn't quite make it out but it sounded like *llama azul*.

I didn't know what *brujo* meant but all the same it frightened me. Perhaps it was the tone in which the word was uttered, which sounded like a long out-breath, so soft that it might have been designed for my ears alone. But that made no sense since I didn't understand the message.

It was a warning. I didn't know how I knew that, but I was quite certain.

It was a relief when the steady increase in the sounds around me suggested the morning's work had begun. People in the dormitory were stirring, some already out of bed and packing away their belongings. Gurdyman was sitting on his little bed, his blankets neatly folded. He was putting on his boots.

The smell of warm bread came sneaking along the passage, and as if this had been the signal, almost everyone in the dormitory hurried off to find its source. Gurdyman joined the rush, looking at me with his eyebrows raised as if to invite me to join him, and I did so. I wasn't hungry, however: I hadn't slept again after that sinister warning whisper, and the fear that I couldn't seem to quell had robbed me of my appetite.

After breakfast Gurdyman announced we were going out. Angry with myself for my continuing meek acceptance, I vowed to demand some sort of explanation from him. He led the way further up the hillside to where a church stood on a patch of flat ground overlooking the valley below, and we went inside. I wondered if he was going to pray, and I stepped back to allow him a moment to himself. But he made no move towards the altar, merely standing still and looking about him. Then he turned and went outside again.

'You remember it all?' I asked as we wandered round the humps and mounds of graves circling the church.

'Oh, yes,' he replied.

Presently he spotted whatever it was he had been looking for, and I followed him to a section of the burial ground where there were perhaps ten or a dozen graves, perhaps more, close together. They must have been quite old, for their outlines were indistinct.

Gurdyman stood in silence, staring down.

'Are your parents buried here?' I asked gently.

He turned to me with a slight start, as if he had forgotten I was beside him. 'I believe so,' he replied. 'I asked Iago, and this seems to be the place he described.'

'There are quite a lot of graves all together,' I observed. 'Did your parents die in some sort of epidemic?'

He shook his head. 'No, not that.' He gave a very deep sigh, as if contemplating the manner of their death troubled him profoundly.

Perhaps I should have backed away and left him to his thoughts. Perhaps I should for once have restrained my curiosity and, out of respect, asked him no more. But I was angry that morning. He had brought me all this way with barely a word of explanation. We had a very long way to go and I still had no clear idea of where we were going and why. It was cold and there was snow up above us in the high mountains; as people would keep telling us, it was the wrong time of year for travelling. And, as if all that wasn't enough, very early this morning I had been badly scared by a sinister whisper right outside the window beneath which I slept.

So I said, with rather more asperity than was appropriate, 'So how did they die, Gurdyman? And why did these other people die with them?'

I thought he wasn't going to answer and I gathered my courage to repeat the question. But then he sighed again, and said very quietly, 'There was a fire.'

'A fire?'

'In the inn. My parents' inn. There used to be a room off the yard where people would gather in the evenings. Travellers would exchange their stories and sometimes there would be singing. The inn was famous for these gatherings, almost as much as for the quality of my father's ale, and many of the villagers would look in when there was a good crowd. There was no harm in it!' he added with sudden passion. 'Perhaps a little too much ale would be drunk, but my father brewed a fine drop and it was too tempting to deny. Besides, those enjoying the company and the ale were for the most part pilgrims, and the remainder were hard-working locals, and did they not have a right to snatch a little pleasure at the end of an exhausting day?'

I realized he didn't expect me to answer.

'The fire took hold swiftly,' he said softly. 'It's said the flames were bright blue, a shade of such unlikely brilliance that people whispered of supernatural origins.' He paused, and I could see that reviving the memories was very painful. 'There was no hope for those trapped inside,' he went on softly, 'for the doorway was narrow and swiftly blocked by people pushing to get out.'

I touched his arm. 'I believe the smoke and the fumes very quickly render people unconscious,' I said. 'Where a fire blazes fiercely, it is the inability to draw breath that kills.'

He turned to me, tears in his bright eyes. 'It is what I have been telling myself,' he said. 'I pray you are right.'

I hesitated, for what I wanted to ask him now was very delicate. 'This is – have you not returned before? Did you not . . .' But I couldn't find the words.

'Didn't I come hurrying to the village when news of their deaths, and the manner of them, reached me?' he supplied. 'No, Lassair. I did not.'

The silence became painful and I forced myself to break it. 'Why not?'

After what seemed an age, he whispered, 'Because I was afraid.'

Afraid! I almost laughed. Gurdyman afraid? But he was powerful, he knew spells and defensive incantations, he—

But he *was* afraid. I could see it now as I stared at him, and hadn't I been sensing it all these weeks?

I said, 'Gurdyman, what does *brujo* mean?'

He spun round so sharply, his face full of fury, that I thought he was going to strike me. 'Where did you hear that word?' he hissed. '*Tell me!*' He grabbed my arm, shaking me.

Angry in my turn, I pushed his hand away. '*Gurdyman!*' I cried. 'It's me, Lassair! Let go of my arm! You forget yourself.'

He muttered an apology, dropping my arm, but then repeated, 'Where? Who said it?'

'Somebody whispered it outside the dormitory window around dawn,' I replied coldly.

He had gone white.

I felt very scared. 'Gurdyman?' I whispered.

He let out a long breath. '*Brujo* means magician,' he said shortly.

'But why should someone speak the word just there?' I asked. But then I thought I knew.

He was watching me closely, and I think he saw understanding dawn. 'Go on,' he commanded. 'Answer your own question.'

'Because somebody knew you were within,' I whispered. 'And that somebody knows what you are.'

He straightened, staring down the hillside to the village. 'Only one person, let us hope, and so we have a little time. We must make ready to leave, child, and be away as swiftly as we can.'

'But we can't, not yet, I've asked Iago to—' I stopped. I hadn't told Gurdyman about trying to acquire a cart.

'To what?' he demanded. We were already striding away from the church.

He'll have to know very soon, I thought. So I told him.

To my relief he chuckled. 'So you do not think me capable of walking all the way?'

My anger resurfaced. 'No,' I said bluntly, 'although you still haven't told me how far we must go. But on the way here we were slower than the slowest of our companions. It's late in the year now and it's getting cold. Wherever we're bound, we should make the best speed and make sure we are safely settled in before the winter really bites.'

He said, 'How do you propose to pay for this horse and cart?'

'I have money.' I lifted my chin, proud to be able to make the claim, warmed once more by the thought that I was in this happy situation because Rollo had endowed me with his wealth. But hard on the heels of that came the reminder that he was dead, and my momentary pleasure vanished.

Gurdyman understood. He put an arm around my shoulders and said, 'It is a high price to pay. You would say, no doubt, like all those who lose people they love, that you would far rather have the person than the wealth.'

He gave me a moment to dry my eyes, then went on. 'Assuming that Iago has fulfilled his mission, we should purchase all the provisions that we can.' He added something else, and it sounded like *Before word goes round the whole village.* But when I asked him to repeat it, he shook his head.

Iago had acquired a short-legged, stout-bodied pony and a cart that was exactly the same in size and form as those I had been noticing. It was about a man's height in length, a little less in breadth, and the planks of its base rested on a frame attached to which were four spoked wooden wheels. The space was enclosed by raised sides and front formed from crudely-hewn planks to roughly shoulder height for someone sitting in the cart, and it was open at the back. Set sideways across the plank at the front there was a sack stuffed with straw for the comfort of whoever held the reins.

As we approached I saw that our bags were already stowed on the cart. In addition there were three or four thick blankets and a couple of pillows, a bulging bag of provisions and a small barrel of either ale or water.

Gurdyman stared levelly at Iago. 'You want us gone.'

Iago protested, but it was half-hearted. Then Maria came out to join him. 'I am sorry,' she said, 'but people are talking. They know you are here. It is bad for business,' she added bluntly.

'I have made no secret of my presence,' Gurdyman said mildly.

'Then perhaps you should have!' Maria hissed back. Quickly recovering herself, she turned to me, holding out some coins. 'You gave Iago too much money,' she said, and her tone was chilly. 'He has paid for the pony and cart and I have taken the cost of the provisions and for your accommodation last night. You pay full rate because we all know you are not here as pilgrims,' she added, although neither Gurdyman nor I had protested.

'Thank you.' I put the coins away in my purse.

My failure to be stung to a sharp reply seemed to mollify her. Coming to stand close to me, she muttered, 'You must understand, we have our livelihood to consider. We need our guests and we cannot afford to become—' She paused as if searching for the right word. 'Unpopular,' she said, but I didn't believe it was what she had originally intended: *outcasts* had leapt into my own mind, although I wasn't quite sure why.

'I do understand,' I replied. 'I am sorry we have inconvenienced you.'

Then, before she could answer, I helped Gurdyman up onto the cart, sat myself on the straw-filled sack and, clicking my tongue to the pony, set off along the narrow street.

I tried to control my fear but I couldn't. Thankfully there were not many people about, but the few that there were seemed hostile. Somebody hissed. There were mutterings, and I saw one woman make the universal sign against the evil eye. We emerged into the square, crossed it and, on a wider road now that went steadily downhill, I slapped the reins on the pony's backside and he increased his pace to a trot.

Now the fear was racing through me, for ahead of us four men stood right across our path. I hesitated, unsure what to do, and from behind me Gurdyman shouted, '*Go on!*' So I slapped the reins again, yelled to the pony and, faster now, drove straight at the quartet blocking the way. Perhaps they thought I would pull up, and when I didn't – when, far from doing so, instead I urged the pony on – their eyes widened and one by one they leapt off the track. As we flew between them, two on each side, there were cries of '*Brujo! BRUJO!*'

But we were past. We were, I hoped, safe.

I risked a glance back over my shoulder, and saw two of the men shaking raised fists at us. One of the others, just like the woman in the village, was making the sign. I kept the pony at the canter, for the slope was still to our advantage, and only when we were down in the valley and the track was levelling out did I slow him down.

I tried to slow my breathing, tried to calm myself and steady my terrified heartbeat. The pony decreased his pace from a trot to a walk. We were ambling along, both Gurdyman and I still silent from shock, when I heard him chuckle.

'For the life of me, Gurdyman, I can't see that it is anything to laugh at!' I snapped.

'You are quite right, child, and I apologize,' he replied. But he chuckled again. 'Their faces!' Then, in a far more sombre tone, 'You did well, Lassair. You got us away, and you have my gratitude.'

He said no more.

All things considered, it did not seem the right time to demand answers to all my questions, and we went on our way in silence.

SEVEN

The cart and the sturdy, calm-natured pony were like a gift from heaven. Gurdyman made himself comfortable, padded with blankets and with a pillow behind his back, and, after our dramatic exit from the village, I found that driving the little conveyance on reasonably good roads was quite straightforward. The best of it, however, was that whereas on foot we had been the laggards, now we overtook all other traffic save people mounted on good horses.

To begin with we were on one of the main pilgrimage routes across northern Spain. It was obviously very well-used, and there were hostels and little stalls selling food and drink at regular intervals. I couldn't help noticing, however, that many of the hostels seemed dead. In places, too, there were signs of destruction, as if there had been fierce fighting in the area. If that was so – and I didn't dare ask Gurdyman – then the deteriorating weather must have temporarily put a stop to it and sent the soldiers home. Along with the snow now visible on the mountaintops to our north, these were further unwelcome reminders that we were now into winter.

During the four days it took us to reach the next waymarker in this journey into the unknown – unknown to me, anyway – the temperature rose a little, and in the main we travelled in sunshine. But the days were short now, and neither Gurdyman nor I had any wish to go on after dark.

We reached a place that Gurdyman said was called Astorga, where there was a bifurcation of two major routes. The one we had been on continued eastwards; the second branched off to the south.

'This is the Via de la Plata,' Gurdyman said as we turned towards the noon sun. 'It is an ancient road that leads to the great cities of the south: to Seville, Granada, Cordoba, and, beyond them, to the sea.'

There was a dream-like note in his voice. 'You have been this way before,' I said.

'I have. I told you, child, I went into Moorish Spain and I lived there for . . . oh, for many years.'

'You saw those cities?'

'I did. I remember Granada in the early morning, with the long rays of the rising sun turning the stones to orange, to ochre, to gold. It became the capital of the region and accordingly the vizier renovated the old fortress, making structures of such beauty that you could not believe they were made of stone.'

Much as I had wanted Gurdyman to draw back the veil and begin to tell me more about his past, there were matters I was far more eager to have him explain. I had secretly been hoping that this day, when we left the west–east road and turned south, he would at last be open to questions about what had happened back in his parents' village. In truth, he ought to have told me straight away, as soon as we were out of danger. But he had not so much as mentioned what had happened, and I had felt uneasy about pushing him. I had gone on reassuring myself that he would tell me in his own good time, once we were on the next phase of our journey.

But now here he was telling me about the travels of his youth, so it looked as if I was going to have to prompt him.

'That all sounds very beautiful, Gurdyman,' I said in my firmest voice, 'but before you go on, I'd like you to explain why back in the village they called you *brujo*, why being named a magician when that's what you are should cause you such fear, and why we had to run away.'

There was a short silence, as if he was framing the words with which to answer me. But then he said, 'Moorish Spain was a land to fall in love with, and that is what I did.'

And I realized with dismay and a grim sense of foreboding that either he had not heard or he was choosing to ignore me. I turned round and looked at him. His eyes were staring into the distance, right *through* me, and it seemed he couldn't see me, which supported the alarming idea that he wasn't hearing me either.

My anxiety increased.

I wondered what to do. There were other people on the road, although no longer that many. Since we had turned off the west–east road we had passed a couple of quite large groups and been overtaken by a few horsemen. Those we met were all going south: no pilgrims were risking the roads to Santiago now. There were hostels on this track but they did not crop up with nearly the frequency that they had done on the previous roads we had travelled. If Gurdyman became unwell, I thought with a shiver, it was likely I would be caring for him by myself.

You're a healer, I reminded myself. *You'll know what to do.*

I gave him my full attention, listened to him as he continued to describe the beauties of the places he had known in his youth. To judge by the strength of his voice and the sense of his delight in what he was relating, there wasn't much wrong with him at this moment.

If he wasn't going to provide the answers I so badly wanted, I thought, I may as well listen to what he *was* revealing. So, giving myself up to his tale, I did.

'I could not believe the extent of the Moorish scholars' knowledge, or the limitlessness of their curiosity and their imagination,' he was saying now. 'They were the heirs to ancient knowledge, for they knew the lands of the Greeks and the Persians, and their wise men had translated the old texts into their own language. It was as if there had been a series of locked boxes full of what the people of earlier civilizations had discovered, and the Muslim sages prised them open and let it all out, looking further, deeper, absorbing what had already become known and pushing it ever onwards. And where they were faced with the limits of their own eyes, they invented instruments to help them. The astrolabe, for example, enabled them to make a map of the skies, and they named the stars in their own beautiful tongue: Aldebaran, Betelgeuse, Deneb, Altair, Sirius.'

A map of the skies. A wonder indeed, I thought.

'In the field of medicine, too, they were intelligent practitioners and far-seeing innovators, writing books on their work for the benefit of those who would learn from them, and developing precise and clever instruments to aid them in the art of surgery. And medical texts were not all they wrote, for literacy is widespread among the Moors and they have collections of manuscripts in their major cities which everyone may read.'

He was painting a new world for me. I could hardly believe what he was describing.

'Oh, but they were heady times for a young man born in the cold, unlearned north!' Gurdyman exclaimed. 'I went from the most basic of shelters which, while it was the best that my parents could contrive with limited funds and by no means any worse than what everyone else had, nevertheless was cramped, dark and not very clean. What a revelation it was to live in a southern house! Men and women there are clean and sweet-smelling, their dwellings are cool, despite the great heat, and sparsely furnished with objects that are pleasing to the eye. People's manners are elegant, they prize learning and they strive to dispel ignorance and superstition. They—'

But, stung by his slur on his childhood home and the parents who had done their best for him, I interrupted. 'Did you never spare a backward glance for your ignorant, superstitious, not very clean parents?' I demanded.

He didn't say anything for quite some time. Then, in a very different tone, he said, 'I wish I could say that I did. But it would be a lie.'

I was about to say something but he went on, 'And I did not intend my description of my former life with them to sound so critical. They worked hard, and by the standards of their own people, they did well. Haven't I told you many times of my father's skill at brewing ale? That was what people came for, and it didn't matter in the least if the beds had vermin and the floors were always muddy, for that was what they were used to.'

'But you didn't go back.'

'No.'

I was realizing very quickly how little I really knew of his past.

For some reason it gave me a shiver of alarm.

Quickly, trying to banish my apprehension, I said, 'Did you go to see them on your way from the south back to England?'

'Back to . . . Oh, I see. You imagine, I suppose, that I went straight from the City of— straight from Moorish Spain to Cambridge?'

'Yes,' I replied. 'I don't believe you have ever suggested otherwise.'

'Did I not?' He sounded distant, as if in his mind he was far away. 'I thought I had told you something of my travels, but perhaps I didn't. But I did not go straight from the one home to the other, child. I became a wanderer, and my journey extended for many years and thousands of miles.'

'But did it include a visit to your parents?' I repeated with irritated impatience.

He grew irritated in his turn. 'Once. I went back once.'

And something in his voice told me not to pursue it.

It was hard to keep track of the days, but I think we had been travelling south for about a week when I first became seriously worried about Gurdyman. He was pale, at times he struggled for breath and occasionally his lips had a blueish tinge. In happier times he had occasionally given up his place on the cart to walk for a few miles, sometimes to let somebody whose need was greater have a ride – a very old man with a sore hip, a young woman with a baby at the breast – and sometimes merely to stretch his legs. Now, I reflected as I shot yet another anxious look at him, there would have been no possibility of that, even had there been people around in need of respite from the endless miles of the road.

For we were on our own.

We had long ago left the last town behind us. It had been a poor sort of place, or perhaps it was merely that it was showing us its winter face; whichever was true, the result was the same, and we'd had a struggle to find supplies. I had recently realized, with a sinking of the heart, that we had barely enough for a couple of days.

We had neither passed nor been passed by anybody for a long time. We hadn't come across a hostel that was open for business since the day after we had left the last town, and we faced the dismal prospect of a third night spent in the cart. Not that it was too bad, for we had cloaks, blankets and pillows, and while the food lasted we would not starve. I was eking it out now, and it seemed a long time since either of us had eaten our fill. I could, or so I hoped, replenish our water from streams. If there were any.

I was worried about the pony, however. While we were still in the northern regions there was grass and other vegetation, and I had discovered a sack of feed tucked away beneath the cart. Water hadn't been a problem either, for we had come across plenty of streams and even a river or two. Now the land was changing, and the landscape was far less verdant. Moreover, the terrain through which we now passed had clearly suffered from a hot summer and it was arid and inhospitable.

We were travelling across a plateau: dry, underpopulated and high. Presently I began to make out rising ground ahead and to the left; to the south-east of us, I calculated. As we drew steadily nearer, I saw heights climbing in the distance and peaks topped with white.

And, behind me in the cart, for all that he had not exerted himself at all since he clambered aboard after our last brief stop, Gurdyman was panting.

The air, I realized with a frisson of alarm, was getting thinner.

I made up my mind that we would stop in good time that evening. I would make a fire – *with what?* I wondered – and try to serve up something hot and appetizing instead of the dried meat and crusts of old bread that we had been subsisting on. Then I would prepare a remedy to restore Gurdyman. As we went on, I pictured the contents of my satchel and wondered what would be best.

The fire was a total failure. Our evening meal was the same as it had been for far too many days, and we ate the last of the bread.

Without the fire I could not heat water to infuse herbs. I had a small jar containing a digitalis preparation, and I gave Gurdyman a few drops in half a mug of cold water. He grunted his appreciation, and I thought a little colour came back into his deathly pale face.

He pointed at his own pack and I nodded, thinking he wanted me to take out his cloak and blanket and help him settle down for sleep. But he shook his head and pointed again, waggling his hand up and down for emphasis. 'Reach inside the pocket at the side,' he gasped.

I did as he told me. My hand closed on a little glass bottle, and my heart gave a lurch. For it was one of my aunt Edild's, and I knew it by touch even before I brought it out into the fading light. I wondered how many times I had handled it, or one just like it; washed it, refilled it, checked it as I counted supplies on her neatly arranged shelves. Edild! An image of her filled my mind and for a moment the wave of homesickness and longing that rose up in me was almost unbearable.

You have to bear it, a voice said clearly in my head.

To distract myself from my misery I wondered how Gurdyman came to have one of my aunt's remedies in his possession, and instantly I thought, Hrype must have given it to him. Hrype, presumably, had described his old friend's symptoms to his wife, and Edild had diagnosed the problem from afar and provided help. I took the stopper out of the little bottle and sniffed, then poured the smallest drop into my palm.

Belladonna.

Gurdyman had been watching me and now he held out his hand. I poured water into his mug and put in two drops, but he shook his head and mouthed, 'More.'

I didn't know how much it was safe to give him. I shook in one more drop, then firmly put back the stopper and returned the bottle to its pocket in his bag.

He sat for a while staring out into the darkness. Then, with a sigh, he lay down and soon he was asleep.

I was far from sleep, for I was far too worried. About him, about the food supplies, about the pony, about being all alone with a sick man in an alien land with no concept of where we were heading and no idea of how to get there even if I did. I was totally dependent upon Gurdyman, and now he was failing.

What in the dear Lord's name would I do if he died?

Go back, I answered myself. *You may not know the way forward, but it would be easy enough to retrace your steps and return the way you have come.*

It was reassuring.

But what about food?

If he dies, you will no longer have to share what remains.

The reply came, I think, from somewhere outside myself. It was ruthless, but it was sound.

I was wide awake.

I kept watch over the lonely, empty lands all around, Presently the moon rose.

I wondered if I should turn round straight away, as soon as it was light. Was it not far too risky to go on with Gurdyman as he was?

An image floated into my mind. Light striking black water, setting off flashes of green and gold in its mysterious depths.

And then, cursing myself for not thinking of it before even as my spirits soared, I knew what to do. I reached deep down into the depths of my satchel and took out a leather-enclosed shape. Carefully, trying not to jolt the cart, I climbed down and walked a few paces away. I sat down cross-legged, spread my skirts on the hard-baked ground and took the object out of its bag, folding back the soft protective layer of sheep's wool.

Then, holding it in my hands, I stared down deep inside the shining stone.

As so often happens, at first there was nothing to see. I waited, for I had learned to be patient. Then all at once it was as if the moon had grown brighter, so that now I saw its reflection clearly in the blackness of the stone. And I saw that it wasn't the light of the moon but the stone's own interior flame. As if it felt my attention, the shining stone had awoken and was joining its energy with mine.

I saw a series of swift images. I saw buildings whose architecture was alien. I saw men with brown faces under clean white headdresses, and women in graceful robes and veils that covered them and hid them from view. I saw a long road, stretching out behind me and forging on ahead. I looked along the road ahead, and saw that it began to climb. Up, up, becoming narrow and twisting, winding its way up into the mountains.

And then I thought I saw, just for a heartbeat, a city made of creamy-white, shining softly in the moonlight. A voice seemed to say, *Hush! Do not speak of it, for its location is secret and it remains ever hidden.*

But I could not speak of it even if I wanted to, for there was nobody to tell.

I stared down into the stone, my eyes searching, but the picture had gone. I thought I might have imagined it; that it had been born of my extreme need.

There was something still visible in the shining stone, however, and I narrowed my eyes to focus upon it. It looked like an afterglow of some sort, and I realized it was just a vague round shape, its edges undulating slightly. It resembled a large and very beautiful pearl.

And, once again, I heard that deep hum of summertime insects and, faintly, the musical, resonating chime of metal on stone.

I sat with the shining stone in my hands for some time, deriving profound comfort simply from touching it. After a while I wrapped it up and put it back in its leather bag. I stood up, walking a few paces to and fro to get the stiffness out of my legs.

It seemed to me that the stone had been encouraging me to go on.

Should I comply?

I trusted it. It was my ally, and I knew it would not lead me astray.

But was it thinking only of what was good for me? Had it borne in mind the ailing Gurdyman?

I stood indecisive.

I knew I must make up my mind before I returned to the cart, for I would not sleep until I knew what we would be doing in the morning. After quite a lot more pacing, I reached a decision. We would go on for at least one more day. There was enough belladonna in my aunt's bottle to last a while, and if it had improved Gurdyman's condition as much as I hoped it would, then for sure he wouldn't hear of us turning back. But I would insist – absolutely insist, before even I hitched the pony to the cart and set off tomorrow – that he tell me where we were going and how to get there.

With the resolution firm in my mind, I settled down in the cart in my blanket, shawl and cloak, and was very soon drifting into sleep.

Next day as we set off again, the air felt different.

The weather had turned colder.

The pony was stumbling, and for long stretches I got down from the cart and walked beside him, a hand on his bridle, speaking softly to him. I was rationing out food with an even meaner hand now, and our noon meal was disappointingly meagre. I filled our water barrel from a stream, miserably aware that if – no, when – the water froze, that resource would be lost.

Gurdyman sat huddled in the blankets. His breathing was laboured and he barely spoke, and I had to abandon my plan to make him give me the information I so badly needed. He had more drops from Edild's bottle first thing in the morning and again at noon.

We stopped for the night. We seemed to be on a wide, treeless, shelterless plain, with the mountains away to the east. They looked much closer now, and it occurred to me that we had probably been climbing steadily all day, although the slope had not really been apparent. The pony and I, however, were exhausted, which suggested I was right. Gurdyman got out of the cart and tottered a short distance away to relieve himself. Had the exercise not been of such an intimate nature, I would have rushed to help him.

I had never seen him look so frail.

When he was settled and wrapped in his blankets once more I climbed up after him and presented the sparse amount of food that constituted our evening meal. He had turned away to rummage in his bag, and he muttered, 'In a moment, child. First I will take a dose of—'

He gave a sort of gasp. I spun round and saw him holding Edild's little bottle between fingers and thumb.

It was empty.

'But there was plenty left!' I cried. 'When you dosed yourself at noon, I made sure to check!' He watched me steadily, not speaking. 'Didn't you put the stopper back properly?' Still he didn't reply. I lunged towards him, blind fury soaring through me. 'You *stupid* old man!' I yelled. 'How could you be so careless? We needed that medicine – *you* needed that medicine! I have nothing so potent in my satchel and I was relying on Edild's potion to last until we find help! And I don't know when that will be, because I haven't any idea of where we're going and if we're nearly there, because *you won't tell me!*'

I screamed the last words, my voice so loud that I felt something in my throat burst. I swallowed my own blood, clamping a hand over my mouth in case he saw.

The devastating, destructive anger had gone. I stared at him, his face so pale, his eyes so troubled, and an agonizing pain ran through me. 'I'm sorry!' I whispered. 'Gurdyman, dear Gurdyman, I'm so sorry. It was an accident, I know, and not your fault, and I had no right to shout at you like that.'

He put out his hand and I took it. It was icy cold.

'You are quite right to be angry, child,' he said. His voice was a breathy whisper. 'I am indeed a stupid old man, for in taking on a task that was over-taxing for someone of my age and in my state of health I have not only endangered myself but you too, and that is unforgivable.'

'*No!* I forgive you, of course I do!' I cried in protest. I had never seen him weak, defeated and humble, and it felt as if my world was rocking on its foundations. If he wasn't the strong, decisive, dependable Gurdyman I knew, then what was going to happen to us? Who was to lead us on if he couldn't?

You.

I had no idea who spoke the word but it certainly wasn't me.

He was struggling for breath, and I sensed he wanted to say something more. He raised his hand and feebly pointed towards the mountains over on our left. 'The place we are bound is just there,' he said, and I had to strain to hear him. 'We climb quite a long way, and we come to a narrow little track that is all but invisible unless you know it is there.' He paused to catch his breath. Then, so softly that I barely heard, '*I* know it is there.'

'And what will we find at the end of it?' I asked.

But he shook his head, silently indicating the water barrel.

I gave him a brimming cup, and he drank it in slow sips. I offered him a strip of dried meat and he took it, but the tiny inroads he made suggested he had done so for my sake and not his.

I gave him digitalis, as much as I felt it was safe to do. I helped him to settle down, propping him up with his pillow resting on his bag. He breathed more easily in a more upright position. I watched him until he fell asleep.

I got down from the cart and went to see to the pony. He had wandered some distance off and found a small stream, on whose banks there were some patches of grass. He was tearing at them desperately and I wanted to tell him, *Slow down, make that last, for there's nothing else.*

I left him to it. I didn't even bother to hobble him. I wasn't worried that he would run away – where would he go? – and just then I didn't much care.

My legs were shaky, and I knew it wasn't just from the long day's walk. Like everyone else, I was used to walking. I wasn't suffering from too much exercise but from not enough to eat.

My stomach was growling with hunger, and if I moved my head too quickly I felt dizzy and saw stars before my eyes. I wondered how long it was since I'd eaten a proper meal, and gave up when I got to five days. Or was it six?

I stood quite still, looking over towards the mountains. My eyes were playing tricks, for sometimes the lower slopes and the distant heights seemed to be very close and I thought I could make out the narrow track snaking its way deep into the heart of the range. Then all at once a huge gulf seemed to rush in to separate me from our goal, and the mountains seemed so far away and so tiny that I knew I would never reach them.

Perhaps I was going to die there, on that wide, desolate plain. Perhaps Gurdyman's bones, the pony's and mine would be found in the spring, when the snows cleared and the first of the new season's pilgrims set out along the trail. I wondered what I should do about the shining stone. Should I leave it for its next guardian to discover? Should I bury it? I didn't know, and the problem was far too great to deal with.

Presently I wandered back to the cart.

Gurdyman looked very peaceful, and it was good to see him deeply asleep. I didn't want to disturb him. Trying not to make any sudden movements, I collected my satchel, my blanket and my cloak and settled down under the cart.

I dozed for a while, in the border land between being awake and being asleep. Thin threads of dreams danced and flowed through my mind. I thought I heard a voice, speaking kindly. I thought it might have been my father's. 'I wish you were here, Father,' I said. I didn't know if my waking self or my dreaming self spoke the words. 'I'd so like to tell you how much I love you before I die.'

I was so cold.

I slept, woke to utter darkness, slept again; so deeply that it might indeed have been death.

Now my dreams were vivid and incredibly realistic, for I thought I could even feel the thump of footsteps on the hard ground beside me. I opened my eyes and saw a whirl of stars overhead, and I said, 'How beautiful!' The starlight was brilliant, lighting the land in shades of silver, and my dreaming mind conjured up a small knot of people filing down from the foothills, singing some lovely, soothing chant, the white of their voluminous garments flowing round them as they walked.

'Pilgrims,' I said.

And from somewhere very close, a deep voice murmured, 'Too late for pilgrims.'

Then I heard the echo of every person who had warned Gurdyman and me of the folly of setting out on such a journey in the late autumn. *It's late in the season for such a voyage*, said the master of the *Amethyst*. And *It is late in the year to be on the roads*, added Maria with a shake of her head. Then they all joined in, a great chorus of them, telling us disapprovingly that we had been foolhardy, taken stupidly irresponsible risks, and that our fate was our own fault.

'I wanted to get away,' I whispered. 'Gurdyman believed he was helping me by taking me with him. I was desperate to set out!'

It is Gurdyman who was desperate, said the quiet voice in my head. *But he could not achieve his purpose alone.*

His purpose? What did that mean?

And what was this about him not being able to do whatever it was by himself? Did it mean – oh, did it mean that he had used my grief and sorrow for his own ends? That, aware of how miserable I was back in Cambridge, he had craftily proposed this alternative, knowing full well I would jump at the chance to be anywhere but where I was?

No, no, I thought wildly, it cannot be so, for he cares about me, he is my teacher, my guide, my mentor, and he would not treat me in this way!

Would he?

And the quiet voice said, *Yes.*

I thought of my family, my friends, the places where I had been happy, the landscape of the fens that was my home and that was deep in my heart. I thought again of my father. I thought of Rollo, his spirit gone on ahead of me.

I thought of Jack.

Then, so cold now that I could not feel my feet, no longer knowing if I was awake or dreaming, I turned my face into the soft folds of my cloak and prepared for death.

EIGHT

It was some weeks after Jack discovered the island and the blackened remains of the fire that had destroyed both the dwellings and Rollo's body, and Cambridge was in the grip of winter. There had been hard frosts for many a morning now, and often the frozen ground did not thaw all day. Snow had threatened several times, although so far there had been no more than a few light coverings.

The gammers and gaffers hurrying out to buy provisions in the market square muttered darkly about conditions getting worse before they got better: far worse, seemed to be the consensus. It was no weather to be outside unless you had to, and then only for a short spell. Jack had changed the times of the watches so that the hours spent out in the harsh conditions were briefer than usual, and his men were grateful. Not that gratitude stopped them grumbling, and Jack had quite often found too many men huddled round the hearth in the castle guardroom when they ought to have been outside.

Without anybody actually ordering or even approving it, Jack had quietly risen to a position of greater power and influence within the ranks of the lawmen of the town. The day of the Picots – the deeply unpopular sheriff, his relations and the corrupt circle of those who had thrived on his patronage – was largely over, with the sheriff himself remaining in his post (there was after all nobody within the city to remove him from it) in name only. The real strength lay with Jack Chevestrier. The men knew him and they trusted him. The townspeople recognized him as a man of integrity. Life should have been good, but it wasn't.

He was perched on a stool in the guardroom one icy December morning, alone after having just shooed out the morning's patrol, when word came from the guards on duty at the outer gate that somebody wished to see him.

'He asked for me specifically?' Jack demanded. 'Who is he?'

He had assumed the caller was male. Just for a moment he thought about the alternative, but that was not something upon which to dwell.

'Yes, he did,' the messenger said. 'As to who he is, he didn't give a name. He's tallish, wearing a heavy dark cloak with a deep hood. Got strange eyes. Sort of silvery.' The man shot Jack a sideways glance. 'Odd, if you ask me. Look out at you like they can see through you.'

Jack had trained his men to be observant and the brief description was perceptive, for if the visitor was who Jack thought he was, then the eyes were his most remarkable feature. 'Tell the men on the gate to send him up,' he ordered.

A short time later, Hrype came into the guardroom. He walked swiftly across to the hearth, holding his hands out to the blaze. Jack let him be, for it was bitter outside and he looked half-frozen. Then, as Hrype's stiff posture began to relax, Jack stood up and poured out a pewter mug of hot, spiced ale.

'You do yourselves well up here,' Hrype remarked after he had drunk a few deep mouthfuls.

'The refreshments are not a regular feature of the guardroom,' Jack replied. 'The barrel of small beer in the corner is a gift from a grateful townswoman whose little son my men fished out of the river when he fell through the ice. She also sent the spices, which she said would liven it up a little and put heart in us.'

Hrype raised his mug. 'She was right.'

Jack indicated a bench pulled up beside the hearth, and Hrype sat down. 'What can I do for you?' Jack asked, settling beside him. He had lowered his voice, sensing already that whatever had brought Hrype to him was not for sharing. The guardroom might be empty, but within the warren of the castle's rooms, passages and hidden corners, there was always the likelihood of someone hearing voices and quietly stopping to listen.

Hrype studied him intently for some moments. Then, equally softly, he said, 'I know you've been concerned about Lassair and Gurdyman's continuing absence.'

'Her whereabouts are nothing to—' Jack began.

But Hrype interrupted. 'Your behaviour would suggest otherwise, for I have observed you checking on Gurdyman's house, as well as at – as well as other locations with which she is familiar and where you might reasonably have expected to find evidence of her presence.'

'They are both townspeople of Cambridge and hence my responsibility,' Jack said stiffly. 'If harm has come to them, if they are in danger, then it is for me to go to their aid.'

'Laudable,' Hrype murmured. He fell silent, watching Jack's face, then said, 'No use searching for them at Aelf Fen and on the burned-out ruins on Mercure's island, however. You won't find them in either location.'

'You know where they are, then?' Jack said, furious with himself at the eagerness in his voice.

There was another, even longer pause. Then Hrype said heavily, 'He has taken her away. They have gone by sea to Spain.'

Jack knew it was the truth. For one thing, why should Hrype have sought him out simply to lie to him? For another, it was in fact no great surprise, since somehow he had already known that Lassair was far away and out of his reach. He thought of the dangers of travel, of the long sea voyage, of the worsening weather. Slowly he shook his head. 'Why?' he said softly. 'Why has he taken her on such a risky venture?'

'More risky, more perilous, than you can understand,' Hrype replied angrily – although Jack knew the anger was not for him – 'unless you know much more than I would imagine about what is happening in Spain.'

'I know people regularly go on pilgrimage to Santiago de Compostela,' Jack replied. 'That some take the short crossing and travel over land, others go by sea to the north coast of Spain. I know the route is long and arduous, whichever method is selected.'

Hrype shook his head. 'They have not gone as pilgrims. The reasons are buried deep in Gurdyman's past, and as yet I am not entirely clear as to the full story. However,' he pressed on before Jack could question him, 'the peril I refer to has nothing to do with the pilgrim roads, which are presumably no more or less dangerous than they have always been. But there is war across the land, for the Christian armies have at last united and they are driving out the invaders.'

'The invaders?' Jack tried to pull together what sparse facts he knew. 'The Muslims from the south?'

'Yes, the Moors,' Hrype said, clearly trying not to show his impatience. 'Their presence originated centuries back, when the leader of one of the indigenous tribes fighting among themselves made the mistake of calling in Arab mercenaries from North Africa to help him out. They fought far too well, however, and soon they were so powerful that they drove the defenders as far north as the Pyrenees, even beyond, before finally they were halted. After that they contented themselves with the land to the south of the mountains, which they largely made their own and which became, under their rule, a great Muslim civilization, its capital cities the sparkling jewels of the world. The Moors prize learning and wisdom, and believe it is every man's duty to share his knowledge. Scholars are honoured, as are those whose talents are in their hands and their creative skills: the craftsmen who work in leather, precious metals, fine cloths. Theirs is a beautiful world.' He sighed.

'You sound as if you have been there,' Jack said.

Hrype glanced at him. 'I have.' It seemed to Jack that he was about to say more, but he stopped himself. Instead he said, 'The attempted reconquest, however, began almost as soon as the Muslims settled themselves in.' He spoke hurriedly, as if eager to forestall any questions about his own time in the southern land. 'The fighting has continued over the decades and the centuries, and both sides have advanced and retreated. The main problem of the Christian armies is that there are far too many differences of opinion over how best to achieve their purpose, as well as an over-reliance on paid soldiers who will fight for whoever is the most open-handed and who have little or no commitment to the cause. Nevertheless, ultimately they will win; they are already winning, for their fervour has been steadily increasing and it has introduced a new spirit of aggressiveness which is overcoming the natural tendency of the Christian armies to squabble amongst themselves.'

'They are uniting in the face of their common enemy,' Jack observed.

'They are,' Hrype agreed, 'which of course is what they should have done in the first place. But the trouble is that men's hearts appear to be divided over whether or not the reconquest is to be desired, for many Christian rulers have learned to appreciate the mixed culture of the south, where a man's faith is respected as his own business and the desire is for a life lived in harmony, where there is room for all to learn and grow. They—'

'But you just said there is war across the land,' Jack interrupted impatiently. He did not want to hear the details of life in this faraway land; he wanted to understand the dangers to Gurdyman and Lassair.

Especially Lassair.

'Yes,' Hrype said quietly. 'Yes, I did.' He paused, clearly thinking, then said, 'In brief, a few years back there was a powerful advance of the Christian forces, which led immediately to the arrival of a new wave of militants from North Africa determined to reverse those advances, which they did, only that led to renewed efforts by the armies of the north, so that the Christians are now pushing the Moors back again.' He met Jack's eyes. 'It is no place for a girl and an old man,' he said.

'But why are they there? What in God's name does Gurdyman think he's doing?' Wanting to shout it out but constrained by the heavy presence of the castle bearing down upon him, the words emerged in a suppressed hiss.

Hrype looked at him, an expression of commiseration on his face. 'Well may you ask,' he muttered. 'As indeed I have been asking myself.' He paused, and his eyes fixed on Jack narrowed. 'It was not my original intention to speak to you of this,' he said abruptly, 'for I considered it none of your business.'

'But—'

With a sharp look, Hrype stopped the protest before Jack could utter it.

'In addition,' Hrype went on, 'I have repeatedly asked myself why I am so concerned for Lassair, since far too often she has been like the prickle of a thorn in the sole of my shoe.' Sensing Jack's intent gaze, he looked up. 'What took me years of hard work and sacrifice always came so easily to her,' he said baldly. 'In short, I resented her. I'm not proud, but there it is.'

There was a brief silence.

'But I am tormented with the thought that Gurdyman may have taken her into danger,' he went on. 'You are too, and so here I am, sharing what little I know with you.'

The silence was longer this time.

Then: 'You said it was to do with Gurdyman's past?' Jack asked.

'Yes, yes, I did.' Hrype sighed. 'But much of what I suspect is guesswork, for he keeps his past a secret and he has drawn a heavy veil across it, so that even with the aid of—' He stopped abruptly, and his expression suggested he had already said too much.

'With the aid of your own special ways of looking into the mind and heart of another, you cannot penetrate his defences?' Jack suggested quietly.

Hrype looked at him but did not speak.

'Well, even if you don't know the details, you seem to recognize the danger,' Jack went on. 'And again I ask: why did he take her with him?'

'If I am right,' Hrype said, 'then Gurdyman has been waiting a very long time for this moment, for the task he sets out to do has its roots in the far past; at a time when he was a young man in Moorish Spain and learned his craft.'

'His craft.' Jack repeated the words dully. He had a feeling of foreboding, for they could only mean one thing. 'When he acquired the information and the skills that force him to do his work hidden away in a crypt deep in the ground.'

'The fact that this work must remain hidden does not in itself mean it is evil or wrong,' Hrype said gently, 'merely that it is open to misinterpretation; that its practitioners are men – and women – feared and shunned by ordinary people. But very often the acquisition of new knowledge is with the intention of doing good. For example, when he—'

Jack had no wish to endure a lecture. 'So he's gone to Spain because of some event that happened when he was learning the arts of the magician.'

'Ye-es,' Hrype said guardedly.

'A wrong was perpetrated against him, perhaps, that now he must put right,' Jack went on.

'It is what I too suspect,' Hrype agreed. 'If the suspicion is correct, then I believe that he could not make this journey, and achieve this end which he appears to desire, without her. Without Lassair.'

'I don't understand.' But even as Jack spoke the words he had a dread sense that he did.

Hrype sighed. Then, with a brief wry smile, he said, 'I am sure you don't. If I am to attempt an explanation it will, I fear, entail my speaking to you of matters on which I know full well you prefer to remain ignorant.'

'I'm quite prepared to—' But the hot words of protest died away, for Hrype was quite right. 'Very well,' Jack said. 'I will try to set aside my prejudice and listen with an open mind.'

Now Hrype was smiling openly. 'I could not ask for more,' he said, and there was clear irony in his tone. Then, hurriedly, as if he needed to speak while Jack's unexpected tolerance lasted, he went on, 'You probably are not aware, but in general men like Gurdyman need a second person with similar gifts in order to achieve their full power. It is called animus and anima, and it seems to work best if the two are of opposite sexes. Usually the master is male and the apprentice female, although I knew a pair where it was the other way round, and the alteration seemed to make no difference. The important factor is to have both male and female elements present, and—'

'It's why he took her on,' Jack interrupted, the words harsh. 'From what she has told me, it appears she believes he did her a great kindness in seeking her out as his pupil and sharing his vast knowledge with her. But she's wrong, isn't she? He didn't do it for her.'

'He did in part,' Hrype replied. Then, with sudden fierce emphasis, 'I *have* to believe he had her interests in mind as well as his own.'

'Why?'

'Because it was I who told him of her existence.'

'*You?*'

Hrype nodded. 'I have known her all her life. I watched her grow from an awkward colt of a child into girlhood, and I saw, even as her aunt did, that she had potential, and not only as a healer. Edild – her aunt, and now my wife' – Jack nodded impatiently, for he already knew – 'taught her, and Lassair went to live with Edild. She fulfilled all of Edild's hopes; perhaps exceeded them. We both saw that there was more to her than a village healer, and I began to understand that a very particular path had been decreed for her. Although Edild was not then aware of the truth about her bloodline, I was, and it encouraged me to believe there was something . . . extra in her nature.' He glanced at Jack. 'I will not elucidate, save to say that long-guarded secrets were finally revealed, and Lassair had to face some deeply unsettling facts about her family.'

Jack nodded. 'I would not ask you to betray any confidences.'

Hrype studied him, a half-smile on his face. After a moment he continued. 'In the course of these revelations, it came to pass that Lassair's inheritance was put into her hands. As soon as we – Gurdyman and I – saw how she was able to interact with the power that lies within this object, there was no longer any room for doubt.' He glanced at Jack. 'She has in her guardianship something very special,' he said, lowering his voice, 'and it—'

Jack nodded. 'I know.'

'You *know*?'

'I have never seen this object,' he admitted, 'but I've long suspected there is something she carries about with her that has power.'

'You have, have you?' Hrype murmured. He was looking at Jack with an expression of deep interest. 'Strange. Most people have no awareness of it whatsoever.' His eyes narrowed suddenly, then it seemed to Jack that he nodded infinitesimally, as if something had just been confirmed to him.

'So, when you judged that she had potential beyond what her aunt was capable of teaching her, you introduced her to Gurdyman. He too saw what you had seen and he took her on as his pupil. His apprentice,' Jack said. His voice was harsh now, for he was impatient suddenly with Hrype's air of mystery; with his knowing expression that said he was able to understand arcane matters that were far too deep for ordinary men. 'And while it might have appeared that the gratitude should be all hers, for Gurdyman was introducing her to a far wider world than that encompassed by a remote fenland village, in fact it was he who needed her, for even back then he was looking ahead, into the future, and knew that he could not progress to this – this task, or mission, or whatever it is, that they have set out on without her.'

'That, I fear, is about right,' Hrype agreed. 'He has, I believe, been delighted and somewhat amazed at what she can do; at how swiftly she learns.' Abruptly he shook his head, as if forcefully stopping that line of thinking. 'But this is irrelevant, for what you are concerned about is her safety. As am I,' he added quietly.

'Gurdyman has taken her into danger,' Jack said dully.

'Yes. I do not like to think that my old friend is capable of such ruthlessness, but I fear very much that he is.'

A heavy silence hung between them. Then, breaking it, Jack said softly, 'Gurdyman has been waiting a very long time for this moment.'

Hrype looked at him sharply. 'What?'

'It's what you said, a few moments ago.'

'Yes, I did, I did,' Hrype said slowly.

'So, why now? After waiting so long, why did he decide to set out now? I don't know precisely when they left, although I suspect you do, but when I last saw Lassair the days were already shortening and the temperature growing colder. It's not the time to set out on a long journey across the seas, and anybody who had a choice in the matter would wait until spring. So, I repeat: why did Gurdyman leave when he did?'

Hrype nodded slowly. 'Yes,' he murmured. It sounded like a sigh.

'That's no answer,' Jack said impatiently.

'No, I'm aware of that.' Hrype paused. 'I might have known you'd notice,' he muttered.

'That it's no time to go travelling?'

'Yes.' Then, talking swiftly and lowering his voice even further, Hrype said, 'Something happened. A dead man was found propped up in the alley outside Gurdyman's house – against the wall of his house, in fact – and Gurdyman found him. He was a vagrant, thin, dirty and ill-looking, and there was something in his hand: a single, fine, beautiful pearl.'

'A pearl? But why—'

'Don't interrupt!' Hrype said sternly. 'I don't know why this discovery upset Gurdyman so very much but I can swear to you that it did, for I went to visit him later that same day and found he had taken to his bed. He was deathly pale, his lips were blueish, he complained of pains in his chest and said his heart was not beating properly.'

Dear Lord, Jack thought, not only has that old man taken Lassair off into the wild on some unknown and dangerous mission, but he's unwell. What will happen to her if he sickens again when they are far from help? If he dies?

Hrype was watching him, sympathy in his eyes. 'She's a healer, don't forget,' he said. 'She carries many remedies in that satchel of hers, among them ones for what ails Gurdyman. He too carries a remedy – a powerful one – provided by Edild. If the worst happens and he has another collapse, Lassair will treat him just as I did.'

'You knew what I was thinking,' Jack said neutrally.

Hrype grinned. 'It wasn't very hard to work it out.'

Trying not to think about Lassair desperate to save a dying Gurdyman, out in the wilds of some strife-torn land with no friend to turn to, nothing to help her but her own wits and her own courage, Jack said, 'So why should a dead beggar with a pearl in his hand cause the old man such distress?' Hrype watched him, waiting, and, letting the thought that was developing in his mind come to completion, after a moment Jack added, 'And why does the very mention of the vagrant – or perhaps it's the pearl – make me so uneasy?'

'Because I've just told you the effect it had on Gurdyman,' Hrype said.

'No. I was already worried, for—' He stopped. His instinct had been not to reveal to Hrype that he'd been keeping an eye on Gurdyman's house, but now he changed his mind. 'I've been watching the old man's house,' he admitted. 'Even when it became clear they'd gone away, I've persisted. And—' The next part was difficult, but he was determined to explain. 'And I've sensed that someone else has been doing the same.'

'You have perhaps seen, or sensed, me?'

But Jack shook his head. 'No.' Noticing Hrype's brief smile, he said. 'Oh, I'm sure you saw me, but I imagine you are far better at melting into the background than I am. What I sensed was deeply disturbing, for it felt – it felt as if it wasn't really there. It was like a breath, or a sudden breeze through an opened door. More than once I have been quite sure somebody was standing close behind me but, when I turned to look, there was nobody there.' He looked at Hrype, searching for understanding. 'This sounds unreasoned and illogical, but it – whatever it was – didn't seem fully human.' He managed a short laugh. 'No doubt you'll tell me it was my imagination.'

'It may well have been,' Hrype replied, 'but if so, it was something that was also in my imagination. Yes,' he added, as Jack gazed at him in surprise, 'I've experienced the same thing. I've even been inside the house,' he said in a whisper, 'and I fled in terror.'

Jack watched him, not speaking. He understood what it must have taken for a man like Hrype to confess his instant of fear to someone like himself. The realization made him feel that Hrype might after all be somebody he could work beside.

He reached for the warmed ale and topped up their mugs. 'I think,' he said, raising his in a silent tribute, 'that we should try to discover more about this vagrant, how he met his death and how the pearl came to be in his hand.'

And, raising his own mug to clink it softly against Jack's, Hrype said, 'I agree.'

They drank. Jack knew, as he suspected Hrype did too, that the task had been taken on and would not be abandoned.

For the first time since Lassair had disappeared, he felt a flicker of hope.

NINE

I was so cold.

I woke – or I thought I had awakened, although I wondered if I was dreaming – to find myself curled in a ball, desperately trying to conserve my body warmth. I looked up, thinking to see the rough wooden planks of the bed of the cart immediately above me. Perhaps I was seeking comfort from Gurdyman's presence; perhaps merely from the cart's own solidity.

It wasn't there.

Above me was the black sky, with the vast and brilliant scattered arc of the great band of stars right over my head. I thought I saw a shadow pass between my eyes and the dazzling spots of light. It was as if a veil had wafted briefly across my vision, or the long, dangling sleeve of a voluminous robe.

My mind didn't seem to belong to me. I fought to reason what was happening – had I rolled out from under the cart in my sleep? Had Gurdyman woken up and tried to rouse me? – but each time I was on the point of some sensible explanation, it was as if my concentration was slowly but inexorably being undone. *You are dreaming*, I heard in my head. Did the words originate with me? Or was someone else insinuating them into my mind?

The images went away.

Then suddenly I was wide awake – or I thought I was – and I was shaking so hard my teeth rattled.

Right above me was something right out of the most lurid fenland horror tale. Something from deep within the dark part of my soul, or an image seen for an instant in malignant nightmare.

A single eye, but huge . . .

Its iris was light brown, its pupil wide and profoundly black. The white was clear, and patterned minutely with tiny scarlet trails radiating from the corner.

It was incredible, alarming, and what made me shudder in amazement was the size.

It was far, far bigger than any human eye could be.

It blinked out, but the effects of its appearance did not dissipate. For I could feel a presence; something was close, so close that I felt breath on my cheek. The breath was warm, dry, and it smelt of . . . of something I vaguely recognized as some medicinal herb . . .

I tried to put up my hands to shield my face and cover my eyes. My death was near, for an eye of that dimensions must surely betoken a gaping mouth, strong, wide jaws and teeth capable of tearing flesh and crunching bone.

I thought I was screaming – I was trying so hard that I felt the sinews of my throat contort and cramp – but all that I could hear was a strangled sort of whimper.

I waited.

Nothing happened.

And presently I opened my eyes again and there was the base of the cart, a foot or so above my head, just where it ought to be.

My mouth was dry and I was shaky and nauseous. I wriggled out from my bedding and stood on trembling legs holding onto the side of the cart while I dipped a mug in the water barrel and had a drink. The water was very, very cold; so cold that the odd taste I'd noticed once or twice before was no longer detectable. Or perhaps I was getting used to it.

I looked at Gurdyman. He lay on his back, hands folded on his chest. I touched them and they were icy. I managed to unwind a fold of his cloak and cover him right up to his chin, and I held his hands for a while until they felt less cold. Not warm; merely less cold.

Then, once again feeling that I might be about to throw up, I went back to my place beneath the cart.

I dreaded falling asleep again for fear of what my dreams would show me next. I lay there for some time, fighting sleep, fighting nausea, and in the end the nausea subsided and exhaustion won the battle. I slept.

I'd been right to be apprehensive about sleeping.

The images I saw now were the worst of all.

I saw the inn that Gurdyman's parents had owned. I saw in my sleeping mind the buildings and the yard that I'd recently seen in life, but now there was another room and it was full of people, talking, eating, drinking, laughing, singing, flirting, enjoying themselves. But there was someone – or I think some*thing* – that did not enter into the festive mood; that stood alone outside and bent its malice upon those within. Upon two of them in particular, or so I thought.

I *saw* the malice, like a dark beam that seemed shot through with something that glittered. It was aimed straight at the heart of the happy gathering, to where a man raised a barrel of ale, filled a jug and handed it to a smiling woman. Then the dark beam was no longer dark, for the glittering substance within it suddenly glowed brilliant red, orange, yellow, white, and burst into bright blue flames.

The woman was engulfed first. Her hair and her clothes caught fire, and she was screaming. The man threw the contents of the ale barrel over her, but the glittering substance did not relent and almost instantly he was on fire too. The flames now leapt and danced like will-o'-the-wisps, landing on the throng already trying frantically to get away, and in no time barely a soul within the room was spared. Those who tried to fight the flames fared the worst: those who surrendered died very quickly.

Then there was a new horror, for in the narrow doorway people were piling up, their passage out to safety blocked by the bodies that already lay inert on the ground.

With a whoosh and a screaming draught of air, the whole building was on fire.

It was so fierce that the destruction was over in no time.

The malice seemed to withdraw back inside itself.

The fire had gone without a trace. There wasn't even the smell of burning. There was nothing but the balmy night air, and the sweet scent of grass with a faint tang of cow muck.

In my dream I twisted and turned, trying not to see the blackened remains of the room: the charred timbers, the occasional white of bone.

They are all dead, a sonorous voice intoned. *See how easy it is to annihilate, where there is the power?*

I wanted to protest: to say that power can be good as well as evil. But my mind didn't work any more.

Wake up, I told myself. Then, more urgently, *WAKE UP!*

I really didn't know if I was awake or not. I felt sick, feverish, my skin on fire even as I shivered in the icy air, for I had somehow crawled out from my blankets and from beneath the shelter of the cart, and I was lying out in the open.

Then I thought I saw claws on the lacings of my gown.

They were long, black, hard, curved like talons, and they picked at me like a scavenging bird on its dead prey.

Was I dead, then?

But I couldn't be, for my head thumped and banged with a pain I had never known before. And now the huge, single eye was back, its fierce intelligence focused on me so that I felt myself wither under its scrutiny.

It was as if I was pierced by it; as if everything within my head, my mind, was wide open to its scrutiny and I couldn't beat it off.

And then, as I gave myself up, I heard a sound in the far distance.

I heard a voice cry, 'Hoi! *HOI!*', and swiftly it was taken up by others. I thought I heard, or perhaps felt, running feet, swiftly coming nearer. And then the eye was withdrawn and the malign presence abruptly shut itself off.

I lay there, half-naked, burning like a furnace.

And after what seemed an eternity I felt a cool hand on my forehead and somebody spoke softly in a language I didn't understand.

I thought I heard my name spoken. Was it my father, come to carry me home? Was the cool hand that of my mother, tending me as she had done through the illnesses of childhood? I said in a voice that cracked and broke, 'Mother? Father?'

And strong arms picked me up, wrapped something very soft and warm around me and bore me away.

I thought I might be awake. Either that or I had died and was in paradise. If so, it was a fragrant paradise where golden sunlight shone through strangely shaped, elegant windows and soft musical sounds permeated the air.

I closed my eyes and all went dark again.

Then – I had the impression it was a long time later – there was an arm insinuating itself behind my head, gently but insistently, and the hard edge of a cup was held to my lips. 'Drink this,' a quiet voice said.

I hesitated. I still had no idea where I was, although on balance I thought I was alive and not dead. The light had changed and now wherever it was I lay was in darkness, lit only by the flame of a candle in a very ornate lantern made of pierced metal. But I was warm, comfortable – whatever I was lying on was very soft but also it managed to support my sore body exactly where it needed to be supported – and I thought my fever had gone down a little. But I was still utterly weak and quite unable to defend myself, so I was at the mercy of anybody who meant me harm. They could have killed me already if they wanted to, I reasoned, so it wasn't very likely that whatever was in the cup was going to poison me.

I took a sip, then another.

It was cool, and both felt and tasted a little like milk, although it was thinner than what I was used to and it had a sharp tang to it. It was good. I tried to gulp down some more, but the cup was withdrawn.

'Slowly,' said the quiet voice. 'Too much too soon on an empty stomach will not stay down.'

It was the same advice I had given countless times myself. The thought that I could well be in the hands of a healer was reassuring, and I felt myself relax. As I did so, I realized that this healer had spoken in my own tongue. Had he, like the people back in Gurdyman's parents' village, had somebody to instruct him? Someone to 'teach good talk', as Gurdyman's mother and father had done for Iago?

The owner of the voice moved away from the bed, and I had the impression of someone quite small, slim and upright. I waited. I heard the sound of a metal spoon on glass, stirring briskly, and then the figure came back and this time held a smaller, glass vessel to my lips. 'Now drink this,' he – or she – said. 'For sleep,' he added.

Again, it is what I would have done. A half-starved, sick, dehydrated body needs water, of course, and nutrition, but above all sleep. Nature is the best healer, as my aunt Edild used to say.

The potion tasted bitter under the sweetness of the honey. I drank it to the dregs, and almost instantly the dark curtain of sleep was drawn across my eyes. I turned on my side, sighed, and gave myself up to it.

Next time I awoke, bright sunshine once again filled the room. Feeling considerably more alert, I lay still and looked around. I was on a narrow bed with clean white sheets and a cover neatly folded back at the foot: perhaps it had been necessary during the chill of the night but it was now not required. The temperature was indeed comfortable, and I could feel the warmth in the rays of sunshine crossing my bed. I looked again at the odd-shaped windows. They were basically narrow rectangles, but at the top the sides drew together before curving outwards and coming back to a point. I raised myself up a little and tried to peer out. Then instantly I wished I hadn't. I'd begun to feel dizzy the moment I lifted my head from the pillow, and now, staring into nothing but blue sky, the vertigo increased. I moaned softly, hoping I wasn't going to be sick.

A dark-clad figure came hurrying into the room. 'Lie back!' she said. The voice was that of whoever had attended me before, and I now saw that she was a woman. Her gown hung in graceful folds around her slim body and her head was covered with a white veil that framed her face, artfully arranged into pleats and tucks. Her skin was smooth and darker than mine, and the fine lines around her mouth and eyes suggested she was considerably older. Her eyes were dark brown and they shone in the sunlight.

'I am Hanan,' she said, coming to sit on the bed and taking my wrist between her fingers and thumb. 'The name means tenderness.'

'Then you are well named,' I replied, for her touch was gentle and I sensed a caring nature.

She smiled. 'Thank you.' She laid my hand carefully back down on the bedclothes and looked straight at me. 'Your eyes!' she exclaimed.

I put my hand up to my face, feeling all around my eyes

and eyelids. What had happened? I blinked rapidly a few times, but there didn't seem to be anything wrong with my vision. 'What about them?'

Hanan had seen my anxiety and she hastened to reassure me. 'Nothing! But I have not seen eyes of this colour before.' She leaned closer and obligingly I opened my eyes as widely as I could. She laughed. 'I thought they were blue, like his, but they are not. They are purely green, but they are pale, bright, like polished silver.'

I was intrigued. I had never seen my own eyes as clearly as she obviously could. Then a thought struck me: she had just described my grandfather's eyes. 'I have an ancestor from the far north,' I said, trying not to let the sudden surge of emotion and homesickness show. 'He, and many others of my northern kin, share the same feature.'

She nodded. I think she had picked up my distress for, businesslike now, she got up from the bed and went over to a small table set just inside the doorway. 'You must eat,' she said, 'if you have the appetite.'

I had, and I did. I consumed fresh bread, cheese, dried meats, some sort of pickled vegetables, more of the tangy milky drink, an apple, some sweet biscuits in which I tasted honey and that sharp tang again.

'It is lemon,' Hanan said. She had been watching me closely as I ate.

'It's delicious,' I mumbled, but my mouth was full and I doubt if she made out the words.

I was chasing the last crumbs around the platter when I suddenly thought, Gurdyman!

Oh, *oh*, how could I have forgotten about him? In anguish, I pushed aside the tray of food and cried, '*Where's Gurdyman?* He was so sick, and the belladonna was spilled, and I could do nothing for him! Oh, I must—'

I was trying to get up even as I spoke, but my legs had already begun to wobble and it was easy for Hanan to push me back again. 'He is being tended,' she said.

'I thought he was dying!'

She nodded. 'Yes, we believe he was close to death. But he is strong, and already he begins to improve.'

She knew who I meant when I called him by the name I'd always known, I thought. And just now she had said she'd thought I had blue eyes *like his*.

'You know him,' I said. 'He has been here before, and you recognized him.'

'Yes,' she said.

Then – then we had reached our destination!

The realization was joyful. We didn't have to struggle on, we hadn't got to face worsening weather and fighting soldiers and a total dearth of welcoming inns, we weren't going to starve.

We weren't going to die.

Hanan was watching me, a kind, sympathetic expression on her face, and I had the impression she had followed the rush of my thoughts. She reached forward, picking up the tray. 'Now, more sleep,' she said, and there was something in the soft, hypnotic tone that instantly made me feel drowsy. 'Already you are better, and the heart beats strongly. Food and drink will hasten the recovery, but best of all is sleep.'

She stood in the doorway watching as I settled myself down. Then, with another of her beautiful smiles, she glided away.

When I next awoke it was evening and I knew straight away that I was a great deal stronger. Hanan was perching on a little stool beside the window, and came over to me as I sat up.

'No dizziness?' she enquired.

'No.'

'Good. More food, more sleep, and tomorrow' – she looked at me, her expression wry – 'perhaps we bathe you.'

As I ate my evening meal – as good as the earlier one, and more of it – I looked down at myself. I was clad in my under shift and it was filthy and stiff with dried sweat. My hair had come loose from its braid, and I raised a lock. It was lank and greasy, and looked several shades darker than it usually did. My hands were the only part of me that were clean, and I remembered Hanan bathing them. Presumably she had also washed my face.

I was embarrassed at my state, especially as she was so very clean.

Hanan came back to settle me for the night, and I slept deeply. Then suddenly I was wide awake. I sat up cautiously: all was well. Then I put my feet to the smooth, cool stone of the floor and tried to rise up. I wobbled violently at first, but then my sense of balance returned and I stood up straight.

One hand on the bed, I walked very slowly over to the window.

I gasped.

It was the middle of the night, and all was quiet and still. The building I was in was set on the steep side of a hill, and I thought we were possibly in the foothills of the mountain range towards which Gurdyman and I had been heading. The long lower slopes stretched out before me in seemingly endless descending folds, and there was a glimpse of the plateau far below. I turned my head to look at what was to the rear, and gasped again, for there were the mountains, soaring up to the starry sky, their snow-covered peaks dazzling white in the moonlight.

The buildings of the town covered the hillside to right and left. If the plain was before us, I reasoned, then the town faced west. I leaned out to stare at the walls of the town's houses, entranced suddenly by the moon shining on whatever material had been used in construction. For the effect was to make cold, hard, inert stone shine with a soft, pearly glow that was dazzling.

If this was the place where Gurdyman had been as a boy and a young man, where he had begun on the course that made him what he was, then no wonder he had wanted to return.

It was utterly beautiful.

In the morning, Hanan was as good as her word. Two men carried a tub of some sort of metal into the room, courteously averting their eyes and careful not to look anywhere near the bed. Then women began arriving, two by two, bearing large jugs of steaming water which they poured into the tub. Hanan added oils from delicate little bottles, and I sniffed with pleasure.

'Jasmine,' she said, noticing, 'and lavender I expect you know.'

'Yes.'

Now the tub was full, and only Hanan and one of the women remained. There was one last jug of water, and the woman set an empty bowl on the floor. She handed a sponge and a block of something white to Hanan, who nodded her thanks. Then she and the woman helped me out of bed and took off my shift. They must have been surprised at the money belt next to my skin, especially when I took it off and they realized how heavy it was, but they set it aside without comment. I wondered fleetingly how it was that I knew without a doubt that it would remain precisely where they had put it, untouched, until I reclaimed it.

Then, holding me carefully, they made me stand in the bowl.

'You are very much in need of bathing,' Hanan said matter-of-factly, 'and so before you sit in the good, clean water, we will first wash off the grime of travel and the sweat of sickness.'

And, enthusiastically but with gentle hands, that is what they did.

I had no knowledge of the white substance in block form, but when it was put in water, rubbed on the sponge and applied to my filthy body, it foamed up and somehow seemed to loosen the dirt. In addition, it smelt delicious. When a jug of clean water was poured over me, the foam ran off and so did the dirt.

And then I was allowed to get into the tub.

The warm, fragrant water came up to my chest, and the sensation was like nothing I'd experienced before. I sank down below the surface, feeling the water run through my hair, and the woman put something from a different bottle on my head and massaged it into my scalp, then rinsed it off with another jug of water.

I would happily have stayed there all day.

But the water cooled, and Hanan said I must not take chill, so she and the other woman helped me out, wrapping me in a thick towel. They rubbed me dry, then dressed me in a robe similar to Hanan's but in sea-green. The woman brought a comb and set about the tangles in my hair. She sat me in the sunshine, and it finished off the drying process.

She said something to Hanan, who nodded. Turning to me, she said, 'She remarks that your hair is the colour of new copper.'

I picked up a lock, just as I had done last night. But now my hair was no longer greasy, dull and dark: it shone.

I hadn't seen it in its true colour since I'd been a child.

TEN

Bathed, sponged all over, clad in clean garments, with a fresh white veil arranged in intricate folds and pleats over my head and hair and my skin smelling of jasmine, I would have liked to go on sitting in the healing sunshine. But impatience to see Gurdyman – to verify with my own eyes that he was neither dead nor about to die – would not let me.

The men came back to remove the tub and the women wiped away the splashes of water and tidied the room. One of them held my filthy under shift, and, seeing my eyes upon it, said something to Hanan. 'She says to tell you that it will be laundered, with the rest of your clothes, and returned to you,' she said.

'I'm most grateful,' I said.

Hanan's fine black eyebrows lifted. 'It is her job.'

'Please thank her anyway.' I wasn't used to anybody doing my washing except myself.

Hanan murmured something to the woman, who looked even more surprised than Hanan. But she gave me a wide smile.

'To say thank you, the word is *shukran*,' Hanan said.

I repeated it several times. One of the departing women giggled.

'To respond to somebody's thanks, we say *al'afw*.'

My attempts with that were even more risible. Laughing along, I was nevertheless pleased to have acquired my first two words.

When Hanan and I were once more alone and it seemed she was about to persuade me back into bed – 'You must be fatigued after all the exertion!' – I said firmly, 'Now, if you please, I wish to see Gurdyman.'

She looked dubiously at me. 'He is being well looked after,' she said.

'I have no doubt about that.' She smiled faintly. 'But, you see, his care has been in my hands since we began our journey, and I find it hard to rest until I have seen for myself.'

I was hoping to appeal to her as one healer to another and it worked. She gave a brisk nod and then, taking my arm and with many imprecations to let her know the instant I felt faint, or nauseous, or light-headed, led me out of the room and down a narrow little stair to the outside world.

The street was busy with morning traffic, and I was glad of Hanan's support as we were hurried along by people busy on their own affairs, many carrying heavy loads, and what seemed to my bemused eyes a constant stream of darting children. There were also donkeys, laden with packages, boxes and barrels, their small feet daintily negotiating the narrow alleys. I wasn't watching where I was going, for this was my first sight of the town other than the narrow glimpse from my room, and I was trying to look everywhere at once. You would know instantly that you were no longer in England, I reflected, for the architecture was utterly alien: the elegant shape of the window in my room that I had noticed and admired was repeated everywhere, and reproduced in a much-magnified size in archways over the street. Again and again I saw the stone that had shone like pale cream pearl in the moonlight. This morning, in full sunshine, the pearls were golden.

We had only gone perhaps a dozen paces before we turned in beneath one of the curiously shaped arches and into a courtyard encircled with arcades. Fountains played, the drops of water catching the sunlight and sending out rainbows of colour. Hanan led me to an open door at the far end, and we went down a cool, shady stone passage. It twisted this way and that – it struck some deep chord of memory – and then suddenly we were in the sunshine again, in a little enclosed court surrounded by high walls. A vine grew up one wall, and the few of its leaves that still clung to it in this winter season were a rich, rusty red. Jasmine grew all over a second wall. A rose climbed a third one, a few last huge pink blooms scenting the air. In a pot grew a very healthy-looking bay tree, its leaves large and glossy, glinting with a recent watering.

And I knew, of course, why the passage had seemed familiar,

for this little courtyard chimed even more chords of memory: it was an exact replica, apart from the jasmine, of Gurdyman's inner court at the back of the twisty-turny house, hundreds of miles away in Cambridge. No: instantly I corrected myself. The Cambridge courtyard was the replica, for of course Gurdyman had modelled it upon this one.

He was sitting in a chair with a sloping back, armrests and a footstool, his head on a pillow and a soft, fluffy blanket over his knees. A second, identically furnished chair was placed beside him. Like me, he was in clean clothes of local design, but I thought he looked far more comfortable in them than I did.

I dashed over to him and, kneeling by his side, took his hand. I stared up into his face. The bright blue eyes were shadowed with fatigue and the residue of illness, but I could see that he was there; his spirit had come back to him, and he was Gurdyman once more.

I was surreptitiously trying to feel the beat of his heart in his wrist, but I wasn't nearly subtle enough.

He patted the top of my head with his free hand and chuckled. 'I am better, child,' he murmured. 'You did your very best for me, I understand, and it was enough, for here I am!'

'There was no more belladonna,' I mumbled. 'I didn't know what to do.'

'You gave me digitalis, you made me comfortable, you kept me warm.'

'We had used up nearly all the food!' I cried, my anguish bursting out of me as I recalled those desperate days. 'I was able to replenish the water cask, but—'

As I'd said that, I noticed Gurdyman look up, frowning. Turning, I saw a man in the doorway. He was tall, slim, he stood with the elegance of a dancer and he was dressed in black, from the headdress to the hem of the robe pooling over his bare feet. His eyes too were black. His expression was stern as he met Gurdyman's gaze, but then he turned to look at me and his entire face changed.

He advanced towards me, his hands held out palms upwards. His smile was warm, and it flooded the intense dark eyes with . . . with love, was all I could think.

'You are Lassair,' he said, and his voice was a deep rumble. 'You are very welcome, and not only because you return our old friend to us.' He bowed deeply, and, not knowing what else to do, I did the same. Straightening up, he was close enough to take my hands, which he did. His were warm, and I noticed how long and shapely they were, the nails beautifully kept. I was ashamed of mine, so square and with the short-trimmed nails that were the only practical way for someone who did my work.

'I am Salim,' he said. 'This was my father's house, his father's before him, and so on up the generations. It is where Gurdyman came when he was a young man, to be the pupil of my father and my grandfather, and he and I were as brothers.'

I nodded. I had already guessed as much. My attention had snagged on the way he said *Gurdyman*: it was quite obviously the same name, but it didn't sound the way I was used to.

'Please, what did you call Gurdyman?' I asked him.

'Gur-dy-man.'

I couldn't help grinning, for now he was deliberately pronouncing it the way I did.

'Yes,' I said, still smiling. 'But that isn't what you said the first time.'

He quirked his head in a gesture I was to come to know very well: a sort of amused recognition that somebody had just said something, or done something, that impressed him. 'You hear well,' he observed. 'And you are right, for originally the name bestowed upon young Juan the Englishman when first he came to us was Gudiyyema.'

'Gudiyyema.' I repeated it softly once or twice, then a few more times, gradually letting it turn into Gurdyman, which, on the last pronunciation, I said in the broad accents of the men of the fens. Behind me, Gurdyman chuckled.

'What does it mean?' I asked. Salim frowned. 'The woman who has been tending me' – I turned to look for Hanan, but she wasn't there – 'is called Hanan, and she told me it means tenderness.'

'Ah, I see.' Salim smiled. 'Indeed, yes. My name means safe. As you appear to suspect, most of our names do have meaning. If we were to bestow a name upon you, we might select Fizza, which means silver, for the light that dances in your pale eyes. Gudiyyema is not precisely the same, for it is only obliquely that it pertains to your friend here. Gudiyyema is the name of a genie in one of our favourite legends, and his magical powers were manifested in the form of a dazzling beam of light from his brilliant blue eyes. We are for the most part a dark-eyed people, and when Juan came to us, we were amazed that anybody could be so different. The only example we knew of eyes like his was the genie Gudiyyema, and this is the name that attached itself to him.'

I turned to Gurdyman, who I thought was looking rather smug. To be named for a powerful genie in a much-loved legend was no small thing, I reflected, so perhaps the self-satisfaction was no surprise. Still looking at him, I whispered, for his ears only, 'Gudiyyema,' and he had the grace to look abashed.

Now Salim said something to him in his own language, and Gurdyman responded, fluently and at some length. I waited until Salim had replied, then said, 'You know each other's language.'

'Indeed,' Salim said. 'Many here speak your tongue, for they are eager to learn the ways of strangers. It is one of our most treasured beliefs, that every man and woman possessed of knowledge must share it with others.'

'I do not think it is a belief that my countrymen share,' I said softly.

'It is not,' Gurdyman said, and I thought he was being careful to keep his tone neutral. 'Our church, in particular, likes to keep its mysteries to itself, and that has led to the widespread misunderstanding that education – literacy, even – is the prerogative of the rich and powerful.'

'It is every man's birthright,' Salim said softly.

Gurdyman held my eyes. 'You see why I love this place?' he murmured.

'Yes,' I replied. This place . . . 'Where are we?' I demanded, swinging round to Salim. 'What is this town?'

His beautiful smile spread once more across his face. 'It is a city where men and women live in harmony with one another; where they celebrate their similarities and respect their differences. It is not known to many, for the world is not ready for our ways. At least three faiths live here and thrive: Muslims, Christians and Jews each have their places of worship and their traditions, yet they take an active enjoyment in learning about each other, in sharing the knowledge that is peculiar to their own faith and history. The city has three different names in three different tongues, but most of us who call it our home simply refer to it as the City of Pearl.'

I thought of the very different lights of moon and sun and how they had each brought out the beautiful glow on the city walls. City of Pearl was precisely the right name.

'Our city has of necessity some dealings with the outside world, for we have found it impractical to live in total isolation, but, as I just implied, we restrict these dealings to a minimum.' Salim hesitated. 'Other people do not share our tolerance,' he said simply. 'We prefer to keep ourselves to ourselves, and the fewer outsiders who know our location, the better. We like to be hidden.'

Yes.

I already knew that.

I heard again the voice that had spoken inside my head, the night I had sat under the vast black sky and looked into the shining stone: *Hush! Do not speak of it, for its location is secret and it remains ever hidden.*

I was about to ask more questions – I had so many – but, as if he read what was in my mind, Salim held up his hand. 'Naturally there is much that you wish to know, Lassair, and we are happy to help you learn.' He glanced down at Gurdyman. 'It is why you are here.' I wanted to question that, too, but straight away he spoke again. 'But today is for you and Gurdyman to spend quietly together, for both of you are convalescents. Your bodies and, even more vitally, your spirits need to recover their strength. Take pleasure in being together, talk when you wish to, rest and sleep when fatigue overcomes you.' He indicated the empty chair beside Gurdyman. 'Food and drink will be provided and, when night falls, Hanan will return to take you to your bed.'

It didn't even occur to me to argue with Salim's plan for our day, for it was precisely what I would have chosen. I wasn't at all sure how I would deal with an entire day of leisure, for I couldn't recall ever having had one before. As Salim made his graceful farewell and glided away, however, I was already making up my mind that I was going to enjoy it.

Left by ourselves in the cool, jasmine-scented courtyard, it was some time before either of us spoke.

Then, when I couldn't contain myself any longer, I said, 'It is time, dear Gurdyman, for you to explain yourself. More precisely, to tell me why you have brought me here – or perhaps I should say *I* have brought *you* here, for it is certain that you wouldn't be here had I not been with you and looked after you.'

'You could not have brought me,' he said crushingly, 'for you knew neither our destination nor the road that leads to it.'

His remark stung. 'Oh, don't be so *logical*!' I said. Until I heard the echoes of the fury with which the words emerged, I hadn't realized quite how angry I was. Then, to my shame, I felt tears prickle my eyes.

He reached out and took my hand. 'I apologize,' he said quietly. 'I underestimate, perhaps, the distress of the last few days, and the demands it probably made on you.'

Perhaps? Probably? Oh, he had no idea. 'We almost died, Gurdyman,' I said, trying to keep my voice level and unemotional. 'You were very unwell and steadily deteriorating, I had nothing strong enough to treat you, we were nearly out of food, I was sick and had a high fever and—'

'You were poisoned.'

The coolly-spoken words cut across my increasingly distressed outpourings and at first I didn't take them in.

Then, in the sudden silence, I heard their echo in my head.

You were poisoned.

'*What?*' In my alarm I wrested my hand free. 'But there was barely any food left, and what there was we'd been eating for days! And we'd run out of water, so I had to find a stream.'

He nodded. 'Yes. The poison was in the water with which you topped up our cask.'

'Was it – was there something bad in it?' I thought back, trying to picture the scene, trying to recall my own actions.

'But it was from a narrow little stream that came rushing straight out of the hillside! I tasted it, I did that test you taught me where you put a tiny drop on the lip and wait to see if there is any reaction? Then you—' He nodded impatiently, and I realized I was wasting words in repeating to him his own instructions. 'I was so careful, and I really can't see how it could have been contaminated.'

'The water was pure enough,' he said heavily. 'Or it was until somebody put poison in it.'

'But there was nobody there!' For a moment I was back in the loneliness and the frightening isolation. I stared at him, and I began to read the truth in his face. 'Somebody was watching us?' I whispered. 'Following us? Waiting till we were all alone and vulnerable?'

'Yes,' he said.

And then like a blow over the head I remembered my nightmare vision.

The single, huge eye.

And for a heartbeat I heard the summertime drone.

'I saw something,' I said. I was speaking so softly that he had to lean closer to hear, but even in that serene place I couldn't bring myself to say the words aloud. 'When I was lying out in the open, I thought something was there. A presence, a huge, single eye, and black, shiny talons on the lacings of my gown.' I fought to control my voice, but I could hear it trembling.

'What you saw, or thought you saw, might have been the result of the poison,' Gurdyman said gently.

But I shook my head. 'Some of it, yes, but there really was someone – something – there,' I insisted. 'Besides, whatever it was had the power to put visions in my head, and they were very specific, as if chosen especially for me. I saw—'

I had been about to tell him I'd seen the night when his parents' inn had burned. That I'd probably witnessed his mother engulfed in flames, his friends and neighbours fighting each other to try to escape out of a narrow doorway and trampled to the ground before they burned. Just in time, I bit the words back.

But I think he knew anyway. He gave a deep sigh and

muttered, 'It is a horror that I too have seen in my mind, too many times.'

'I'm sorry.' I reached for his hand again.

He managed a thin smile. 'For what?'

'For being the means by which you have to see it, or at least think about it, again.'

'Child, it is never far away,' he said sadly.

'And it – what it depicts – is why we're here?' I asked timidly.

He was silent for a long time. Then he said, 'There is a power, and it is alive and growing stronger.' Briefly I heard the hum again. 'It comes out of the past, and I have long known of it. Known *it*, once,' he added, the words more to himself than to me.

I wasn't sure what he meant. He knew it, once? In the past, then? In this place? But surely nothing so frightful could emanate from the City of Pearl?

'You're not – you can't be saying that this evil comes from here?'

The faint smile creased his face again. 'No, it did not have its origins here, for it is far more ancient than the first occupation of this city. And you are wrong to name it evil, although I understand that what was put into your mind would make you think so.'

I shook my head in confusion. He noticed – of course he did – and his grip on my hand tightened. 'Child, power in itself is neither beneficial nor harmful; it just *is*. It is what men and women do with it when they learn how to access it that results in what we call good and evil. And few who gain that access can claim always to have acted for the good.' He released me and put his hands up to his face, so that when he spoke again the words were muffled.

But what I *thought* he said was, 'Myself included.'

I saw that he was tired and I let him rest. I lay back in my chair, fluffed up my pillows, drew the soft blanket over my knees and closed my eyes. When I opened them a short time later, he was asleep.

A white-clad servant brought us food some time around

midday, then left us alone. The meal seemed to refresh Gurdyman and when we had finished, he spoke to me of the City of Pearl, of its varied peoples, of its traditions of tolerance and its belief in the sharing and the dispersal of knowledge. He told me of the wonderful things that had been invented here and in the wider region; of how they advanced learning and made life so pleasant and comfortable. By the time dusk began to fall and Hanan appeared to take me away, he was tired again and so was I.

I bade him goodnight and wished him a sound, restorative sleep. He nodded his response. Then Hanan took my hand and we left.

Back in my little room, the sheets on the bed had been invitingly turned down and the lamp with the intricate metal cover was burning, sending pretty patterns dancing on the white walls. My clothes, I noticed, had been returned, and lay across a wooden chest at the foot of the bed. The garments had been beautifully laundered, and some kind hand had expertly repaired the various tears, holes and worn patches acquired through the weeks of travel. I picked up the white linen cap that I usually wear over my braids, and it felt slightly stiff. I didn't think I'd ever seen it so bright.

'I am very grateful,' I said, indicating the clothes.

Hanan nodded. 'You may wear them tomorrow if you wish.'

I looked down at the sea-green robe I'd been lent. 'Might I also keep this for a little longer?'

Hanan smiled, clearly pleased. 'Of course. It is a gift, for you to wear or not as you choose.'

'Thank you.'

She nodded again, already backing out of the room. 'Now I wish you goodnight,' she said, and softly she closed the door.

I had thought that, after my lazy, self-indulgent day and the long nap I'd taken after Gurdyman and I had eaten, I wouldn't sleep. I was wrong. Perhaps the hardships, the worry and the fear of the long journey had taken more out of me than I realized. I remember getting between the smooth, cool sheets, putting my head down on the blissfully soft pillow and blowing out the lamp. I remember someone – a man – laughing softly in the street below, and someone else hushing him. I remember the smell of jasmine. Then I fell asleep.

The days passed. Lazy days of convalescence to begin with, when Gurdyman and I rested in the sunny courtyard in our comfortable chairs, ate, slept, talked. Then, as I recovered my strength and began to get restless, one morning Salim asked hesitantly if I would like to meet some of his townspeople.

I almost cried *Yes!* there and then.

'What about Gurdyman?' I asked; he was dozing in his chair, and I kept my voice down.

Salim looked at his old friend.

'I think he should rest for some more days yet,' he replied. Then, as if he had sensed my sudden anxiety, he added, 'Both of you have suffered an ordeal. You who are young naturally recover more swiftly.'

I wanted to ask for reassurance; I wanted to hear Salim say that Gurdyman would definitely get better, in time. But I was a healer and I knew it wasn't wise to make such promises.

'Should I not stay with him?'

Salim shook his head. 'No need,' he said. 'He will be watched over and cared for.' Then he held out his hand and I took it.

On that first day he took me to meet a doctor. He had realized, I suspect, where my main interests lay and he could not have chosen better. The doctor was a small, wizened man with very dark skin and immaculate white robes, his rooms were shiny-clean and smelt sweetly of herbs, and he opened my eyes to a world I had barely imagined. Using beautifully-coloured images, he took me on a tour through the interior of the human body, and so many things that had been a mystery to me suddenly became clear.

When we stopped to eat a simple meal – warm bread, olives, goat's cheese and a lemon-flavoured drink – he sat looking at me, gently smiling. 'You like to learn,' he observed. 'You are like a . . .' He paused, searching for the word. 'A sponge,' he said.

A sponge.

Yes, that was exactly what I was. And I went on being it for the rest of that day and the one that followed. When my small doctor had to turn me away and see his patients, Salim took me instead to a large, cool room where there were more scrolls, manuscripts and books than I'd imagined could exist in the world and left me in the charge of a handsome young man with perfect manners who did his best to describe the motion of the planets. In numerous successive sessions up in that cool room I was taught the rudiments of mathematics, geometry, something called algebra, and as the days and then weeks went by I began to feel that the sponge had absorbed all it could for now.

Then I spent a day with Hanan, who took me to her house to meet her family. After the endless hours of study, it was good to chatter and laugh. Hanan's ancient grandmother showed me how to cook some of their favourite dishes.

That evening, as I did every evening, I went to see Gurdyman before bed. His colour was better, I thought, although he wasn't improving as quickly as I'd have liked.

'You look well, child,' he said with a smile.

'I am well,' I replied.

'You like it here in the City of Pearl?'

'I love it,' I said with total honesty. 'But—' I stopped, for even as I'd said the word, I saw a shadow pass over his face. It was surely not right to worry him, when he was still recovering his strength.

He watched me, still smiling faintly. 'Always questions,' he murmured.

He was quite right. The questions I very much wanted to ask him just then were, *What are we doing here?* and *How long are we staying?*

The same questions, really, that I'd been so anxious to ask since our journey had begun.

He leaned back in his chair, his eyelids drooping. 'Goodnight, Lassair,' he said. 'Sleep well.'

I tiptoed away.

It was dark when I woke up.

I was afraid, although I didn't know why because the

moonlight was sufficient to show that nothing in the room had changed: I was in my bed, safe, warm, and all was quiet.

No it wasn't.

I had heard something, and now I strained to hear it again.

Shouting, some way off. And a crackling sound.

I leapt out of bed and ran to the window. I leaned out, and some stray breeze from the valley far below brought the smell of smoke. Even as I stood there peering out, trying to see its source, it grew stronger; now I could see white clouds billowing up from an area on the fringes of the city, where a road came curling up from the vale.

Then there was a loud bang, and a great shower of sparks flew up into the night sky. There were screams, more shouting, the sound of voices calling and crying out in horror.

The sparks had turned to flames; wild fire, roaring so loudly that I could hear its menace as it leapt up in a high arc above whatever building was its source.

The flames were bright, brilliant blue.

ELEVEN

The dreary days of a cold fenland winter were slowly passing. Jack had made no progress in his search for any word about the vagrant Gurdyman discovered dead outside his house with a pearl in his hand and, as the weeks passed and the beggar's death faded further into the past and the back of people's memories, he began to believe he never would.

Although he had assumed Gurdyman took the pearl, he hadn't managed to discover what had happened to the body. He guessed its presence had eventually come to the notice of those lowly men whose job it was to dispose of the city's refuse, and that it would have been loaded onto a cart and tipped into some common grave, perhaps with a few words muttered over it by a priest with more important things on his mind. That was what usually happened.

None of which was any help whatsoever in tracing the dead man's last movements . . .

Jack had been optimistic at first, methodically visiting all the places where the poor gathered for succour and shelter, from the clean but basic refuges run by the monks to the filthy hovels at the far end of the quayside that were the haunts of the truly desperate, and that most people avoided as if they feared some frightful sickness or a knife in the guts. He had spoken with thieves and pickpockets, following up the vague thought that the vagrant had stolen the pearl and might therefore be known to other men who lived by the same uncertain and dishonest craft. He had called on the women and the men who ran the taverns and the brothels beside the river; in particular, he had briefed his friend Magnus, who with his pretty young wife ran the tavern Jack had always used as an unofficial meeting place for his group of loyal and trustworthy lawmen, telling him who he was looking for and asking him to pass the word and keep his ears open.

The problem was that he was only able to give such a loose description of the dead vagrant that it could have fitted almost any male from fifteen to fifty. Gurdyman could have provided helpful details about the man, but Gurdyman was far away. The only distinguishing feature about this particular vagrant was that his body had been found in the alleys off the market square and he had stolen a pearl.

The paltry description was proving to be useless. After all the endless trudging and the countless questions, Jack had discovered precisely nothing.

Now it was some weeks since he had seen Hrype, and as he trudged off through ankle-deep snow towards the castle, he wondered if he was faring any better. On an impulse, he decided not to report to the guardroom – there wasn't any real need for him to pay a visit, since the bad weather was keeping most people indoors and had apparently frozen any criminal tendencies out of those who did venture out, and he'd only been going for the company – and instead headed over the Great Bridge, turning off the road towards the market square and diving into the warren of passageways within which Gurdyman's house was hidden away.

He had little hope of finding Hrype there; it would have been far too much of a coincidence. He had a vague idea of leaving a token of some sort that might prompt Hrype into coming to see him next time he was in town, but he was already dismissing it as he approached the house. For one thing, Hrype would undoubtedly seek him out anyway if he had anything to report and probably even if he hadn't, and for another, Jack had nothing on him which could be spared to serve as such a token.

As he reached Gurdyman's house, with its shallow stone steps leading up to the stout wooden door, all thoughts of leaving messages and talking to Hrype were driven out of his head.

The snow on the steps had been disturbed; it looked as if something like a wing had passed over it in a narrow arc, and there was one small footprint.

And the door was fractionally open.

Standing in the alley so as not to disturb the marks in the

snow, Jack leaned over and very gently pushed the door. Silently it opened further, then it caught on something. When there was a clear space for his feet, he leapt over the steps and landed with a thump in the dark passage. His elbow banged into the door, sending it crashing back against the wall.

So much for not alerting whoever was inside.

Glancing down, Jack saw a shattered lantern lying on the floor.

He advanced down the passage, one hand on the hilt of the large and very sharp knife that he kept in a thick leather sheath attached to his belt and concealed under his outer garments in the small of his back. In the enclosed space, it was a handier weapon than his sword.

Whoever was within, he was sure it wasn't Hrype. The footprint was far too small.

He went on, light from the enclosed court at the far end of the passage now illuminating his way, for a door had been left ajar. He looked in the small room to the left that served as a kitchen, and went up the first few rungs of the ladder in order to peer into the attic room above.

The bed had been turned on its side, the wooden frame cracked, the mattress ripped open and the bedding, torn and shredded as if with giant talons, scattered all over the floor. It was as if whoever had done it had, in Lassair's absence, taken out on her bed the violence they would have hurled at her.

Descending, very shaken, Jack went out into the courtyard. There was nobody to be seen, and the house was too sparsely furnished to afford places of concealment behind cupboards or beneath elaborate beds and chairs.

He turned, gathering his courage, for now he had to check the crypt.

He had been down there briefly a couple of times before, when he and Lassair had been searching for Gurdyman. He had not got much further than the steps, but even there he had sensed something about the deep, dark space. It smelt odd, and the shelves and benches had borne a selection of strange objects and heavy leather-bound tomes, but it had been the sensation of quiet power thrumming steadily from some unknown source that had most set his senses on alert.

Now, as he descended the second flight of steps and jumped down into Gurdyman's workroom, he felt the power again.

But this time it was subtly altered.

He had a sensation of someone, or something, suddenly very close – far too close – behind him. In a heartbeat he smelt something sharp but quite pleasant and refreshing – he didn't know what it was – and he felt the whisper of breath as someone muttered soft words just below the level of hearing. Before he could do anything to defend himself – before he could even turn round – he found himself breathing in a different smell, one that wasn't in the least pleasant and that, far from being refreshing, instantly made his head reel and nausea rise in his throat.

He said, the words no more than a choked hiss, 'I can't breathe!'

He felt small hands on him, supporting him with surprising strength as his legs gave way, lowering him carefully so that his head did not crash against the stone floor.

As his eyes began to close and consciousness fled, he thought he heard the soft whispering voice again. 'Do not come here,' it said now. 'This is not your concern.'

Then his head filled with pain and he blacked out.

It was Hrype who found him. Hrype who was there, some unknown time later, when he opened his eyes and woke to pain, puzzlement and an urgent need to empty his bladder.

He muttered this most immediate need to Hrype, who helped him along to the rear of the house and waited, then took his arm and guided him back to the crypt. 'Lie on the bed,' Hrype commanded.

Jack did so. He felt slightly better when he was lying down. He looked up at Hrype. 'How long have I been here?'

'When did you arrive?'

Jack thought. 'This morning.' But which morning? he wondered. As if the same thought had occurred to Hrype, he raised an eyebrow, arms folded as he stood before Jack. 'Er – two days have passed since the last heavy snowfall.'

'Ah.' Hrype nodded. 'That was in fact yesterday morning, then.'

'How did you know I was here?'

Hrype studied him for a long moment before answering. 'If I said I sensed it you probably wouldn't believe me, but in fact I can offer no other explanation.' As if he knew it wasn't enough, he added, 'There was a good friend of mine who lived nearby, close to the sacred well. I use the old house when I have occasion to stay here in the town overnight, for I no longer care to remain in Gurdyman's house after darkness falls.'

'I know what you mean,' Jack muttered fervently. Then the sense of what Hrype had just said penetrated his dazed mind, and he said, 'I've been to the place by the sacred well.' He could have added, *Lassair and I discovered two recently dead bodies there*, but he decided not to. Hrype would know only too well what happened to the house's occupants, and there was enough to worry about in the present situation without dragging up the horrors of the past.

'The friend of whom I speak,' Hrype was saying, 'remains in some form within the house. I cannot say how, only that I have evidence of this. Thoughts have been put into my head; again, I do not explain, only to tell you what I have experienced. On the first occasion, I had just come from here – from this house – and I was afraid. The thought that arose in my mind then was that there was indeed a threat, but that it was not to me. The second time was soon after dawn today. I woke from a dream, and I knew I must come to Gurdyman's house.' He paused. 'Of course, it might have nothing to do with any outside agency, and merely my own conscience telling me it was high time I checked on my old friend's dwelling again.' The expression in his light eyes seemed to say, *I know what I believe, and am not much concerned with your opinion.*

Jack smiled. 'However you came to be here, I'm glad to see you.'

'Do you recall what happened?' Hrype asked.

Jack shrugged. 'I came to the house, I found the door open, the merest crack. I saw a small footprint and other marks in the snow on the step. I searched up above, on the ground floor, and there was nobody there.' He paused. 'Someone has been up in the attic room. The bed's been destroyed. It could be they were searching for something,' he went on before Hrype could comment, 'but I don't think so. I felt violence and—' He stopped. It was better not to put what else he had sensed into words. 'I came down here. I smelt something, I heard a whisper of breath, then I was collapsing. I would have fallen like a stone, for all power had left me, but somebody lowered me down. I heard a voice telling me not to come here because it wasn't my concern, then nothing.'

Hrype nodded. 'Did you feel afraid?'

'There wasn't really time,' Jack replied.

Hrype smiled thinly. '*I* felt afraid,' he said. 'I came here, alone, and my fear began even before I stepped inside. I thought there was someone in the house; a listening, watching, silent presence, waiting to see what I was going to do. It intensified once I came down here, and then I thought I heard a very soft whisper, in another tongue. It was too much for me and I fled back up the steps. I was fumbling to open the door and I dropped the lantern, and in the sudden darkness I had a very clear image.' He glanced at Jack. 'Of a pearl.'

'I'm surprised, then,' Jack said after a while, 'that you came back.'

Hrype smiled again. 'I'm not sure I would have done without the prompt.'

All at once Jack wanted more than anything to get out of the crypt; to get out of the house. He realized as he struggled to stand up that he was both extremely thirsty and very hungry. Pushing Hrype's restraining hand out of the way – 'I'm all right!' he muttered – he strode over to the steps, along the passage and up to the door. Turning to Hrype, he said, 'Come with me. I know a tavern where they serve up good food and even better ale.'

He emerged onto the alley, watched as Hrype locked the door, and then, with Hrype's footfalls right behind him, set off for the quayside.

He paid for the bread, bacon and mugs of ale. He felt that, Hrype having come to find him, it was the least he could do.

When they had finished the food and the mugs had been refilled, he said, 'So, now we know that a small, slight but nevertheless strong person who speaks words in a foreign tongue in a very soft whisper haunts Gurdyman's house.'

'Small, slight but strong?' Hrype queried.

'The footprint in the snow was small, and I had the impression that whoever came up behind me was short and slim. But he was strong, because he bore my weight as I fell.'

'And you are neither short nor slim,' Hrype agreed.

'It's all muscle,' Jack muttered.

'You have done better than I,' Hrype said, 'for, although I have felt this man's presence in other places, I perceived no sense of his size.'

Jack shot him a look. 'Where else have you sensed him?'

Hrype met his eyes. Jack sensed he was reluctant to answer. Then, with a sigh, he said, 'Once out near Aelf Fen. Once on the track that leads from the fens into the town.'

Jack felt a stab of alarm. Both were locations he associated with Lassair.

'He's looking for her,' he said.

But Hrype shook his head. 'No. I do not believe he is any danger to her. She is far away in any case, and I cannot think he doesn't know it.'

'So what's he doing here?'

Hrype didn't answer for some time. Then he said, 'I have given the question endless thought, and there is one answer that has occurred to me. Well, many have occurred, but all the others I have rejected.'

'We'd better have the one you've held on to, then,' Jack said. He hoped his impatience hadn't been detectable.

Hrype's brief look of apology suggested it had. 'I think this person came here for a purpose, which was to prompt Gurdyman into setting out on his journey. Why he has to make it, who wants him to go and why he had to leave precisely when he did, I still cannot say. This person perhaps came as the agent of somebody else, and his role was complete once he'd put that token of the single, beautiful pearl in a place where Gurdyman would spot it.'

'So why didn't this person leave as soon as he'd achieved his purpose?'

'Yes, that is the question,' Hrype agreed. 'He was delayed somehow – perhaps he was injured, perhaps he was sick – and by the time he was able to go, it was no longer possible.'

Jack, nodding, saw what he meant. 'Because there were no more ships,' he said. 'Winter had tightened its fist, and few if any boats were setting out even for the coast, never mind for destinations further away.'

Hrype was watching him with a strange, eager light in his eyes. 'What do you think?' he demanded. 'Does it make sense?'

'Yes,' Jack said simply. He picked up his mug, drained it and stood up.

'Where are you going?' Hrype asked.

'The weather is still bad, but it's warmer than yesterday and soon, maybe, the snow and the ice will clear. River traffic will start up again as soon as it's at all feasible – commerce doesn't wait any longer than it must, and there are livings to earn – so there's no time to lose.'

'You're going to find him.'

'I am going to try. Even if he manages to elude me, I'm going to look for the place he's been putting up. If you're right, and he was indeed sick or injured, then it may be he'll have kept out of others' way. I've been doing the rounds of the better-frequented places but I've been asking for news of the dead vagrant with the pearl. But now we know he was merely incidental. I'm going to search again, widen the area and change the description of the man I'm looking for.'

'He attacked you,' Hrype said softly. 'He administered some substance that put you out cold on the floor of Gurdyman's crypt for a day and a night.'

'He won't do so again.' Jack stared down at Hrype. 'I'll be here tomorrow evening, so you can come and find me if you have anything to report, and I'll return at the same time on all subsequent days until we find him.'

'Very well.'

'In the meantime, if you need me I'm sure you know where I live.'

'I do.' Then, as Jack turned to go, Hrype added, 'Good luck.'

It was only after they had gone their separate ways that Jack realized he had omitted to ask Hrype what he was planning to do.

It took Jack almost a week but in the end he met with success, of a sort.

Methodically he did the rounds of all the places he'd been to before. The taverns, the brothels, the houses of charity run by the monks and the nuns. He spoke to the boatmen, shut up in their boats while they waited on the weather. He spoke to the apothecaries and the healers. Everywhere he asked the same question: have you seen a slim, slight, foreign man who was laid up injured, or sick, some time in the late autumn?

And it was a healer who gave him the first clue.

It gave Jack a stab to the heart to stand in the tiny shop where the healer made his preparations and advised his patients, for the smell of herbs, spices, ointments and sweet oils reminded him so forcefully of Lassair that he almost felt she was right there beside him.

But this healer was, in all important respects, entirely different. He was a very old man, his long white hair and beard were tangled and not very clean, the black cap and gown stained with ancient food. He was impatient and irascible, and as soon as he understood that there was no money involved in this interaction, that Jack was only there to ask for information, he tried to shoo him out through the door. Jack was obliged to tell him he was a man of the law and threaten him with obstructing a legitimate enquiry before he would relent.

'Why d'you want to know about this little foreigner, then?' he demanded. 'Done something wicked, has he?' He gave a hoarse, malevolent chuckle, which loosened phlegm in his throat. He coughed, spat, then added, 'Attacked someone, has he?' He chucked again, with the same result. 'Some fine specimen like yourself, and him a dainty little runt of a fellow?'

'You know who I mean?' Jack said, pouncing on the last few words.

'I might and I might not,' replied the healer. 'Oh, very well!'

Jack had taken a step forward. 'I did treat a man who sounds like the one you're after, although for the life of me I can't imagine what you want with him, nice, polite, innocuous sort of a fellow that he was.'

'What was wrong with him?'

'He was sick, like you said. He had a cough and he couldn't breathe. Soon as I saw him I reckoned it was the cold and the damp, and he said that was so, and that he was used to warmer, drier weather, even in the fall of the year.' He chucked again, and the malice was even more noticeable. 'I told him, I did, then you don't want to go visiting the fen country in the autumn or the winter, because warm and dry conditions are not what you'll find!' He laughed uproariously at his own wit, and Jack thought that the ensuing coughing fit was well deserved.

'When did you last see him?' he asked, once the old man had recovered enough to speak.

'Oooh, two, three weeks back. He came in for more supplies of horehound, and he asked me how soon the boats'd be running again. I told him it'd be a while yet.' He nodded as if in verification of his words.

'Did he say where he was bound?'

The old man shook his head. 'Up to the coast, I'm guessing, if he was waiting here for a boat, as that's where they mostly all go.' He chuckled again. 'But that won't be the final destination if I'm any judge, what with him being foreign.'

'Foreign,' Jack repeated. It was no more than he already knew. 'You can't add anything to that? Hazard a guess as to where he came from?'

'How should I know?' countered the old healer. 'One accent sounds like another, far as I'm concerned. I don't like foreigners,' he added with sudden venom.

'I expect you like their money,' Jack observed.

The old man spat again, which seemed to be his eloquent comment on the matter.

Reasoning that a man who wished to leave the town on the first boat that would take him to the coast would probably try to put up close to the quay, that was where Jack went next.

And there too, increasing his frustration, he met with the man's trail and not the man himself.

At a dim, dark little place tucked away almost at the end of the quay, beyond the last of the brothels and hidden by a large warehouse, Jack learned that a short, slim foreign man had indeed been staying for perhaps six weeks and probably longer. Nobody seemed quite sure when he had arrived – the management of the place appeared to be fairly haphazard, with nothing in the way of a record of who had stayed and for how long – but the consensus was that it was well over a month, according to a woman who did the laundry, and that the man had arrived around All Saints', according to a fat man whose role, judging by the broom in his hand, appeared to be to sweep the floor.

'He was sick, wasn't he?' Jack asked the woman, who seemed to be the more intelligent of the pair.

'Oh, that he was,' she replied. 'He'd have gone weeks ago otherwise, or that's what I thought. He gave the impression he couldn't wait to leave.'

'He was frightened, he was,' put in the man with the broom. 'His big brown eyes used to widen with fear, and you could see the whites all the way round. He was wary of everyone as was put in with him, and when she – not *her*,' he said, jerking a thumb at the washerwoman, 'I mean her, the mistress – when she said his coughing was that bad it was keeping folks awake and putting off the customers, and he'd have to move to the outhouse, he were *glad* of it!' His eyes rounded in amazement at anybody preferring an outhouse to a communal sleeping chamber.

'Show me this outhouse,' Jack ordered.

Still holding his broom the man did so, leading the way out of the low, dark building, around its end and across a dirty, stinking yard to a short row of lean-tos on the far side. 'In there,' he said, pushing at a door whose planks were rotted at the base.

Jack stepped inside.

The room was very small, and there was little within except a straw mattress, a neatly stacked pile of cracked platters and a few small items of furniture too far gone for repair, presumably chucked out from the inn. There was a circle of stones in the middle of the floor, the earth black with ash. The occupant, he reflected, had done his best with his meagre accommodation.

'Mistress said he could light a fire,' the fat man said. He pointed at the pile of broken tables and stools in the corner. 'No shortage of fuel, if you weren't fussy. And he had his own blanket – good and thick it was.'

A blanket. A straw mattress. A fire. Dear God, Jack thought, even so it was no place for a man with a bad chest to overwinter.

'Where is he now?' he asked.

The man had begun to move his broom to and fro across the floor, but in such a desultory fashion that you couldn't really call it sweeping. 'No idea,' he replied.

'But he's settled up? He's paid you and he's gone?'

The man nodded. A sly smile spread across his huge face. 'Gave me a tip,' he said, reaching into a pouch at his belt. 'I fetched him food and drink when he was too poorly to go out, see, and he remembered.'

He was holding up a pale object between finger and thumb.

It was a very small pearl.

During Jack's week of searching, Hrype had been out of town.

The more he thought about it, the more certain he was that he'd guessed correctly concerning the elusive figure of the slight foreign man: that only mischance had kept him in Cambridge over the winter.

He will leave very soon, Hrype thought as he trudged along.

On an impulse he stopped, left the track and forced a way through snow-laden trees and undergrowth until he came to a small area of clear ground. It was too cold to sit, so he squatted down instead, then took his rune stones out of their bag, cast them on the piece of cloth he kept with them and, for some time, simply stared at them.

They confirmed what he already suspected.

After the moments of silent thanks to whatever spirit empowered them, he put them carefully away.

Then, his mission on the fen fringes all the more important now, he went on his way.

With so much to tell Hrype, Jack found it immensely frustrating that, evening after evening, he failed to show up in Marcus's tavern. When finally he did, looking wet, cold and tired, Jack restrained his impatience until he had drunk and eaten, then succinctly outlined all that he had learned.

'The pearl,' he concluded, 'seems to suggest he's the right man. Maybe he had a small supply of them, and used them in payment as well as for throwing Gurdyman into a state of panicked alarm.'

Hrype said nothing for a while. Then, with a sigh, he muttered, 'The right man, yes, so it indeed appears. But where does that take us, if we can't find him and still have no idea where he came from, who sent him and why they had to make Gurdyman set out on his journey? And if he—' He stopped.

'We can't find him *yet*,' Jack said, concentrating only on the first part of Hrype's complaint.

'But you think we will?'

'He's desperate to leave,' Jack replied. 'We'll just have to watch the boats, once they start moving again, and wait till he approaches one.'

'And how do we do that?'

Jack grinned. 'I'm not without resources,' he said. 'I'll set men to watch.'

'And what if he sets out over land?'

'He won't. He needs to get to the coast, and travelling by water is the only option in this season when the land is flooded.'

Hrype was watching him with a peculiar intensity. 'Impress on these resources of yours how important it is,' he said very softly. 'He's restless now. You tell me he's left the place he's been lodging, and you don't know where he is now. He'll leave soon, Jack. Very soon.'

'He can't go unless there's a boat,' Jack pointed out.

Hrype muttered something that sounded like *There will be.*

Deciding not to ask how he could be so sure, since the answer would undoubtedly take them into realms where he preferred not to trespass, Jack reached for their empty mugs and went for refills.

That night as the town slept, the thaw that had set in a few days ago, slowly building momentum, suddenly increased its pace.

Residual floes of ice on the river grew smaller and disappeared. Drifted snow on the banks of a hundred tributary streams and ditches melted. Soft rain began to fall.

And the river that had been all but unmoving since the freeze set in slowly came back to life.

On the quay in Cambridge an old and experienced shipman, uneasy and wakeful as he lay in the storage space of his boat, felt the alteration. He got out of the huddle of blankets and skins with which he'd kept himself warm and clambered up on to the deck. Yes, his instincts had been right. He stood watching as the water flowed strongly past, and something in him responded to its joy in this release from deep winter's hard grip.

'Getting moving at a pace now, aren't you?' he muttered softly. 'Well, I reckon I'll go along with you.'

He had a cargo of salt pork, herbs and spices waiting for him at Lynn, and buyers who would shove each other out of the way with desperation-born ferocity the moment he brought it back upriver. He'd be able to add on a coin or two to the going rate. He smiled to himself.

As soon as it grew light, he went back into the hold, kicked awake his three-man crew and told them what was happening.

A little over an hour later, with an even stronger current flowing, he was ready to leave. He'd sent the lad to draw in the plank they'd set up to enable them to fetch last-minute supplies from ashore, and the boy already had his hands on it.

Then a cloaked, muffled figure came hurrying up. The lad let go of the plank and rubbed his eyes. 'Now where in God's name did *you* come from?' he muttered. 'I was looking right at the spot where you're standing, and I'll swear you weren't there a moment ago.'

He made the sign of the cross. Then, surreptitiously, added the hand gesture against the evil eye.

A soft voice called out, 'You take passenger to coast?'

The shipman, hearing, paused. He named a price, far higher than the usual rate. The figure looked about to haggle, then nodded. The lad reached out a hand along the plank and the figure took it, accepting the assistance with a courteous smile.

Then the plank was drawn up and laid down on the deck, the ropes that tethered the little craft to the quay were unfastened and, with barely a nudge from the skipper's long pole, she was caught by the fast-flowing water and set off on her journey to the coast.

TWELVE

The fire was burning with a strange intensity. The blue flames soared into the sky. A vast, overpowering crackling noise pulsed out from whatever the blaze was feeding on, unlike anything I'd ever heard before.

There were shouts, cries, screams from all around. Others were awake now. Of course they were – the lower slopes of the little town were close to the blaze, and nobody could have slept through the noise and the brilliant light in the sky. Besides that, there was something unnatural about the fire . . . Even from where I stood, some distance away from and above the inferno, I sensed it. I felt as if my skin was alive, as if soft fingers were brushing up and down my body, sending out tremors and tremblings of reaction.

The strange thing was that the sensation wasn't totally unpleasant.

Hanan was beside me.

'What is it?' I breathed. 'What's happened?'

She shook her head. 'I do not know. I have seen fires before, but not like this.'

'It's blue,' I said stupidly, as if she couldn't see that for herself. 'Why?'

Again, she shook her head.

There were more screams, piercing, horrible, and I thought they were coming from the area around the fire. My healer self took over. I drew on my clothes, braided my hair and covered it with my cap, picked up my satchel and slung it across my body. 'Come on,' I said.

She nodded, understanding. Well, she would, for she was a healer too. As we reached the door and the steps down to the street, she touched my arm. Turning, I saw she had a folded veil over her arm, made from some fairly dense material.

'I don't need— ' I began. But then I realized it was wet –

heavy with absorbed water – and that she had one for herself too.

'I put them in a bucket of water when I first saw the flames,' she said. 'It is our normal practice, when attending the victims of fire. You cannot help others if you are burned.'

If you are burned. It was a horrible thought. I drove it away, took the veil and flew down the steps.

Others were making their way down the narrow, steeply sloping streets towards the fire. Some of the more level-headed townspeople, perhaps sensing the incipient panic and observing how the crowd was getting in the way of those who could help, tried to get them to return home. There were shouts and orders in different languages, few of which had any effect.

We were close now.

And then, just ahead, I saw a familiar figure. Short, rotund, bald dome of a head circled with silver-white hair.

Gurdyman, on the arm of the tall figure of Salim, was hurrying to the fire.

I ran on, catching them up. 'You shouldn't be here!' I cried, grabbing his hand as if I would hold him back by force. 'You shouldn't have let him come!' I yelled to Salim. 'You know better than anybody that he's not well!'

Salim gazed at me impassively. We were still moving forward, partly under our own momentum, partly driven on by the crowd. His eyes softened for a moment with compassion. 'I could not stop him,' he said above the noise. 'He is here for the same reason that you are. That she is.' He jerked his head at Hanan. 'That I am.'

I was staring at Gurdyman, trying to see right into his face and read his expression. He was pale, and the blueish tinge around his lips was back. He looked utterly resolute, and I began to see that Salim had spoken the truth when he said Gurdyman wasn't to be stopped. I met his eyes, and he nodded. 'Yes,' he said, leaning close to speak in my ear. 'I understand the danger, and so we will all keep a careful eye upon him.'

And then there was no more time for talk.

We came round a bend in the road and the heat hit us.

People were gasping, crying, screaming as the horrible sight came into view. A long row of low buildings was aflame, the fire roaring with great intensity and, as yet, confined to the structures already burning. There was no wind, which probably accounted for this, but, as if the fire resented being robbed of further fuel, it seemed to burn all the harder.

'What were these buildings?' I shouted to Salim.

'Storage, stabling sometimes when outsiders – when guests have come to the town,' he replied.

I noticed the courteous amendment.

'Not dwellings for people?'

But he only shrugged.

Stabling. Oh, no! I grabbed his arm. 'My horse?' I yelled. My sturdy little pony! Where was he?

He smiled faintly. 'No, he's not down here. He is safe.'

Hanan gave a sudden cry, and a soft wail emerged from her parted lips. I spun round to see what she had seen.

There were two bodies on the ground, still moving despite the terrible damage, still trying to crawl away from the destroying heat.

Together she and I leapt towards them, but strong hands held us back.

'You can do nothing,' said Salim's hard voice.

I tried to pull myself out of his grip. 'We have our veils, soaked in water!' I shouted, shaking my veil in his face.

But he shook his head. 'They would avail you nothing. You would burn and die too.'

He turned to the two men closest to us, muttering a string of instructions. They nodded, then hurried away. They seemed to be going around the burning buildings in a wide circle, keeping a safe distance.

'They are searching for others who might have escaped,' he said. The compassion was in his eyes again, but now it was not for me. He was reaching into a pouch by his side, removing a bundle of soft cloth and a small bottle made of dark brown glass. He saw me watching. 'You wish to help?' he said quietly.

'Yes.'

He straightened his shoulders and walked towards the two figures on the ground. They had stopped crawling now. They had managed to get some distance from the fire, which was starting to die down, but I didn't think that was the reason for the cessation of movement.

They were still alive, but barely. All of their clothing and most of their flesh had burned away.

Salim crouched beside one of the pair. He tore the cloth in two, handing half to me. 'Do as I do,' he said.

He unstopped the bottle and put several drops of a darkish liquid onto the cloth. He gave it to me and I did the same. 'Be very careful not to breathe in the fumes,' he warned.

Then very gently he put the padded cloth over what remained of the nose and lips of the man – or it could have been a woman – lying before him. Equally gently, I did the same with the other body.

Salim's victim struggled feebly for some moments. Mine was probably already dead, for I detected no movement at all.

I didn't realize I was weeping until I felt the tears running into my mouth.

When it was done, Salim stood up, carefully put away the bottle and the pieces of cloth and stood up. He took my hand. He saw my tears and reached up to wipe them away. 'It is an element of healing,' he said gently, 'to understand when the damage and the agony are too great for life to be tolerable.'

'We killed them,' I whispered.

But he shook his head. 'They were already far along the road to death,' he said. 'We merely put an end to the hopeless pain.'

I sensed he was right. My head knew he was, anyway. But as we slowly walked away, I knew it would take my heart some time to catch up.

And then all thought of the two dead bodies flew out of my mind.

Because Gurdyman sat slumped on the ground, Hanan's arms around him and her worried face staring up at Salim and me in desperate appeal. 'He collapsed!' she cried. 'He put his hand to his chest, gave a cry and fell!'

I dropped to my knees in front of him, taking in the half-opened eyes, the blue lips, the pallor of the plump face from which so much flesh seemed to have fallen away. 'Oh, Gurdyman!' I whispered.

In that moment I was not a healer, not a potential source of help for him. I was simply someone who loved him, thrown into a panic of anxiety and horrified distress because she thought she was about to lose him.

Then the calm tones of Salim were giving orders. Somebody brought a door from a nearby house, removed quickly from its very basic hinges, and eager hands were raising Gurdyman up and carefully laying him on it. A woman handed me her shawl, and I bundled it up and put it under his head. Someone else provided a cloak and I wrapped him in it, for already his hands felt cold.

Men stepped forward to bear him, one at each corner, and slowly, as if he were a king of old on his bier, he was borne away up the sloping street and back to Salim's house.

Gurdyman didn't die.

He was very ill, and I think it was only Salim's profound knowledge and incredible skill that brought him back. It was his heart, of course, as it had long been, and Salim was quite right when he said that Gurdyman had been very unwise even to consider the journey all the way from England to the City of Pearl.

'He would not be stopped,' I muttered when he repeated this for perhaps the tenth time.

Salim touched my hand. 'It is not your fault,' he said. 'There are – other forces are at work.'

But I was struggling with my guilt, for in my heart I believed I must be to blame – I should have *made* him go back! – and I barely heard him.

I tried to suppress my emotions by observing everything that Salim did. I watched Hanan too, for she adopted the role of Salim's assistant, and I came to understand that she knew almost as much as he did.

In my time with the people of the City of Pearl I had already been astounded many times by the things they could do; by the answers they had worked out to the questions common to all human beings; by the love and the compassion they poured into everything they made and everything they did, as if in each moment of the day they were determined to do their very best; by their insistence on using the talents and the abilities they had been born with for the benefit of each other and for the community.

And constantly, all the time, all over the city, they shared what they knew. There were schools and libraries like the cool, shady room where I'd been taught, where the older and the wiser men and women were happy to instruct others, and no question was too silly (I knew that from personal experience) and nobody was ever made to feel ashamed because they didn't know the answer.

In those days and weeks when Gurdyman lay so close to death, I learned more about the nature of the heart, the failings to which it is prone and the best way to treat them, than I had ever dreamed was possible.

On the first day that Gurdyman sat up in his bed, Salim left him in Hanan's care and took me off to his workroom. He had the heart of a stillborn calf in a bowl of some sharp-smelling liquid and, after removing it and patting it dry, he proceeded to cut it open.

'I am dissecting it,' he told me. 'This is in order to show you how it works.'

'Are you allowed to do that?' I breathed. I didn't know then that the heart had come out of a calf.

He laughed. 'Yes. It is not human, Lassair, but the anatomy and the method by which the organ operates are similar enough for our lesson.'

Then he showed me the chambers and the little tubes, demonstrating the pumping motion which made the blood flow. He unrolled a long scroll of parchment on which there was a drawing of a human body – it was similar to the drawings my dark little doctor had showed me – and pointed out the blue and the red tubes that went all through it, explaining how the beat of the heart made the blood flow right to the tiniest of them.

It was all but impossible to believe him, but he insisted it was true.

He showed me what happened if something made a blockage within the heart. 'We believe this is what occurs when men like Gurdyman collapse in great pain and clutch at their chests,' he said. 'Those who survive say it is like a very severe cramp.'

'Yes, I have treated such patients,' I said.

He nodded. 'Well, the heart is made of muscle, so perhaps we should think of a cramp in our leg, reflect on how painful it is, and then multiply the intensity by ten.' While I was still thinking of that, he went on, 'You treat this condition with belladonna?'

'Yes, but only when it is severe. Otherwise with digitalis.'

'Yes, just as we do,' he remarked. 'I believe,' he added, as if confiding a great secret, 'that the drug thins the blood somehow, so that the proper flow is restored.'

I wasn't sure I believed that, either.

Gurdyman was improving, but slowly. Salim had told me that this had been a bad attack, and that it was highly likely my beloved mentor and teacher would not recover fully. I was still struggling to accept that. For me, Gurdyman was invincible. I found it very hard to understand he wasn't going to live for ever.

But he was getting stronger. Now he was at last able to get out of bed and walk to the pail behind the screen in the corner that was kept for bodily waste. It was an important moment, and all of us – Salim, Hanan, Gurdyman, I myself – felt a lifting of the spirits.

Then one day everything changed.

I'd been given some time away from the sick room – both Salim and Hanan said I must have a rest from the anxiety and the work – and I was out in the city, exploring. I knew the central area well by now, after all the weeks and months, and today I planned to venture further. I'd dressed accordingly, putting on my own clothes and, instead of the soft little leather slippers we usually wore, my stout boots. As ever, I carried my satchel, in it my sister's shawl and the shining stone. At the last moment, I picked up my cloak; although the morning was warm and sunny, I knew from experience that the wind often shifted round to the east later in the day and sometimes it even brought flurries of snow.

I believe I knew even then, as I prepared for the outing, that something was about to happen.

I went down to where a big bridge spanned the great gorge

separating the city and the foothills from the plain, staring down into its depths and at the river that ran fast through them. I thought about home, and my heart gave a lurch of pain. I'd been far too busy and far too worried about Gurdyman to be homesick, but now he was getting better the longing flooded back.

I thought about Jack. I wondered if he was thinking about me. No, I told myself. Of course he isn't. *When I get back, I'd like you not to be here.* His hard words and the icy tone in which he'd uttered them were graven in my memory.

I wandered back into the city, pausing to stare at the burned-out buildings. They hadn't got to the bottom of what caused the fire. The bright blue flames, and the fact that they hadn't spread to any nearby structures, remained a mystery. There had only been the two casualties, for the buildings were old and deemed unsafe and usually deserted. The bodies had been those of a young couple who had gone inside for some privacy, away from society's stern eyes. I liked to think that their last moments before the flames took them had been happy, even joyful ones. Not that it was much consolation.

I was still haunted by that moment when I had put the soaked pad over the burned face and known that life was extinguished.

Abruptly I turned away from the ruins and began the climb back into the heart of the city.

I went on past the shady corners where people congregated to eat, drink and talk. I went on past every street, alley and square that I knew, ever upwards through increasingly narrow lanes and passages until the houses grew sparse and were set further and further apart and the foothills rose up before me. Here were the pastures and the small fields where crops grew, where little streams tumbling down from the mountains soaring behind the city watered the sun-warmed, south-west-facing land so that it provided in abundance for the people of the City of Pearl. Here cattle, sheep and goats grazed, and in places horses raised interested heads to see the stranger walk by.

I'd been climbing for ages and I had lost all track of time. I paused to drink from a stream, and suddenly remembered

Gurdyman saying we'd been poisoned; that someone had put some substance into the water I'd fetched from the stream down in the plain.

The drama of his collapse and sickness had driven it, as well as so much else, from my mind. My life in the City of Pearl had become all-important, almost as if the recent past had been obliterated.

Now, perched on a rock high above the city, I turned my mind back to what had happened on our awful journey.

Who had wished to harm us?

Who had whispered outside our lodgings in the village where Gurdyman's parents' inn had been? Where it had burned down with just the same blue flames, if the accounts were to be believed, as those that had recently destroyed the old buildings in the lower reaches of the City of Pearl . . .

Brujo. That was the word that had been whispered. Gurdyman had told me that *brujo* meant magician. But what about *llama azul*? I had heard that whispered, too, outside the window and again as we were driven away.

Why had they thrown stones?

Was it the same person – or people – who had poisoned the water? Who had caused me to see that terrible vision of the single huge eye and the claws scratching at my clothes and my flesh?

Why? *Why?*

I folded my arms on my knees and dropped my head on them.

And, some time later, I sensed someone sit down beside me.

I raised my head, turning to see who it was.

It was a man, his age difficult to determine. He was older than me, younger than my father. He had an oval face beneath a broad forehead, and his eyes were a clear golden brown. He was lightly bearded. His features were regular, and the overall effect was of a handsome man. I could not accurately determine his height and size while he was sitting, but the impression was that he was neither tall nor short; neither fat nor thin. His brown hair was worn long, to his shoulders, and it was streaked with white; it was the contrast of this with his smooth, unwrinkled, tanned skin that made it hard to decide how old he was. He was dressed, as were many people in the City of Pearl, in a long brown robe beneath which I could see the white of his undershirt. He smelt clean; he smelt of lemons.

He sat in quiet patience under my scrutiny. Then he said – and his voice was quiet, soft and with an accent I did not know – 'You were thinking, among many other things, of the water from the stream.' He shook his head, and the small gold coins that hung on a chain from his ear jingled together gently. 'Do not be frightened. There is no need, for no harm will come to you now.'

I digested the strange statement. Did he mean he knew I'd been made sick by some substance added to the water I'd found when we were so desperate, and it wasn't going to happen again? But I hadn't imagined that it would, for the stream I had just drunk from emerged straight from the side of the hill, clear, fast-flowing and so cold it had made my head ache. Unless it was poisoned at source, it was impossible for anyone to have introduced something harmful into it.

'I am not concerned. Well, not about that,' I said.

'What *are* you concerned about?'

'I'm worried about Gurdyman' – somehow I knew he would know who Gurdyman was – 'and I fear Salim is right when he says he won't ever recover his full health.'

'He will not,' said the man. 'A portion of his strength and his power has gone out of him.' He was looking at me with a peculiar intensity as he said this. 'It is this rather than any intrinsic problem with his heart that has made him so unwell, and now he is trying to adjust to living as he will be from now on.'

'So he's not going to die?' Until I asked the question, I hadn't realized how much the possibility had been preying on my mind.

The man smiled. 'We shall all die, some sooner than others. Gurdyman has a good number of years left to him.'

I was so glad to hear it that I didn't think to ask him how he could be so sure.

Then he said, 'The substance that was put into the water cask made you sick?'

I thought back. 'I wasn't actually sick, but I felt nauseous and my head was swimming.' I turned to him. 'I saw visions and they were very frightening.'

He nodded. 'Yes, that is to be expected.'

'You know, then, what the substance was?'

'Oh, yes, for it was I who put it in your water.'

I don't know why I wasn't horrified. Why I didn't get up and run away or, at the very least, leap up to remonstrate with him for what he'd done and demand to know why. But I did nothing, other than to say calmly, 'I see.'

'The fact that your body did not reject the substance is the proof that was required,' the man said. 'And that, indeed, was the reason for administering it.'

'Did not reject . . . you mean I didn't vomit it up or purge it via the bowels?'

'Yes.'

'But . . . What was it?' Now I was alarmed. I'd worked with Gurdyman long enough to know the risks of ingesting substances that altered the mind, which it seemed was what I'd been given.

He shook his head. 'I will tell you and, in due course I hope, demonstrate to you how it is acquired and the method of preparation. For now, though, the name would mean nothing, for it is not found or, I believe, used in your land.'

'You know where my land is?' This was becoming more weird by the moment.

'Of course!' He smiled again. 'You live in a house in a narrow little alley off the town's market place, and originally you come from the wet, watery fens – you have a strong affinity with water, in fact – and—'

'I haven't!' I protested. 'My web of destiny shows me to be a being of air and fire, and—'

'How, then,' he said with relentless logic, 'do you account for your ability to see the safe ways across the marshland?'

I had no answer.

He knew so much about me. He must be a friend or acquaintance of Salim, and learned all the details about Gurdyman and me from him.

I have never understood my extraordinary willingness to accept such flimsy explanations . . .

After quite some time he said, 'I am called Itzal.'

'Lassair,' I responded.

'I know,' he breathed

Of course he did.

He stood up, raising a hand to shade his eyes as he looked out down the long slope of the foothills to the city below and, beyond it, the plains and the sunset. The sun was low, I was surprised to see; I – we – had been sitting there far longer than I had thought.

Itzal turned and held out his hand. 'Come on,' he said. 'It is time to go.'

'Very well.'

He jumped down from the rocky outcrop where we'd been sitting. Instead of turning downhill towards the city, however, he headed off the other way. He was still holding my hand, and willingly I went with him. Very soon the climb became steep and difficult, and I began panting.

He stopped and reached inside the leather bag slung over his shoulder, pulling out a silver flask. 'Would you like something to help?' he asked.

I stared into his light brown eyes. I didn't answer; couldn't answer, for I had no idea whether or not to accept.

He studied me. 'It is the moment, I think,' he said. 'You must now decide if you can trust me. It is my intention – my duty – to take you on a journey; one that will change you for ever and that is the next stage in your path. This has been laid out for you.'

'Laid out for me?' I whispered.

He nodded. 'Just now, I am offering you nothing more than a draught that is an old stimulant long used by those who live in the mountains, but you have only my word for that. You will, I hope, accept, and discover that I am telling the truth. This will, I further hope, confirm to you that I truly mean you no harm: quite the contrary.'

We stood there face to face for what sometimes in retrospect seems an age; sometimes no more than a few heartbeats.

And then I saw my own hand reach out for the silver flask.

I held it for a moment, then put it to my lips. The liquid within was quite sweet – a touch of honey? – but it also had a refreshing sharpness. There were other tastes, too, but I could not identify them. I drank a sip, two, three, four, and it felt as if a great source of energy was all at once flooding through my body.

'Enough, I think,' Itzal said, taking back the flask. He too took a mouthful, and his lips were where mine had just been. No doubt they had been there before, and the thought of that small intimacy between us did not in the least dismay me.

He was looking at me again, the clear brown eyes catching the dying sun and shining now with little lights of gold.

When he turned away at last and resumed the climb, it didn't occur to me for an instant not to follow.

My path had been laid out for me.

We were walking by moonlight now. We stopped to rest briefly and I looked back the way we had come. I gasped, for I hadn't realized we had climbed so high. We were out of the foothills and in the mountains, and if I hadn't been so hot from the exertion, I would have been shivering with cold.

I opened my satchel and took out my shawl, wrapping it close around me beneath my cloak and tying the ends in a loose knot. The soft wool against my skin brought my beloved sister Elfritha to mind, and I felt her there beside me. She gave me a hug.

I thought, *She is not concerned for my safety. She is happy, smiling.*

It was a further reassurance.

Itzal was watching me. He offered the flask again and I took another few sips. Then he handed me a piece of bread in which there was a chunk of cheese and some onion. It was delicious, and I wolfed it down as swiftly as if somebody was threatening to take it away. I wondered how far we would walk, and where we were going.

'We have completed the climb,' Itzal said in reply; had I asked him out loud? 'Now we descend, on the north side of the mountains, to the place where I left the horses. It will be very late when we get there, however, and so we shall sleep then and go on in the morning.'

'Go on where?'

He studied me for some time. 'To what awaits you, deep within the painted darkness.'

THIRTEEN

When I woke up, dry and warm in one of the stalls in a small stable block on the edge of a little settlement, whatever influence had held me the previous afternoon, evening and night had eased off. My first thought, even before I had properly taken in my surroundings, was, *Oh, dear Lord, Gurdyman will be so worried! And Salim, and Hanan too, they will—*

'They know where you are going,' said Itzal.

I turned in the direction of his voice. He was sitting on a straw bale, looking refreshed and smiling gently.

'They don't,' I protested. 'They can't!'

'Do you wish to go back?'

'*Yes!*' I cried. But then almost instantly, as an irrepressible flare of excitement shot through me, 'No.'

'Have some food, then.' He handed me warm bread, a slice of ham, a small and wrinkle-skinned apple. There was also a mug of milk, still slightly warm. I took the food and the milk from Itzal's hands, glancing around as I did so. Edild's stern training made it hard to eat and drink amid filth, but the stable block was well-maintained and reasonably clean. Raindrops fell in a steady rhythm from the low-sweeping roof, and my heart sank at the thought of setting off in wet weather.

Again, Itzal read my thought.

'It is a fine morning,' he said. 'There was a heavy dew, that's all.' Then, with a nod, he got off his straw bale and left me to my food.

I wondered how long it was going to take me to get used to him.

As I ate, I was thinking. Trying very hard to make sense of the extraordinary. Gurdyman had brought me here, not explaining why we were making the journey, and naively I had believed that it was because of my sorrow and distress; that his intention was to take my mind off grieving for the two men I had lost and give me something exciting and challenging to do. I knew now that this wasn't the truth; or, at least, not the whole truth, for it had become clear that Gurdyman had a purpose in returning to this land, and that this purpose – vitally important to him and somehow connected to the terrible fate that had befallen his parents – had summoned him back to the City of Pearl. The place and at least some of its inhabitants were involved in the mystery, for they were part of his past.

The entire trip wasn't at all what I'd thought it was.

And now it seemed there was also a hidden plan for me.

Had Gurdyman known what would happen, then? Had he understood that I would meet Itzal – whoever Itzal was – and go off with him to whatever awaited me?

Yes, a voice said in my head.

I did not know who had spoken, but it was comforting.

It meant, apart from anything else, that I didn't have to visualize Gurdyman's shocked horror when he discovered I'd gone.

Because it was rapidly becoming clear that this was what he'd intended for me all along.

I had finished the food. I went outside to find a private place to pass water, and when I returned, I bathed my hands and face in a trough outside the stable. Itzal was leading out two horses, already bridled, and now he went back inside to fetch their saddles. The horses were similar in build to the pony that had drawn the cart I'd purchased for Gurdyman, only these were a little longer in the leg and considerably more elegant.

I returned to the place where I had slept to gather up my belongings. On impulse, I drew the shining stone out of my satchel. I sat down in the clean straw and crossed my legs, resting my open palms on the folds of my skirts with the stone upon them.

It was dark and quiet at first. Perhaps it wasn't going to respond.

Ask something, my inner voice prompted.

Am I doing the right thing? I said silently.

A single flash of brilliant, dazzling gold lit the stone.

Perhaps it was simply the early sun striking a spark, but I chose not to think so.

I'd rarely had such instant, certain confirmation.

Carefully I wrapped the stone and put it away in its habitual place among the remedies and simples I always carry. I packed my folded shawl on top. I stood up, straightened my skirts, brushed off the straw and swung my cloak round my shoulders, then went outside to join Itzal and to see what would happen next.

'We shall be crossing what is in effect a high bowl-like plateau, its sides formed by the range of mountains we have left behind us, the Pyrenees far away to the north-east, and the long range of the coastal mountains straight ahead,' Itzal said as we rode down the last of the slopes and set off across level ground. 'Our destination is in those mountains' – he pointed dead ahead – 'and we have rather more than two hundred miles to go.'

'Two hundred!' I could barely envisage such a distance.

He smiled. 'You have travelled more than that already in the journey to the City of Pearl from where you made landfall,' he remarked.

'Yes, and it took days! Weeks!' I cried.

He thought for a moment. 'Three or perhaps four weeks. Certainly not much more. And it was accomplished in the company of an elderly man, who at first walked very slowly on his two feet and was then borne in a cart drawn by a single pony.' He glanced at me. 'Now you travel with someone who is not infirm, and we have horses who are used to covering many miles in a day at a fair speed. We shall reach our destination in ten days at the most, probably less, provided the weather is reasonably kind.'

A dozen questions flew into my mind about this destination, but I knew there was no point in asking them. I'd tried already, as we'd been saddling up and setting off, and Itzal had simply smiled his inscrutable smile and replied, 'There is nothing to fear, Lassair, and, for you, everything to gain.'

He had made quite a lot of those enigmatic remarks, and I'd known him – no, been in his company, for I certainly couldn't claim to *know* him – for less than a day. The weird thing was that I trusted him.

We rode on, an easy silence between us. I quickly discovered that my horse – a bay mare with a long mane and tail – was well-behaved, willing and a very comfortable ride, so I felt confident in losing myself in my thoughts. So I asked myself *why* I trusted Itzal.

My total lack of fear, or even unease, could be attributed to that great flash of brilliant golden light from the shining stone. Over the years I'd learned to put my trust in the stone; to perceive that in some way I didn't understand, it and I were linked. It *knew*, was the best I'd ever been able to come up with. It was my ally, and it would not let me go too far wrong.

That, anyway, was my belief and my hope.

The other factor that contributed to my absence of unease was that I was warming to my strange companion.

He had all but admitted he'd been following Gurdyman and me as we made our slow and, latterly, painful way from the village where his parents' inn had been to the vale before the City of Pearl, and it was very possible he'd picked up our trail as soon as we left the ship at Corunna. A dark little voice in my head reminded me that he knew all about the fens, and Cambridge – even the location of Gurdyman's house – so it was at least possible he could have been watching us even before we set out.

And he had also admitted to putting some substance into our drinking water; perhaps not the poison that Gurdyman said it was, but something designed to test me, as Itzal had claimed, to see if my body had the power to deal with it . . . It was an unpleasant thought, and I could still recall all too vividly the dreams, visions and hallucinations I'd suffered.

But when I really thought about my various emotions on that long journey, I couldn't honestly say I'd felt true fear; not, at least, once we'd left the village where they'd driven us out with sharp stones and hissed words. Now, with some new depth of understanding I hadn't had before, I could see that the villagers had been a lot more frightened of us than we were of them.

They remember the fire, the voice in my head said. *They*

were terrified that it would come again. That the magician all at once in their midst, uninvited, unwanted, would make the terrible blue flames and everyone would die.

But Gurdyman wasn't there when the fire happened!

They thought he was.

Brujo meant magician. I knew that from Gurdyman. And *llama azul* – I knew now with utter certainty and without anyone telling me – meant blue flame. Oh, yes, it made sense; the villagers, suspicious and afraid, saw someone they had once known come walking back into their lives. His reputation had no doubt grown in the course of the decades since he'd last been seen, augmented and exaggerated by scary fireside tales told on dark winter nights. They'd have gossiped, muttered behind their hands, reminded each other of the peril he brought with him, and then the whispers would have begun, shortly followed by the hostile confrontation that had driven us away.

Once we were far enough away for the fear of the villagers to be just a nasty memory, the mood had subtly changed.

I had worried about our lack of food, about Gurdyman being so sick, about having absolutely no idea where we were or where we were bound, but I hadn't felt frightened.

It was quite a realization, and it told me very firmly that I was right to trust Itzal. I'd been helpless as I lay beside the cart lost in visions and he could have killed me if he wanted to. Instead I'd just seen a panoply of horrors prompted by my own mind. And, I reminded myself, also by whatever he had put in the drinking water.

Trust him, my inner voice said. *But be wary.*

For now, it was the best that my inner voice and I could come up with.

Our days passed comfortably enough. The tracks and the occasional larger roads we travelled on were in reasonable repair, and the many rivers we crossed offered either bridges – some of them alarmingly fragile-looking and rickety – or fords. Itzal had provided us with a good stock of food from the stores in the stable where we had collected the horses, and occasionally we passed through small towns and villages where we were able to augment our supplies with fresh produce. The weather varied between warm, damp days when the wind came from the west or south-west and bright, cold ones when it shifted to the north and the east, sometimes bringing snow, for we were high up on our mountain-enclosed plateau and here winter had not yet passed.

All the time the coastal range up ahead grew steadily closer.

When we were perhaps a day's ride from the foothills, Itzal broke a long silence and said, 'Do you believe that our lives have a pattern, Lassair?'

Since his previous remark had been about whether or not we needed to purchase more bread, this took me aback. 'Er—'

'They do, you know,' he went on before I'd had a chance to enlarge on my dim-witted response. 'And the pattern plays out over many lifetimes.' He paused. 'You and I are here today, for example, riding towards our destination and not far from it now, because many years ago a son was born to two people who had given up on parenthood.'

Gurdyman. He had to be speaking of Gurdyman.

'The little boy was precociously intelligent, but the humble little village where he had been born lacked the least opportunity for a poor man's son to receive the sort of education worthy of him. And so fate acted. The infant's parents, who had never once strayed from their village and had previously exhibited no wish whatsoever to do so, suddenly decided to travel to Santiago de Compostela to give thanks for the miracle of their son's birth.'

'But—' I stopped. I'd been going to protest that surely setting off on a pilgrimage to give thanks was quite a common thing to do, for it was what I had thought when Gurdyman told me the story. What, perhaps, Gurdyman had wanted me to think.

Now, however, Itzal had shaded it differently.

'They did not return to their ignorant backwater,' he was saying now, 'for, once again, fate stepped in and it so happened that the woman was too weak for the long and arduous journey. They put up in a village beside the road, intending for it only to be temporary, but they found they liked life in the northern mountains of Cantabria, and instead they stayed.'

'It suited Gurdyman's mother's health!' I said. 'For the first time ever, she didn't spend the winter coughing!'

'But why was that?' Itzal asked. 'The weather in the mountains is harsh in winter, as you have no doubt discovered for yourself. And was it not unexpected, to say the least, for two humble, unsophisticated people no longer young to give up everything and everybody they had ever known and settle in a little village in a distant land full of strangers?'

When he put it like that, I had to admit that it was.

'The plan was thus put into operation,' Itzal murmured, half to himself, 'and the wheel began to turn.' Before I could ask what he meant, he went on. 'Tutors and teachers appeared for the bright young boy, seemingly at random and as and when he needed them. When he had outstripped the village man and the parish priest, the smooth path was laid out before his feet and it took him south, to where the greatest learning of the age was to be found and, after many miles of far-flung travels, finally he was led to the City of Pearl.'

'They loved him there!' I cried. 'Salim told me! His father and his grandfather welcomed Gurdyman into their household, he and Salim were like brothers!'

Itzal gave me a long, intense look.

'Yes,' he said. Then, sighing, 'Yes indeed, that is how Salim would see it, for he too bears the guilt, and it blinds him so that he cannot see the truth that lies beyond.'

'What is he guilty about?'

Now he was looking away from me, up ahead towards the mountains. 'Salim and Gurdyman studied long and hard under Nabil and Makram. Those were the names of Salim's father and grandfather,' he added, apparently perceiving that I didn't know. 'There were many other teachers too, great men who had given their lives to the study of every subject from medicine and the stars to the delights of the table and the wide and beautiful realm of the imagination, which they made tangible in their verse and their paintings. As is their way, these men of prodigious learning understood that their duty was to pass their knowledge on to others; to teach, to inspire, to stretch the minds of their pupils to the utmost. In those young men, one a son of the house, one a blue-eyed stranger, they encountered two of the most eager, receptive minds they had ever known.' He turned to me again, and now something very fierce burned in his golden-brown eyes. 'But Salim and Gurdyman shared the great masters' attention with another. And, when the moment came for the brightest star of the three to be rewarded with the great prize, it was clear to all three who should receive it. Salim stepped back. So, too, should Gurdyman have done. Outstanding though he was – perhaps one of the finest ever to have been taught in the City of Pearl – yet the third pupil was better still.'

He stopped, and he was silent for so long that I thought he wasn't going to continue. The bay mare was all at once uneasy, as if she sensed whatever was humming in the air.

If so, she wasn't alone.

I felt as if a storm was brewing, right overhead, and yet the sky was clear. And, quite clearly, I heard that strange sound like a thousand summer insects, a gentle drone inside my head.

Then, speaking lightly and breaking up the alarming tension as if it had never been, Itzal said, 'But, enough. It is almost midday, and we still have not found anyone who will sell us fresh bread.'

We reached the foothills late that day. I had imagined we would stop and find somewhere to sleep, for the horses needed rest even if we didn't.

We went on.

We paused for over an hour beside a stream as the path began to climb, and both we and the horses drank deep from the sparkling water. Then after another interminable time of struggling up the increasingly steep tracks, we came to a small settlement. It consisted of no more than a long, low building under a very steep roof, beside which were some small areas of rough grass enclosed by sparse-growing, stubby trees and bushes. There was a rudimentary stable on the far side of the grassy area. A mule looked up from its grazing to inspect us. Lights showed within the low dwelling.

'Go inside,' Itzal said as we dismounted. 'They know who you are and they are expecting you.'

Stiff and weary, I did as he said. He had turned away towards the stable, and I was relieved he hadn't suggested I help him to settle the horses. I would have liked to say a grateful word to my mare but I was too tired.

I knew, without his having told me, that I'd finished with riding for now.

Was this, then, our destination? I stared up in dismay at the humble building. If so, I had to admit it was a disappointment . . .

The woman who was within looked up at me as I opened the heavy door and entered. I saw an expression flit across her face that looked very like fear. Then, without a word, she disappeared through a second, smaller door leading into a back room, returning presently with a laden tray containing a basket of bread, a jug of ale and two mugs, and two wooden bowls of stew. It smelt good. She put the food and ale down on a small table, then, with a sort of bow, backed away through the door to the inner room and closed it, softly but firmly, behind her.

I was staring hungrily at the basket of bread and the large pat of golden butter, wondering how long I was going to resist it, when Itzal came in. 'Food, oh, good!' he said. 'The horses also have provender, and someone is tending to them. Eat!' he added.

I obeyed. The stew was very tasty, and consisted of lumps of root vegetables, onions and pieces of lamb in a rich, spicy gravy. The bread was fresh, the butter sweet and creamy, the ale excellent.

When I'd finished the food and was on my second mug of ale, I said, 'Is this an inn?'

'Of a sort, I suppose,' Itzal replied, 'although it is a long way from the frequented paths and tracks and it serves the needs of few.'

Of people like you, I thought, who have mysterious business up in the mountains. *Deep within the painted darkness.* I recalled the phrase he had used.

Which, he had informed me enigmatically, was waiting for me . . .

* * *

We settled for the night, lying on benches set against the walls. It was comfortable enough, for pillows and blankets had been set out and I had my warm cloak.

I dreamt vividly.

I saw Gurdyman, propped against pillows and saying to Salim, *She will understand. I cannot prevent her from finding out, but she is loving and does not condemn.*

I saw my father, arguing with someone who looked like Hrype. Who *was* Hrype. Hrype seemed to be demanding something of him that my father didn't want to give. *No, you can't! He's far too old!* Father shouted, his face distorted by anger. And Hrype, annoyingly calm as only Hrype can be, replied coolly, *Is that not for him to decide?*

In a flash so brief that I almost missed it I saw Jack, standing over the fire that had consumed Rollo's body. Then he turned around and looked straight at me.

I must have cried in my sleep, for Itzal was beside me, a hand on my shoulder, tucking the blanket more closely around me. 'Sleep,' he said gently. 'It is not yet dawn.'

I must have slept again, this time dreamlessly, and next time I woke the thin light of early morning was coming in through the tiny window.

The woman I had seen last night brought food and a hot infusion, still without saying a word. Itzal gave her some coins. I packed my satchel, put on my cloak and we went outside. I paused to say farewell to my bay mare, who pushed her nose affectionately into me in response.

Then Itzal led the way to where a narrow little path set off up the mountainside, and the next phase of our journey began.

We climbed for most of the morning, stopping frequently to rest. Below us to the south the high plateau we had crossed spread out beneath us. If I half-closed my eyes, I thought I could see the ranges of mountains that contained it to the east and the south, but it was probably my imagination.

We went on.

I lost track of the hours. But there were far too many of them, and the muscles of my calves, thighs and buttocks were hot with pain.

Then, when the sun was starting to tip down into the west, we came to a place where a rocky outcrop hung forbiddingly over a small hollow. Nothing grew but some sparse lichens, for we were above the tree line. I didn't think I'd seen anything moving, except for Itzal and some huge birds wheeling and circling over the plateau so far below, for ages.

Itzal was crouching before a crack in the rocky rear wall of the dell. It was low and narrow, and so well concealed that I hadn't spotted it until his presence in front of it made it apparent. He took the pack off his shoulders, pushing it on before him. Then, turning, he said, 'You are slighter than me, so you should not find it such a squeeze. Wait until I call out, then follow.'

I don't want to! I cried silently.

Oh, dear sweet Lord, I didn't want to. The crack, ominously dark, was like a frown line between two eyebrows clenched in angry disapproval, and the air coming from it was dank and very, very cold. Everything about the place was yelling at me to get away, to return where I'd come from, not to venture any nearer.

But then, as Itzal's legs and feet followed the rest of him inside, it was as if a cool, calm voice called out to me. *You may enter*, it said. *The warning is not for you.*

And Itzal called out, 'Come on!'

I stood undecided. I could go back down the mountain, find the little settlement with the stable, find my mare, hand over enough money to purchase her and ride off south, back to the City of Pearl. Or I could even set out for the coast, which I knew was away to the north, and find a ship to take me back to the fens.

But if I did that – if I obeyed the momentary cowardly impulse to run away – I would never know why I'd been brought here, and what lay within waiting for me.

The painted darkness.

It might have been foolhardy, irresponsible and unwise. But it was also irresistible.

I took my satchel off my shoulder, pushed it ahead of me as Itzal had done, dropped to my hands and knees and followed him through the crack.

* * *

At first the going wasn't too hard. We seemed to be on a path that ran up and down at random, and either by good luck or the work of human hands, there weren't too many rocks projecting from the walls or embedded in the ground beneath to trip or damage the unwary. Itzal had picked up and lit a lamp from a small rock shelf inside the entrance, and in the utter darkness its small flame gave a surprising amount of light.

Sometimes we had to crouch down very low to get under the roof. Sometimes we had to turn sideways and force our way through very narrow gaps. Once we had to get down on our bellies and wriggle like snakes down a long, rocky slope that seemed to go on for far too long, and at the tightest point the roof pressing down immediately above me drove me close to screaming. The entire mountaintop rested there, just over my fragile body, and my mind was filled with images of horror as I saw its colossal, unimaginable weight collapse on top of me.

But just as I thought I would break, I heard an unexpected sound: the rushing of water, quite close by.

I don't know why it should have reassured me and given me such renewed heart; there was no clear reason. But it did. An image of longships flashed into my mind and I thought of my ancestors travelling the length and breadth of their world, full of courage, fighting fear, hunger, injury, illness, homesickness. I was of their blood, through my grandfather. None of them would start screaming merely because they were forced to wriggle through a tiny passage deep in the mountain.

My fast, panicked breathing calmed down, and the race of my rapidly beating heart began to slow. I crawled on.

At last I reached the far end, and scrambled out. Itzal, waiting for me, smiled. 'Well done,' he said. 'Most people cry out in panic the first time they come through, usually at the place where that rock sticks out on the left and you are absolutely sure you can't get past.'

I grinned back. 'I very nearly did,' I replied.

He put his head on one side. 'What stopped you?'

I held back from telling him about my forebears and their courage. 'I reasoned that you got through,' I said lightly, 'and you're bigger than me.'

His laugh told me he didn't believe the explanation but wasn't going to challenge it.

And I realized, with a chilling sort of thrill, that I was beginning to read his thoughts.

We went on.

I was tiring now, and only pride stopped me from asking for a rest.

Time passed.

I was hungry and thirsty, and it seemed at times that the walls all around me were pulsating, coming closer in a cold, hard hug and then receding again.

I noticed that, just in front of me, Itzal had stopped.

'Wait,' he said very softly; just a breath.

I waited.

He blew the light out.

I stifled a cry.

He had stepped away from me. Being robbed of sight seemed to have heightened my other senses and, for all that he had made no sound, I knew he was no longer anywhere near.

I was alone, in the dark, and I had no idea what lay ahead.

I couldn't hear water now. The silence was total, as if my hearing had failed as totally as my sight. Nervously I stretched out my arms, fingers spread wide. They met empty air. Had the sense of touch gone, too? Or had the black, rocky walls of this strange world simply fallen away?

I waited.

Nothing.

Had he left me? Was this a test, to see what I would do?

A small impulse of anger rose in me.

Well, I wasn't going to stand here trembling for the rest of my life!

I took a pace sideways, stretching out my arms again. The fingers of my left hand touched the rocky wall. Good: something solid.

I edged a foot forward. Then another, feeling with my toes before I put my weight down, for in the course of our long progress into the mountain we had come to many places where there were sudden and unexpected drops; where the floor fell away and we'd had to ease ourselves down.

One step. Two. Now the gentle downward slope was rapidly increasing.

I kept my hand on the wall, my other arm outstretched too. Then suddenly my right hand came in contact with the wall on the other side, and quickly I put my left hand above my head to check on the ceiling height. My fingers banged into rock so quickly that I knew the roof was descending.

I was in a narrow funnel, and it was closing in on me with every step I took.

Still I went on. The little spark of anger had grown, and with it my determination not to yield to fear. Well, it was more than fear now, but I didn't let myself think about it.

I went on.

I was crouching now, the walls holding me like a hard, cold birth canal. The air was thick and heavy, making it difficult to draw breath.

I shut down firmly on the images forming in my mind. Images in which I walked into a dead end, in which the rocks fell behind me, in which I was trapped and crushed, dying from broken ribs and smashed limbs and lack of air.

Squeezed all around now, I forced a way on.

And then several things happened all at once.

The rocky prison suddenly relented.

I could breathe again.

Brilliant light illuminated the scene.

Dazzled, I tried to look in every direction at once, and to my horror all around me there were animals – horses, bulls, bison, huge cattle with great curving horns – and all of them were rushing past me and threatening to smash me to the ground and trample me beneath the huge hooves.

Then someone laughed.

A robed figure stepped out straight in front of me, and someone who smelt of musk and lemons held out their hands.

'Welcome!' a voice said.

The figure was slim and not tall, veiled and robed, and in that instant of first meeting, the main impression was of the wide light-brown eyes in which the lamplight picked out bright reflections. No, the eyes weren't brown, they were gold . . .

'You are tired; near to exhaustion, perhaps,' the low-toned voice went on. 'Just a little further to go, and we will help you if you stumble. Then you shall sleep.'

'Sleep,' I repeated. Such was the hypnotic quality of the voice that I felt my eyelids drooping even as I stood there.

Two larger figures, similarly robed, emerged from the darkness and came to stand either side of me. One of them – a big, broad-shouldered man – looked anxiously into my face. 'You walk?' he asked. 'I carry?'

'I can walk!' I replied quickly. 'But thank you.'

He nodded, and I felt his large, warm hand under my elbow. The other man did the same on my other side.

And then, with Itzal walking ahead with the lamp and the figure who had first greeted me walking behind – walking quite silently, I noticed – we left the vivid animals behind. After we had been going for a short time a strange fancy took me, and I wonder if those wonderful creatures were only there when somebody took a light into the tunnel, at all other times time galloping out on the plains.

And such was the mood, on that extraordinary night, that it seemed perfectly credible.

FOURTEEN

'What do you mean, he's gone?' Jack shouted. It was early evening, he was in Marcus's tavern, Walter and Henry sat shame-faced before him. None of them had even touched their mugs of ale. 'You were watching! I told you to keep an eye on all boats leaving the quay – sweet heaven, there's few enough setting out just now – and you assured me you'd see to it!'

'Yes, chief, I know,' Walter said, 'and I've no idea how it could have happened. It's only what we suspect, mind, and we can't say for sure.' He scratched furiously at his head, as if the action might release from some crevice of his mind a plausible explanation. 'I set a watch and the men took shifts throughout the day and night. They're good lads, too, I made sure of that. Only three boats have set out for the coast in the couple of days since you told us to watch, and the lads didn't see any young, slim man go aboard any of them. Not only that,' he added, 'but nobody answering the description has so much as been spotted lurking around.'

Henry, the youngest and one of the more alert and intelligent of Jack's band of loyal lawmen, spoke up. 'We saw crew members going on board,' he said. 'Could your man have pretended to have been someone belonging to one of the boats?'

It was, Jack thought, a bright suggestion. 'Walter?' he said. 'What do you think?'

But Walter shook his head. 'I doubt it, chief. Those boats aren't big and the crews are usually as small as the master can get away with, since fewer wages to pay means more profit. They'd all know each other far too well to be fooled.'

Young Henry, undaunted, was frowning, clearly following a thought of his own. 'Maybe he did disguise himself, though,' he said slowly.

Walter snorted. 'What, as a water barrel or a coil of rope?'

Henry turned to him. 'No,' he said, his indignation not quite suppressed. 'As anything other than what we were looking out for.'

Jack, understanding, said, 'Go on.'

'Well, round about midday yesterday, the second boat that set out had a fat old couple as passengers. Neither of them could have been your slim young man, chief, because I saw them with my own eyes and I'd swear they were exactly what they seemed to be. But Ginger – he was on watch the night before last – said that the first boat to leave went very early, at daybreak, and a young woman went on board at the very last moment.'

Under his breath but not quite inaudible enough, Jack said, 'Fuck.'

'Sorry, chief,' Walter mumbled.

Jack touched his shoulder briefly. 'It's all right, Walter. I should have warned you how slippery he is. I should have been there myself, since it's only I who have a sense of him . . .'

'What do you mean?' Walter said, clearly disturbed at the odd words.

'I can't explain,' Jack said shortly. 'Walter, send somebody up to Lynn after that boat. I need to know if—' But no, he thought. That wouldn't work. The slim man had managed to evade his watching men here in Cambridge, and made his escape when there were few people about and only one boat leaving the quay. What chance would his men have in a busy port such as Lynn, and with a quarry who was as elusive as a wisp of smoke? A quarry that Jack alone had a chance of catching, and that a slender one.

He knew, as well as he knew his own two large hands clutched round his ale mug, that this was their man. It wasn't even that he had doubts and was silently arguing them away: there *were* no doubts.

And there was no time to wonder at his certainty.

'Chief?' Walter asked.

Jack, knowing exactly what he must do, drained his mug in a few swallows and put it down with a thump, then stood up. 'I'm going away for a while, Walter. Probably just for a few days, but I can't swear to it and it might be longer. Much longer,' he muttered.

Walter nodded. 'Right you are. Going after him yourself, are you?'

'Yes.' He went on looking at Walter, frowning.

Henry, catching on to what was concerning him more quickly than the older man, said quietly, 'We could say you've had a flare-up of trouble with your wound.' He nodded towards Jack's chest, where back in October Gaspard Picot's hidden blade had driven into the thick pad of muscle over his heart. The deep wound had subsequently become infected, despite all Lassair's care, and Jack's convalescence had been long and hard.

'Aye, come to think of it, you've been looking right peaky recently, chief,' Walter said with a grin. 'Those nuns out at Chatteris are renowned for their healing skills, although I'm told they like to take their time about it.'

'Yes, I heard that too,' Jack said. He looked at the two of them, moved at their readiness to lie for him. 'Will you keep an eye on my geese?'

'Of course,' Henry said. It was he who had seen to the creatures during Jack's immobility. 'I'll check inside your house a couple of times a week, too.'

Jack nodded his thanks. 'Well, I'd best be off, then.'

As farewells were said, he had a sudden conviction that this was going to be no brief absence.

And that he had absolutely no idea how he knew, or what lay ahead. He only knew that he had to go.

He left the tavern and returned to his house. He went around the two small rooms methodically, picking up the items he would need and setting them beside a worn leather backpack. The house was orderly and clean. That was the way he liked it, and now, when he was leaving for an indefinite time, it meant there was little to do before departure.

He sat down to wait.

And presently there was a soft tap on the door, and Hrype came in. 'You weren't at the tavern,' he said by way of explanation.

'No.'

Hrype's glance fell on the leather pack. He looked quizzically at Jack.

'He's gone,' Jack said shortly. 'Looks as if he disguised himself as a woman and slipped on board a boat that left for the coast very early yesterday morning.'

'So you're going after him.' It was a statement.

'I am. I think—' *I think he means to harm Lassair. I saw what he did in the attic, I believe she's in grave danger and I can't just sit here and do nothing*, was what he almost said. 'I thought probably you would come with me.'

Hrype smiled. 'Yes, I will. I have a ship,' he added very softly.

'You – *what*?'

'We have to get to Aelf Fen,' Hrype went on.

'There's a ship? At Aelf Fen?'

'There's a boat,' Hrype corrected. 'And the boat, or so I am very much hoping, will take us out to where the ship to which it belongs will await us.'

'How did you do it?' Jack asked. 'How in the good Lord's name did you know we'd need it, for a start, and how did you then go about acquiring it?'

'It's not yet certain that I have,' Hrype said warningly. 'I believe, however, that if you and I turn up together and you add your persuasive voice to mine, then some time tomorrow we shall be on our way to the coast, where with any luck we shall pick up the trail of your mysterious fugitive.'

But Jack, recalling his earlier misgivings about Walter and Henry's ability to find their quarry in the hurrying crowds of a busy sea port, said, 'That is easier said than done, and he'll have a two-day start on us. He'll be aboard some ship and on his way by the time we arrive, and we'll never find him.'

Hrype looked at him, and Jack couldn't read the expression. 'We will,' he said very quietly, 'if we know where he's going.'

'And just how can we know that?' Jack demanded. 'More of your mysterious powers of insight, I suppose?'

Hrype smiled, his face full of amusement. 'I'd like to say so, but it would be a lie. But come on! Think about it! I've told you I know where Gurdyman was bound for, and isn't it virtually certain that our lean young man will be going in much the same direction?'

Yes, was Jack's instinctive answer. But instinct was not enough. 'Tell me why I should believe that,' he said instead.

Hrype sighed. 'Someone from Gurdyman's past in the south badly wants him to return, perhaps to atone for some event that happened there. The summons was by means of a sign left where he would find it, and that would have meaning only to him. He left, as quickly as he could despite it being the autumn and a bad time for travelling, and he took Lassair with him. The messenger should have gone back to wherever he came from once his mission was accomplished, but he fell ill and had to remain here until the boats were leaving once again. Now that we assume he's gone—'

'He has.'

'Now that he's gone,' Hrype repeated, 'where else would you suggest he's going except back to the person who ordered him here? The same person,' he added in case Jack had not followed the argument, 'whose command was to send Gurdyman to him.'

It was all very plausible, Jack thought. But was it enough? I can follow my instinct and my heart, he thought dispassionately, pick up my pack and set out, right now, with this strange man who seems to have become my ally and my friend. Or I can listen to my logic, conclude that it's all shadow and illusion with no basis in stern reality, and tell him to go off on his whimsical journey by himself.

Which was it to be?

They walked all night and by dawn they were wet, cold and tired. The water was high throughout the fens and frequently they had to take detours up to higher ground, adding several miles to the journey.

As the sun came up, they were looping round behind Aelf Fen.

'We're not going down into the village?' Jack asked.

'No. There's no need, for what we seek is beyond the settlement.'

Hrype increased his pace, perhaps anxious not to be spotted

by any alert eyes among the early rising inhabitants. Jack hoisted his pack higher and followed.

They had gone a mile or so, keeping to a track that ran on a low rise to the east of the flooded marshland, when abruptly Hrype turned to his right, following the course up a narrow waterway making its way down towards the fen basin. He strode on, faster now, and Jack kept close behind.

And presently he saw a small boat moored up ahead. It was covered with an awning made of skins and oiled cloth, so that the interior was protected from the weather. Hrype approached it and called out. 'Thorfinn? I'm back.'

A gap appeared between two of the covers, and the upper part of a man's body emerged. He was huge. His long, abundant hair was silvery white, as were the heavy beard and moustache. His eyes were a light blue-green like the northern sea, the irises ringed in indigo. They were Lassair's eyes.

He was old, but as he climbed out of the boat and up onto the bank, he moved easily. And there was authority and strength, even a sense of threat, as he stood before Hrype and, eyeing Jack, growled, 'Who's this?'

'Jack Chevestrier,' Hrype said, standing aside so that Jack and the huge man were face to face.

The old man stared down at him. Jack was neither short nor small, but the white-haired man exceeded him on both counts. 'So you're Jack,' he said. It seemed to Jack as if an invisible dagger of ice was aimed right at his heart.

'Thorfinn,' Hrype said quietly. 'It is none of your business.'

And, very slowly, the old man relaxed.

'What do you want?' he said after a few moments.

'You know what we want,' Hrype replied.

'Oh, so it's *we* now?'

'I think it always was,' Hrype muttered. Then, more loudly, 'Will you do as I asked, when I came to see you a few days ago?'

'You presume that it is possible,' Thorfinn said. 'You imagine that I have but to cast off from this sheltered haven and take us up through the narrow byways of the fens until we come to open water, where a ship will await us.'

Hrype gave a barely audible sigh. 'But I know your ship is nearby, because you told me you had seen Einar very recently.'

Einar? This mysterious ship's master? Jack wondered.

'Einar has better things to do than to sail up and down the coast until and unless I have need of him,' Thorfinn said.

'You also told me,' Hrype said, and Jack could hear the effort it was taking to keep his patience, 'that you, your son and his entire crew were all delighted at the prospect of the voyage, and that Einar himself said that it was far too long since they'd faced such a challenge.'

'Yes, I did say that,' Thorfinn admitted. 'And you reckon you're coming with us?' He spun round to Jack.

Jack could only guess at what it meant. If he was right, then Hrype seemed to have foreseen that the slender man would escape from Cambridge and Jack's vigilance and that, when his absence had finally been noticed, he would already be well on his way. By the time anybody had found a craft in which to pursue him he would be long gone.

And, aware of all this, by some miracle Hrype had found a ship. Not only that, but by some insight that Jack didn't begin to understand, Hrype seemed to know where the young man would go.

He met the old man's eyes. 'Yes. I am,' he said firmly.

Thorfinn grinned, a flash of large, regular and slightly yellowish teeth amid the silver white of his beard. 'And you'll not be taking no for an answer, hmm?'

The waters were running high and, once released from its narrow channel, the small boat quickly found a strand of the great current that swept out of the fens towards the greater waterways and the sea. As they left the coast behind them and sailed out into open water, Jack's misgivings about the folly of the enterprise returned, for how on earth were they to find one ship in such a vast waste of water? But Thorfinn seemed to know exactly where she would be: and there *was* a ship, long, graceful, fast, coming into sight right ahead.

Jack, amazed at the unerring instinct that led the old man right to the spot, heard Hrype laugh softly.

'It is not magic,' he said. 'Thorfinn's son regularly comes

to see him, and he always makes sure the old man knows his movements.'

The small boat crept nearer to the larger craft, and Jack stared up at her. 'Her name,' Hrype said, 'is *Malice-striker*.'

Then men were reaching out to receive them, to help them aboard, to raise the boat and stow it. Then, even as Hrype grabbed Jack's arm and pulled him down beside him in a place where they wouldn't impede the crew, the ship was beginning to move, accelerating with unbelievable rapidity, and they were on their way.

Abruptly still after the furious activity, Jack found himself with nothing to do but stare around him. The ship was some twenty paces long, perhaps five paces across at her widest, and tapered elegantly to fore and aft. She looked like one of her warship forebears, as if whoever had built her kept in his mind and his heart a memory of the long, lean hounds that had sailed the northern seas before her. Her hull was strengthened by a series of ribs, with additional ones at the prow, stern and before the mast. The cargo hold yawned in the gap between the fore and aft decks. The only shelter for crew and passengers was that afforded by the ship's high sides.

The crew numbered eight, and Thorfinn's son Einar was the master. He was huge. He had light eyes, a heavy beard and thick reddish-fair hair in two plaits braided with leather thongs. His feet were bare.

Presently Thorfinn came to join Jack and Hrype.

'The very wind we'd have prayed for is filling our sail,' the old man said.

Jack glanced up at the big square sail, tightly angled and filled with wind. The land was dimly visible over to his right, and they were flying along parallel to the shore. 'Is it?'

'We sail around the great lump of land that lies between the Wash and the open sea, eastwards and then south,' Thorfinn said. 'We shall hope the wind remains our friend, but if it doesn't, then our quarry will also be affected.'

'But how do you know what ship our quarry is aboard?' Jack asked in frustration.

Thorfinn reached out a large hand and briefly touched Jack's shoulder. He said, just as Hrype had done, 'We know where he is going. That is all that matters.'

'How *can* you know?' Jack demanded.

Thorfinn spoke with compassion, as if understanding Jack's misgivings. 'Many paths lead to the place where this man is bound, for it is full of ancient echoes and it draws to itself those who feel its pull.' As Jack was struggling with this extraordinary statement, Thorfinn muttered something else; something that sounded like 'It is Lassair's ultimate destination.' He was about to cry out in protest – *You know where she's going? Will she be all right? Is she safe?* – but then Thorfinn said, 'Do not worry. I have been there myself, and I remember the way.'

FIFTEEN

It was hard to tell how long we walked through the dark, rocky tunnels and passages that bore through the heart of the mountain. I felt as if I were in a dream world, and I couldn't tell reality from illusion. I was desperately tired now, and it felt sometimes that I slept as I stumbled along. My two guides did not let me fall, however, even when they had to negotiate very narrow gaps and were forced to pass me from one pair of hands to the other.

Then all at once we emerged from the side of the mountain.

The dark night sky arched above us, glittering with stars. The air was cold and fresh, and I thought it was the sweetest thing I had ever smelled.

We descended a steep little path that twisted this way and that. Presently I saw a huddle of low buildings ahead, set in a valley beneath a long spur of mountain that shot out to the north, so that the valley faced west and a little south. There were fields around the buildings and some trees.

One of the buildings had a light in the window.

We approached it and the door opened to us. Inside there were low beds with thin mattresses, blankets and pillows. 'Yours,' the man on my right said, gently pushing me towards the bed set against the rear wall. Suddenly wondering if the robed figure with the bright eyes was still there, I spun round and stared out onto the darkness.

The patch of worn ground before the dwelling was deserted.

I stumbled towards the bed, fell onto it and lay down. The pillow was cool beneath my cheek. I closed my eyes. Someone drew a warm, soft blanket over me and I snuggled into it. Someone – perhaps the same person – took off my boots. There were voices speaking quietly but I didn't trouble to listen. They were speaking a language I had never heard before.

I was clutching my satchel to my chest and I thought I

could feel inside it the hard, round shape of the shining stone in its wrappings and its bag. I thought it felt warm. It was probably only my imagination, but I was too far gone to care. The stone seemed to say very softly, *Safe.*

It was enough. I let sleep take me.

I woke to soft light and early morning silence.

Several of the other beds were occupied, the occupants deeply asleep. The air was cold, the fire in the hearth now reduced to a few glowing embers in a mass of burned wood. The room was clean and, considering how many people appeared to live here, reasonably tidy. I looked round at the sleeping forms but could not tell whether or not one was Itzal. Couldn't tell even if they were men or women, so well-wrapped in the covers were they.

But I knew with absolute certainty that the robed figure who had welcomed me in the painted darkness last night wasn't among them.

I still had my satchel clasped to my breast. Carefully and silently I unfastened it, taking out the soft leather bag that held the shining stone. I removed the wool padding and held the stone in my hands. It was warm, just as my fuddled and exhausted mind had suggested it was last night.

And, as it had done before in the stables on the far side of the mountain, in answer to my unspoken question it shot out a great burst of golden light. Hastily I tried to cover it, for sudden light can awaken sleepers just as noise can. I found that I was smiling, wanting to laugh. I had no idea why, unless the unexpected moment of joy had originated within the stone.

I wrapped it – the light was beginning to fade now, but still very bright in the dim interior – then briefly held it to my breast. I could have sworn I felt it throb, in time with my heart. Then I put it in its bag and tucked it away in my satchel.

Even as I did so, the door opened a crack and a deeply hooded figure peered in through the gap. 'Come,' a voice said softly.

I got up, folded back the covers, put on my boots and picked up my satchel and my cloak. I moved on tiptoe across the floor, weaving a way between the beds. I pushed the door open just enough to go out, then closed it. All the time, the bright pale-brown eyes with the golden lights were watching my every move.

The robed figure had moved away a little, and now, beckoning, went up a path leading back into the mountain's lowest folds. I was too intent on following to spare a moment to look around me, but senses other than sight were informing me even as I panted after the robed figure. The air smelt wonderfully fresh, as if dew sparkled on new green grass and vegetation, and I detected a faint salt tang. And the air was warm on my face. I knew without looking that the snow had gone from this valley; that spring was near.

After a short, hard climb, the figure stopped. We were on a small patch of level ground; a sort of platform that dipped into the rocky hillside to form a shelf. It was in deep shade, for a great shoulder of mountain stood between us and the rising sun in the east, but the cool was welcome after the climb.

The robed figure turned, pushing back the deep hood to reveal the face.

And I saw, as I think I had already known, that it was a woman.

She perched on an outcrop of rock at the rear of the shelf, patting to the space beside her. 'Sit,' she said. I obeyed. She reached into her pack and produced fresh bread, a pat of soft goat's cheese wrapped in a vine leaf and a flask of cold water. While she divided it between us, I looked around.

The first surprise was that I could see the sea. It was some way off to the north, judging by the position of the sun. We were on the shoulders of the mountain range that ran along the coast, and the green of the plain below shone in the early light. The little settlement where I had spent the night was somewhere down in the foothills, invisible now beneath the pine-cladded lower slopes. I wondered if this track was the one by which we had descended the previous evening.

We shared the food, and the woman did not speak until we had finished.

'I am Luliwa,' she said. I said nothing, merely nodded. *You have had me brought here*, I thought. *It is for you to explain yourself.*

But I wondered if I might after all have spoken aloud, for she nodded, gave a brief, rueful smile, and said, 'Yes, you do just as I would do myself if the positions were reversed. You wait for me to speak. To explain.' She paused, then went on. 'I will; of that you have my word. For now, though, let me merely say that you are safe. You are safer than at any time since you left the house in Cambridge, and possibly for a long time before that, but you already know this for your shining black companion has twice told you.'

She knew about the shining stone. Of course she did.

She was watching me. In the brief silence while she studied me – I could feel her bright eyes on me like a gentle warmth – I did the same to her.

Her skin was light brown, and what I could see of the hair drawn back beneath the edge of the hood was darkest brown, or perhaps black, streaked at the temples with silver. The dark brows arched up over those extraordinary eyes, and the well-shaped, powerful nose bisected the lean cheeks like the prow of a ship. Her mouth was wide, and the lines around it suggested that she smiled more often than she frowned.

But for all that there was a deep sadness in her face. I found myself staring into her eyes, quite unable to look away, and it seemed to me that the pupils slowly widened until they had eradicated the golden irises and become a deep, bottomless black. It was . . . it was like staring into a lightless cave. It was like – the thought came out of nowhere – looking into the past.

And that profound black *did not reflect light* . . .

I felt that I was tumbling, swirling and turning as I fell, and around me walls of hard rock flashed images at me. I saw those huge animals again, and now there were other pictures too, zigzags and dots and a grid pattern, and a great arc like the backward-turning horn of some enormous animal, jagged on one edge and smooth on the other. And then one side of my forehead exploded in a sudden stab of agony, for I had seen these images before, many times, in the onset of the dreadful half-brow headaches that I'd suffered for most of my life.

Luliwa gave a soft sound of distress and instantly the images went away and so did the pain. I was left with the odd empty-headed sensation that always follows the terrible headaches – as if, with the cessation of the torment, the body in its huge relief doesn't quite know what to do with itself – and then that too was gone.

Luliwa reached out to take my hand. With her free hand she stroked my forehead, and her touch was cool, and my flesh seemed to lean into it.

'I did not know,' she said very gently. 'I should have guessed, however, for so often the condition exists alongside.' Just as I began to ask what she meant, she added, 'I am sorry, Lassair.'

'I'm all right,' I said. I hoped I didn't sound as grumpy to her as I did to myself.

She was looking at me anxiously. 'Truly all right?' she asked. 'We have a hard path ahead, and at the end of it much will be demanded of you.'

I stood up, managing to control the momentary dizziness. 'Truly,' I said. 'Lead on.'

Not long after we had resumed our climb we went inside the mountain.

Just as on the southern side, I didn't see the entrance until Luliwa was standing right in it, for all that this time I had been on the look-out for it. This portal was different from the long, narrow crack that Itzal had led me through, for it was low and in form like an almost perfectly-rounded arch. It was hidden behind a rocky outcrop, deep in the shadows and looking like nothing so much as a smooth lump of stone made black and shiny by a rivulet of water that flowed constantly over it. It was only when Luliwa went straight through it that my perception altered and I realized that what had looked like an outward-curving block of rock was actually a dark space.

Luliwa waited while I crouched down and crawled in after her. She had lighted a lamp, and she held it up for me to see that we were in a passage, its roof lowering overhead. There was room to walk upright here, but I knew this would not be the case as we went on into the mountain. She met my eyes and I nodded to tell her I was ready. Then she turned and walked on.

* * *

You lose all sense of time inside a mountain.

I was aware of so many things, but the passage of time wasn't among them. It seemed meaningless here, for such was the sense of antiquity – of being in a place that had been there unchanged since the world began – that whether I spent a day or a decade inside the mountain was quite irrelevant.

Luliwa didn't speak. I imagined she was leaving me to experience the impressions for myself.

Once I had accepted the darkness, and the unyielding nature of the rock, and the silence, and the total unlikeliness of my being there at all, I began to sense other things.

The first and most powerful of which was a feeling that Luliwa and I were not alone: that there were other consciousnesses in there close beside me, sending out feelers that penetrated deep inside me to discover what I was, what I wanted, why I was there. I let them come into me, for I was here at another's wish, not my own, and I didn't feel I had anything to hide. I was, I suppose, innocent.

After a while I think this was understood, for I started to feel less like an intruder. I didn't feel welcome – not yet – but it seemed that some sort of barrier that I'd sensed I was pushing against had begun to ease a little.

And Luliwa, speaking for the first time since we'd come inside, said quietly, 'Good.'

We went on. Sometimes we climbed – once I had to cling onto a rope slung along one rocky wall, hand over hand up a cruelly precipitous little slope that I'd never have managed without aid – and sometimes we descended. At one point the way became a narrow tunnel, and we had to wriggle along it on our stomachs, bending almost in half to negotiate a tight bend.

I was afraid then; terrified.

And Luliwa, who had probably brought initiates this way before, knew it was the moment to give reassurance. 'Nearly there,' came her mellifluous voice from ahead. And, again, 'You are safe.'

And the terror faded.

It was after negotiating a long set of rough-cut, steeply descending steps that I became aware the silence was no longer absolute. I could hear water, and in the instant that I did so I recalled hearing it when Itzal and I had made the journey the other way. In front of me Luliwa had reached the foot of the steps and she turned, waiting for me to join her.

'There's water nearby,' I said very softly.

She nodded. 'Yes. There is a little river which has its source to the south of the mountains, where it appears as a sparkling stream issuing out of a spring, bringing life to the plateau. But it disappears when it reaches the mountains, and men believe it is swallowed up by the earth. Another river emerges on the northern side of the range and makes its way to the sea, by which time it is wide and full with the water that penetrates down through the rocks. Few realize that it is the same river that disappears to the south, but it is.'

She was looking at me with a strange expression. She seemed to be expectant; excited, almost, as if she was waiting for me to gasp in amazement and make some profound comment.

I shrugged.

'I don't—' I began.

But then I saw an image.

And it was the last thing I had expected.

But then moments from my own past seemed to join with it.

I was sitting beside the man I later discovered was my grandfather and he was telling me a tale of his own past, although I didn't know at the time that the sailor called the Silver Dragon was in fact himself. He had taken his ship and his loyal crew into danger; *Into many adventures as they followed the routes discovered by their forefathers* – I could hear his deep, solemn voice – *always pushing on, always discovering new lands. Knowing that the path was becoming increasingly perilous, he persisted in following it when he should have turned back.*

And then, even as I was setting out on my long journey all those weeks – months – ago, he had said of my destination, *It is a land full of marvels and magic.* When I asked him if he'd been there, he said, *I have been everywhere.*

And he had told me not to leave the shining stone behind.

It had been the last thing he said.

I sneaked my hand inside my satchel and sought out the

stone. My fingers loosened the drawstrings of the leather bag and I reached under the soft wool to touch it. Just for a heartbeat, Thorfinn was suddenly right there with me.

'He was here,' I breathed. 'He came in his ship – in his beautiful fierce ship that was the original *Malice-striker*, and that now lies on the shores of the land where it came into being. The ship whose noble name now belongs to another . . .'

Luliwa, studying me, smiled but said nothing.

We went on. Sometimes we walked beside the underground river, and it was dark, and full of power, and I was afraid of it. Luliwa offered me no comfort now. She seemed to be implying that the time had come for me to deal with my fear by myself.

Then we were climbing again, and the noise of the water faded and disappeared. We stopped to drink and to eat sparingly.

A long, long time later, we stopped.

I realized, even as I bent to catch my breath and then stretched this way and that to relieve my aching back – we'd been crouched down in a low-roofed tunnel for a long time before emerging into this space – that this was somewhere Luliwa and her people visited regularly. She reached up onto a shelf and her hand went straight to the lamps, which she lit. The soft light waxed, and I stared around me with astonishment.

I had expected the vivid images on the walls, for I had seen some of them last night, although at times I'd wondered if I'd dreamt it.

Some of the animals were here too. There was a massive bull, and a horse whose head seemed to emerge from the wall, for whoever had painted its beautiful lines had made use of an outcrop of rock in precisely the right place and of just the right shape. There were other horses, many of them, their heads and necks dense black and their hindquarters light, patterned with dark spots. Their legs and feet seemed to melt away, giving the illusion they were standing in some medium other than the firm ground. And now there were other images too: a wall of handprints and another area where paint had been applied – sprayed, I thought – around the outline of hands. I looked from one to the other, positive image and negative image, and they seemed to move.

I shook my head, dizzy suddenly, as the painted walls came alive all around me.

'Sit,' Luliwa said, guiding me to a shelf of rock that might have been put there for this very purpose. She reached into her bag and withdrew a small silver flask, unstoppering it and handing it to me. I took a sip, and knew it to be alcohol. It was delicious but potent. I took another sip, and then with a smile she took it away.

After a moment I said, 'Who did this? Did you?'

'I?' She shook her head, and a look of wonder – of fear, even – crossed her face. 'Oh, no. Not I, not any of my people, although perhaps – just perhaps – it could have been our long-distant ancestors, for our legends and our tales tell us that we have inhabited these isolated lands from far, far back in time.'

'They are old, then? The pictures?'

She stared at me, her pupils wide, and once again I had the sensation that I was looking into a deep, black cave. This time, however, I was ready. I was still fearful but I knew I could not turn away.

'They are old, Lassair,' Luliwa said distantly. 'So very old. Always here, alone, hidden away through the centuries, the millennia, their power waiting to awaken when the time was right.'

'And you – someone discovered that they were here?'

'I, yes, it was I,' she said. She sighed, settling beside me. 'I was running away, fleeing from—' She stopped. 'Evil had been done,' she went on, 'to me and by me, and I was furious at that done to me and already beginning to feel the painful stirring of guilt over that done by me.'

'What did—?' I began.

But she went on as if she hadn't heard.

'I was searching for power – for magic, perhaps you might phrase it, although I did not – and I believe that it was this that summoned me here. The force that lay hidden in the mountains needed to be found, and I needed to find it. The two halves knew each other, and they drew together. I was *led*' – she emphasized the word – 'to the crack through which you were admitted yesterday, for, like you, I came from the south.'

Before I could think about that, she was hurrying on, speaking swiftly now.

'I was sick, exhausted, grieving, and I know now that these factors combined to put me into a quite different state of mind from any I had ever known. This, too, was perhaps predestined: that I should find the painted darkness just at the time when I was most receptive to what was hidden in its depths. I saw with such clarity that first time, and it took me years until I had the sight again.'

'What did you see?' I whispered.

'I saw exactly what you see,' she replied, 'what all of us who undertake the journey into the dark will see, for the images are there on the walls for every one of us.'

'But you saw more,' I said. 'They are not just images, are they?'

And the look she gave me then had triumph in it, for all that she quickly suppressed it.

'Are they not?' she said with a smile.

'You know they aren't.'

'Perhaps, but tell me what *you* know.' It was a command, and her voice was hard now.

I paused, for the whirl of my thoughts was only now beginning to coalesce into something that had any meaning.

I stood up, moving away from her as she sat on the stone ledge. I walked over to the nearest wall – it was the one with the spotted horses – and ran my hands over their flanks. It felt as if they moved beneath my touch; as if they were contracting and releasing the little muscles just beneath their coats, as a horse will do when flies bother it. I moved on, slowly, thoughtfully, and went to the wall on the other side, putting my hand over one of the places where an ancient hand had once been flattened against the rock while its owner had blown a spray of red paint all over and round it.

My hand, as I knew it would, fitted perfectly.

And then it felt as if that long-ago person was beside me, and I was seeing through her eyes. I knew she was a woman.

I saw the rock walls as she had done: as something no longer solid but as a veil between me and the life that pulsed and throbbed, that had its being, on the other side.

Not a veil but a membrane, said a voice in my head.

A membrane.

A layer of tissue such as we have in our bodies; a barrier, that allows some things to pass but not others.

Suddenly, fleetingly, I was back in the City of Pearl with my dark little doctor. Just for an instant, everything came together and I heard that summertime drone again, louder now and far more powerful.

Then it stopped.

A membrane. I went back to where I had just been. It was a healer's term, and I knew that she – this long-ago woman from deep in the past – had been a healer like me.

Yes.

And just as the membranes in our bodies were selective, so was this one. It *chose* who it allowed to see its secrets.

I turned slowly, staring at first at one section of the walls, then another, then yet another. The images were everywhere now. It was as if, having discovered – having been shown – the right way to look, to perceive, everything was now open to me.

For a long, long time, I just stood and drank it in.

And I understood, very dimly and right on the edge of my mind, that the viewer brought something of her or himself. For gradually I began to see images that were not from this ancient mountain world of huge cattle and bears and wild horses, but from a world much nearer to my heart.

I saw the fens, and the sun on the water, and the islands that appeared and then mysteriously disappeared as the levels rose and fell and the land changed. I saw creatures that I had known in my own life: hare, fox, weasel, rat, snake, fish. I noticed that the fox appeared more than the others, and I recalled the fox I had known all my life: Fox, my own spirit animal.

And here he was, waiting for me, and both of us were full of joy at our reunion.

After an age, I turned to go back to Luliwa, sitting silent, watchful and still behind me.

And then, even as I walked slowly across the rocky floor, I saw another vision; it was close, very close, just there on the far side of the veil.

Not animals now, not even Fox and the other familiar, beloved creatures of home.

This was something quite different.

Perhaps it was the presence of the healer woman from the far past that made it happen. Perhaps she was still there with me, her mind somehow in tune with mine across the huge temporal gap between us.

Perhaps it was simply that I had been thinking of home.

In the vision – the hallucination – I thought I saw a parade of figures who I knew, without being told, were also healers. But they were great healers: far above anything I had achieved. I saw many that were strangers to me, wearing their power like a mantle that shone all around them. And, at the end of the line, I saw some that I recognized.

I saw Hrype, and, standing close to him, their love wrapped around them like a blanket, my aunt Edild. Yes, of course, I was well aware my aunt was a healer, and, now that I saw Hrype in this company, the realization came that I'd always known he was as well. I saw Thorfinn, and the power thrumming and pulsing from him was so strong that I flinched. I saw my Granny Cordeilla, a healer too – the best, Hrype had once told me – and now my heart leapt with joy for in a swift blink I saw them together, my grandfather and my grandmother, as they were when they were young, and they too were enclosed in their love. There was another, shadowy figure standing on the fringes of the group, but I couldn't make out the identity. It was someone I knew; there was no doubt of that.

But there was no time to work it out, for all at once I was among them, standing in a circle with them. Lying on the floor in the middle of the circle was a still figure wrapped in a blanket, and I knew from one look that this man, or it might have been a woman, was very sick. I wanted to protest, to say to the healers that I wasn't ready, didn't have their power, but they held out their hands to me and I couldn't step away. Then all of us were raising our arms, and from our fingertips came lines of light which linked into a veil, or a mesh, that wrapped itself gently around the sick person, surrounding him – her – with lines of bright gold.

And then, as the force embraced the figure lying on the ground and reanimated her – it was a woman – I looked across the circle and into the eyes of the figure standing opposite to me: the one I had known but not identified.

It was Jack.

I must have cried out. I don't remember. I had my hands up to my face, half of me wanting to blot out that loved face, half of me wanting to preserve its image, I don't know.

Then Luliwa's arms were round me, she was murmuring kind, gentle words, saying it was enough, it was too much, and guiding me to where she had placed something soft on the hard ground. She helped me to lie down, covered me with my own shawl, cradled my head between her hands and said, her voice low, hypnotic, 'Close your eyes. Rest. Let it all settle down.'

And, finally, 'Sleep.'

SIXTEEN

They nearly caught him in Concarneau.

The skill of Thorfinn's son Einar and his crew had achieved the long voyage from the mouth of the Wash to southern Brittany in excellent time. Jack, spending much of the journey huddled in layers of clothing, rugs and furs and crouched beside Hrype in the meagre shelter of the ship's sides, had at first thought the pursuit hopeless before it had even started. They had learned in a small port on the Kent coast where they had purchased supplies that a ship, the *Holy Mother*, had lately sailed for the French coast, catching a favourable wind that had been blowing hard out of the north-east. But the wind had abruptly changed.

'It'll delay the other ship just as it's delaying us,' Thorfinn said calmly, observing Jack's frustration.

Then, when they were on their way once more, it had been a series of vivid impressions. The cold. The exhilaration – you couldn't sail on a fleet and superbly engineered ship such as *Malice-striker* without wanting to shout aloud from time to time from the sheer thrill of it. Fear. The crew were evidently experienced and highly skilled and they clearly respected and were possibly in awe of Einar, but even their proficiency and air of calm couldn't prevent the fact that sailing far away from the shore in open water with a high sea running was pretty terrifying.

And Jack worried constantly about Lassair, and whatever peril Gurdyman had led her into, and whether or not she would survive. Whether or not she was still alive.

He didn't dwell on that.

They found the *Holy Mother* at St Malo, but she had already taken on her cargo and was preparing to sail back to England. Yes, they had indeed carried a passenger over with them; a slim young man, foreign-looking. Their master said he had no idea where the young man was bound, but a lad who was probably the youngest member of the *Holy Mother*'s crew came running after Jack and Hrype and said he'd heard the man trying to find passage to Bordeaux.

So *Malice-striker* had set out again, rounding the great triangle of land that pointed out into the vast sea to the west like an arrowhead aimed at the sunset. The voyage was awful, and far too many times *Malice-striker* seemed so close to the horrifying array of sharp black rocky outcrops guarding the shore like a vicious army that Jack was amazed they survived. Again, he had to admit, with a silent and fervent prayer of thanks, that the crew knew what they were doing.

But everyone's luck failed at Concarneau. The wind dropped, and old hands looked at the sky with worried frowns and spoke ominously about something bad brewing. The something bad was a storm, blowing in with such ferocity out of the south-west that ships' crews safe in harbour blessed their good fortune and others not so prudent or so lucky tried to outrun it or perished. Most perished, for when the wind was blowing you towards the perilous shore with a fist like iron in your back, there was nowhere to run.

Einar and his crew stayed on board *Malice-striker*, reasonably well protected by the enclosing walls of the harbour. Thorfinn went ashore with Jack and Hrype and they found damp, dirty and unwelcoming lodgings.

And they waited.

On the second night of the storm, with no sign of diminution in the wind's strength, Jack and Hrype sat in damp dejection in a tavern close to their horrible lodgings. Thorfinn was trying to fight the crowds all after the same thing – more ale – and Jack watched as the huge old man bodily lifted a lad who had tried to push in front of him and put him down again out of the way.

Thorfinn returned, three large mugs of ale in his hands.

'I don't envy Einar and the crew,' Jack said as Thorfinn sat down.

'They're probably saying the same thing about us,' the old man replied. 'Crowded taverns full of surly people, filthy, vermin-infested lodgings, townspeople out to make the most of the storm and overcharge for every last thing? They'll all think they're better off on board, believe me.'

There was a sudden commotion on the other side of the taproom. Raised voices, fists flying and a fight that sparked off so quickly that Jack and the others barely had time to pick up their mugs before a body came flying towards them and crashed into the table. Jack reached down to grab the young man by his collar and prop him up against the wall, and he noticed Hrype going to the aid of another, older man with blood pouring down his face while Thorfinn, having carefully put their mugs on a shelf out of harm's way, strode towards the two main combatants and prised them apart.

When all was calm again, the three of them resumed their seats and Thorfinn handed them the ale.

Jack had his mug to his lips when Hrype said quietly, 'Don't drink it.'

Jack stopped. 'Why not?'

Hrype was staring into his own mug, an expression of fierce intensity on his face. 'It's been drugged.' He sniffed. 'Poisoned, maybe.'

Not pausing to wonder why he should instantly believe him, Jack raised his head and stared slowly all round the room. 'Pretend to be drinking,' he said. Thorfinn and Hrype, understanding, obeyed. 'Talk.'

Again, his companions realized why he'd given the command.

As the three of them made the sort of remarks and speculations about the storm that most of the town had been making for nearly two days, Jack went on staring.

And, in a corner near the wide door, he saw a slim shape in a heavy cloak. The figure was in shadow, and Jack had the strange illusion that he was melding with the wall behind him, either coming out of it or flowing into it. He had the impression of a pale oval of face under the hood, but he could make out no details other than, just once and very briefly, a flash of brightness as some stray light caught the eyes. They were looking straight at him.

He turned to Hrype, sitting on his right, as if interested in what he was saying. When he next looked up, the young man had gone.

Jack leapt up. 'I've seen him. Come on!'

Hrype and Thorfinn were close behind him as he shouldered his way across the crowded room, and he noticed that Hrype – careful Hrype, healer Hrype – had the three mugs of ale in his hands. As they hurried out of the door, he bent down and poured the contents into a gutter.

They went out into the wind and the rain and began hunting.

They made themselves unpopular in a dozen lodging houses along the quay, barging in and pulling covers off sleeping people, staring at bemused faces roused to anger by the disturbance, muttering apologies when they were the wrong ones. Then they ventured up into the town and started again. They checked ten, a dozen, fifteen taprooms, but there was no sign of the slim young man. Short of knocking on the doors of private houses and demanding to search them, there seemed little more they could do.

'He's maybe already on board some ship,' Thorfinn said as they staggered back to the harbour against the blustering, buffeting wind. 'Other crews will be doing what Einar's doing, and waiting out the weather on their ships. Could some master have agreed to take our man before the storm hit and permitted him to sleep aboard until they can sail?'

'It's possible,' Jack conceded.

So they approached the line of ships along the quay, asking, looking, and met with no success there either.

'He's a phantom,' Jack said in disgust. 'He's—'

But he didn't finish the remark.

They were fighting their way back to their lodgings, ducking down below the harbour wall to derive what little shelter it could provide, repeatedly soaked by spray blown off the turbulent sea, and suddenly one of the huge stones set along its top came crashing down in front of them, so close that, even with the force of the wind, Jack felt the rush of it as it passed him.

He grabbed at his two companions, securing his fists in Hrype's sleeve and the folds of Thorfinn's heavy cloak, and dragged them back under the wall. Just in time, as a second stone fell right on the spot where they had just been standing with a thump that made the ground shake. The air was filled with sharp and deadly fragments of granite, one of which Jack felt slice across the back of his hand. He glanced down, but it was only a shallow cut.

'*Back*!' he yelled, his voice fighting the fury of the elements. 'Back the way we came, so we can utilize the overhang of the wall, and we'll return to the middle of the town the long way round.'

He tried to look everywhere at once as they fought their way along beneath the wall and off towards the quay, and he sensed Thorfinn and Hrype were doing the same. He felt eyes on him, every step of the way, but whoever was watching them so closely kept himself hidden.

Back in the tavern, they ordered more ale. Recalling their earlier experience, now all three of them kept their mugs in sight, on the small table in front of them.

'Why is he trying to kill us?' Jack said.

Hrype looked at him coolly. 'Because we have succeeded in following him this far, which he cannot have expected, and he is becoming desperate.'

'Yes, I appreciate that' – Jack held on to his impatience – 'but *why* is he so intent on stopping us?'

'Because he's aware we know he killed the vagrant found with the pearl in his hand.' Even as Hrype spoke the words, Jack knew he didn't believe them.

'Hardly!' he protested. 'A lawman and two companions taking all this trouble over one dead beggar? No. It must be to do with his destination, and what – who – he expects to find there.'

Thorfinn was watching him, understanding in his eyes. 'You think as I do. His presence in Cambridge, the trap he set to entice Gurdyman and the way he's trying to stop us, all suggest he knows what Gurdyman's doing in Spain and what has summoned him there.' Then, his voice grave, he said quietly, 'He is making his way back to whoever is the architect of this matter, and he does not want any witnesses to their reunion. Especially not us.'

'We are all agreed that the matter does not originate with him,' Hrype said shortly. 'He is carrying out another's will.'

'Yes,' Jack said. 'This matter is just too *big* for one slim young man.' He paused, another thought forming. 'And, given the lengths he's going to as he tries to shake us off, I'd conclude he fears this other man's wrath.'

'He is right to,' Hrype said softly.

Jack turned to look at him, noticing Thorfinn had done the same. 'Explain,' he said curtly.

Hrype shook his head. 'I am not sure that I can,' he admitted. 'But I am convinced that something very deep and dangerous lies at the heart of the matter. It has its origins in Gurdyman's past; in the years he spent in Spain. It *must* have,' he insisted, although neither Jack nor Thorfinn had spoken, 'for why else has Gurdyman gone back there? He is growing old, his heart troubles him, and perhaps at long last he recognizes that he will not live for ever.' He paused, frowning hard. 'I sense that there is darkness within him. It has lain hidden for much of his life, and the bright intelligence that is typical of him has been in the ascendant. But that beggar's corpse with the pearl in its hand opened the heavy door within him that he locked on the far past, and now he—'

But Thorfinn had evidently had enough. 'You speak of his bright intelligence that hides some dangerous darkness,' he said roughly, 'and while it is clear that you both admire and like him, I can have no opinion, for you speak of a man I have not met.' He paused, breathing heavily. 'You tell me you believe he has set out to right a long-ago wrong, and normally I would say of such a man, well done! Good! What you are doing is admirable, honourable!' He leaned forward, and his eyes were full of both anger and pain. 'But this man has taken my granddaughter with him, and that is another matter altogether.'

Neither Jack nor Hrype made any comment.

But it flashed through Jack's mind that he hoped Gurdyman would have a satisfactory explanation if – when – Thorfinn finally challenged him.

After some time, Thorfinn roused himself. Turning to Hrype, he asked, 'So where was Gurdyman aiming to make landfall?'

Hrype glanced at him. 'Corunna.'

Thorfinn nodded. Then he closed his eyes, and for some

time simply sat very still, his breathing steadily deepening. Jack, watching, wondered if he had slipped into a doze. He met Hrype's eye, about to suggest as much, but Hrype shook his head. 'Wait,' he mouthed.

Time passed.

Then abruptly Thorfinn opened his eyes, blinked a couple of times and said, 'Not Corunna. Oh, your friend Gurdyman may well have landed there, and my granddaughter with him, but it is not our quarry's destination.'

Oh, God, not another one, Jack thought. *First Hrype, now Thorfinn.* 'How do you know?' he said, trying to keep the angry frustration out of his voice.

Thorfinn shot him a quick look, as swiftly looking away again. Then he said calmly, 'You must both understand that I do not care where Gurdyman is; that my only concern is Lassair. She may still be with him, she may not. He may be in Corunna—'

'He did not plan to stay there,' Hrype interrupted.

'—but Lassair is not,' Thorfinn went on as if he had not heard. 'She is in the mountains of the northern range, and at some time very recently, she stood beside an underground river where once I sailed.'

'You cannot know that,' Jack said forcefully. 'I don't believe you.'

Thorfinn shrugged.

And Hrype murmured, 'She has the shining stone.' Raising his head to meet Thorfinn's eyes, he added, 'Which was once in your keeping.'

'In answer to your objection,' Thorfinn said, turning to Jack, 'I do not *know*. All I can tell you is that this place where I once explored has repeatedly been in my mind of late. It may be simply that we are sailing south, towards the coast of Spain, and my memories have been stirred up. It may also be because I am bending all my thoughts on my granddaughter, and some power far beyond my understanding is telling me where to find her.' He looked to Hrype, then back to Jack. 'My vote is one of three, and I suggest we each choose our preference. When we are able at last to leave here, do we sail for Corunna or do we follow my instinct?'

Despite logic, despite rational thought that insisted Thorfinn could not possibly be sure, Jack said, 'We follow your instinct.'

And Hrype said softly, 'I agree.'

There was a brief silence.

Then Jack broke it. 'We'll set a watch from early tomorrow, if the storm abates. We'll take note of any ship that's preparing to set to sea and check to see if our young man is aboard.' He looked at Thorfinn. 'Instinct is all very well,' he said. 'But I'm not yet ready to abandon the more traditional methods.'

The storm died away overnight, and it was the cessation of sound that woke Hrype. He got up, nudged Jack and the two went silently out of the communal dormitory and emerged into the thin dawn light.

In time to watch a cog in the very act of sailing out between the two arms of the harbour wall.

Jack swore, for some time and without repetition.

'Impressive,' Hrype murmured.

'It's *exactly* what he did back in Cambridge,' Jack muttered furiously. 'He seems to know precisely when a ship's about to depart, and he manages to insinuate himself on board before anyone else realizes what's happening. I should have been prepared!'

'If in truth our man is on board that ship,' Hrype said calmly.

'He is.'

Hrype nodded. 'Yes, I think so too.'

Jack turned to him. 'Do you really think Thorfinn knows where he is heading?' he asked. 'Or is it just an over-confident boast to give us a little optimism?'

Hrype didn't reply for some moments. Then he said, 'Thorfinn has a long and colourful past, and he has travelled more widely than anybody I know. He and his kind were undaunted, and endlessly curious. Endlessly hungry, for new people to trade with and new lands to settle. Even if those lands were occupied by other people,' he added with a faint smile. 'So it's perfectly possible he knows the north coast of Spain and has visited ports and sailed up rivers in his exploration of the country. Whether he really can take us to the precise place where Lassair now is, I have no idea.' He met Jack's eyes. 'But I very much hope so.'

Malice-striker was on her way.

Jack and Hrype had raced back inside to rouse Thorfinn and pay a sleepy and very cross lodging-house keeper the money they owed. Hurrying down to the quay, they had discovered that Einar, having felt the change in the weather even as he slept, was in the midst of preparing to sail. Jack sought out the harbour master and discovered that the ship which had sailed soon after dawn was called the *St James*. She was bound for Bordeaux with a cargo of salt and, provided the weather held good, was going on south towards Bilbao, Santander and Corunna.

Einar smiled as Jack relayed the news to Thorfinn and Hrype.

'South,' he murmured. He turned his head a little. 'And the wind comes out of the north-east.' Now Thorfinn too was smiling.

'The *St James* has quite a start,' Einar went on, turning to Jack and Hrype, 'but she will have *Malice-striker* hard on her stern. She is heavily laden and we are not. I do not think she will lose us now.'

SEVENTEEN

The intensity of my initial period of training with Luliwa all but exhausted me. I knew time was passing – weeks, perhaps even a month or more – for even I, who spent so much time underground in the painted darkness, was aware that spring had come.

Such was the force of her influence over me that I didn't have a moment to ask *why* she was doing it: why she seemed so fixated on transferring into my consciousness the things she held in hers. Although I knew we could only be scratching the surface of all that she knew, nevertheless those first sessions with her, when I began to suspect what she was, opened my eyes as nothing had ever done before and made me aware how much I didn't know.

She was a healer, she experienced visions, she had the ability to look right inside a sick person and see the root of what troubled them. She introduced me to the idea that a physical symptom such as headache or cramp in the guts could have its origin in the mind, and she put the extraordinary suggestion to me that the pain would go away if the mental distress was eased.

And, slowly at first, for I was resilient and disbelieving, she told me how to go about it.

She was an apothecary and she made all her own potions, ointments and specifics from ingredients either grown by herself, in the sheltered little gardens beneath the out-flung arm of the mountain, or purchased from the traders whose ships regularly called at the ports along the coast. Her knowledge of the power of plants and other natural substances surpassed that of anyone I'd ever worked with, even Gurdyman.

Gurdyman.

I'd know all the time that one day she would speak to me of Gurdyman. The moment came on a bright day of warm spring sunshine, when the two of us had taken a break from the dark mystery of the caverns and passages under the mountain and had taken our work up to the little platform on the path up through the foothills where we had first shared a breakfast all those weeks before. We were grinding the seeds of fenugreek with pestle and mortar, and Luliwa had been telling me that the powder we were making was used as a digestive aid and to stimulate the flow of milk, and could also be mixed with hot milk to make a poultice to ease the pain of ulcers, boils and bruises.

Now it was afternoon, and the rocky shelf was in full sunshine. It was warm, almost hot, and we were dressed in light clothing.

'You do not ask how he fares,' Luliwa said after a lengthy and, I'd thought, peaceful silence.

I knew who she meant by *he*. And the peace abruptly broke apart as I realized how long it had been since I'd thought of my mentor.

'I should have done,' I muttered. I couldn't even say that I'd been worrying about him in silence, because I hadn't.

'Gudiyyema' – she pronounced it as Salim had done – 'is in no danger. He has recovered from the attack, and as long as he does not exert himself, he is well.'

'How do you—' But before I'd even completed the question I understood how she knew. Since she'd begun teaching me, I seemed to have learned how to make better use of the things I was already aware of; I had become better at working things out for myself. 'Itzal. He goes to and fro between here and the City of Pearl.'

'He does,' Luliwa agreed. 'You will have seen for yourself that it is not an arduous journey, and he is well accustomed to it.'

'Does Gurdyman know I'm here?' I asked in a small voice.

'Oh, yes,' she said.

There was a long silence. Then, gathering my courage, I said, 'Why am I here?'

She didn't reply for so long that I thought she wasn't going to. But then she said, so softly that I strained to hear, 'Because of a . . . a wrinkle, in the natural order of things. There is a plan, you know, Lassair, and it represents the way that is destined for us; the way that ought to be. Yet sometimes people discover they have the power to interrupt this plan, and they ignore the inner voice that tells them it is forbidden; that having the power is one thing, but using it quite another.'

I tried to think what she could mean.

I said after a while, unwilling even to voice the thought but in some way compelled to, 'When you say *people*, you're speaking of Gurdyman.'

And, sighing, she said, 'I am.' She was staring at me now, the gold in her eyes shadowed by whatever troubled her. 'What I have to tell you is deeply disturbing, and it will undoubtedly distress you.' She paused. 'Are you ready to hear?' she asked softly.

I wanted to say *No!* I wanted to shout, to protest that whatever he was, whatever he had done, he was first of all Gurdyman, my teacher, my friend, and that I loved him and I didn't want to hear what she had to say.

But the voice in my head said, *He brought you here with no word of explanation. He allowed you to think it was for your sake, to take you on a thrilling journey so that you would forget your grief over Rollo and your heartbreak over Jack. And he took you into danger, so that you almost died. And he refused to tell you why.*

And I heard myself say, 'Yes. I am quite ready.'

'Salim's grandfather Makram was the greatest teacher of his age,' Luliwa began, 'and from birth he brought up his son Nabil to follow on in the same tradition. You have been in the City of Pearl, Lassair, and you have been told how it is the way of our people to share our wisdom, to propagate the dissemination of knowledge so that every man and woman may be brought out of the darkness of ignorance and into the light.'

She paused for a moment, gazing into the distance as if looking at something remembered with quiet happiness. Then, not waiting for comment – I didn't have any to make – she went on.

'Nabil had a son, Salim, who inherited the ways of his forefathers and desired to absorb all that they would teach him. But the old man, Makram, had an interest in and a great talent for an area of knowledge for which neither his son nor his grandson showed sufficient aptitude, if indeed they showed any at all, and so the decision was taken to seek out some young person who did have such aptitude, and offer them a place in Makram's household and under his tuition. And word came to the City of Pearl that a young foreigner had been found who seemed to be suitable.'

Gurdyman. I thought it, but didn't speak.

'This young man had been born a long way away, and had come to our country as a small child. Quickly outgrowing the kind and philanthropic men of his village who had done their best for him, he set off to the hot south, learning as he went, always learning, uncovering his own rare abilities and in awe of them. Soon he felt that the whole of Spain was not enough, and he set off to travel the world. He went across the narrow seas into the vast and sun-baked land in the south, and worked his way east to Egypt, to the land of the pharaohs of old, where he was introduced to an amazing new world of knowledge that he had hitherto not even suspected existed. Soon that, too, was not enough, and on he went, striding through the Holy Land, on east and north, into the heart of the lands that stretch away into the endless east, following the trails of men who travel halfway round the world to trade and share the secrets of their own people. He turned north, into the lands of his own forefathers, and there was instructed in the powerful magic that is his northern inheritance.'

The very words sent a cold sensation down my spine.

What did she mean?

'In the end, for he had exhausted himself, he returned to the land where he had been raised and grown to manhood, and, in time, his name became known to the great teachers of the City of Pearl. He was known as Juan then, for his parents had named him for the saint.'

'John. Yes, he told me he had been called John.'

Luliwa nodded. 'He was renamed, of course, once he was in the city, for there are many called Juan and not a one is like him. He became Gudiyyema, after the character of our legend who—'

'Yes, Salim told me,' I interrupted. I was far too impatient to learn the things I didn't know to waste time with things I already did.

Luliwa smiled. 'Of course, he would have done. Gudiyyema was very proud of such a name. It appealed to him very much, to be called after a powerful genie.'

'It's the name he's known by in the place where we live,' I said. 'Everyone calls him Gurdyman, which is the nearest approximation.'

'Everyone?' she echoed softly.

'Well, the small group who know of him.' And, even as I spoke, I realized how few they were.

'He is wise, I think, to keep his light shadowed,' she murmured.

My impatience overflowed again. I was desperate for her to get on with the story. 'So, he arrived in the City of Pearl and Makram began to teach him,' I prompted.

'Yes. Makram was delighted to have an adept such as he, and Gudiyyema was like a man in paradise. He absorbed, digested and disgorged everything that Makram taught him, usually with some refinement of his own, and the household stood in wonder at his brilliance, which of course delighted him even more and made him begin to believe that no goal was too great, no achievement too ambitious.'

'But?' I asked, when she fell silent. I knew there would be a *but*.

'Gudiyyema was not the only pupil in Makram's house,' she said very softly. 'There was Salim, but as you will already have realized, the particular teachings that Makram offered were not for him, and in the main he was taught by his father, and a fine job Nabil did.'

'Salim is a good man,' I said.

She gave a wry smile. 'He would, I am sure, be pleased to have your approval.'

I subsided, wishing fervently I'd kept the thought to myself. Who was I, after all, to pass judgement on someone like Salim?

But I sensed that Luliwa was disturbed – distressed, even – and I suspected it had some cause other than my somewhat tactless remark. I reached for her hand. It was cold.

'What is it?' I asked. 'What has upset you?'

She shot me a glance. 'You grow perceptive,' she observed. Then, taking her hand away and sitting up very straight, she said, 'The third young person who shared Gudiyyema and Salim's education was endowed with a talent for precisely those matters at which Gudiyyema excelled, and listened with tightly focused, avid attention, just as he did, to every word that came from Makram's lips. In time, all of them in that place of high intellect and brilliant learning understood that this person's abilities exceeded those of Gudiyyema, and so it was their right, by the most ancient of traditions, to be Makram's natural heir; the person who would be initiated fully into all that he knew.'

She paused, and in turn the darkness of an ancient sorrow and the fire of an old and furious resentment flashed across her face.

I waited.

'But Gudiyyema was not going to allow that to happen,' she said eventually, her voice quite calm. 'He was the better, in his own eyes, and he decided to take what by right and by ancient law belonged to another. He was clever – so very clever – and he knew his rival's weakness. He used it, and the rival was a rival no more.'

She stopped.

The echo of her words seemed to resound inside my head.

So what was she telling me? That Gurdyman had refused to accept that another young man's talent exceeded his own, and that it was this man, not himself, who would be the beneficiary of the great gift on offer?

That Gurdyman had stolen something that by right should have gone to someone else?

I couldn't believe it. I didn't want to believe it.

But I looked deep into Luliwa's golden eyes and I knew she had told me the truth.

My head was bursting with questions and I yearned to demand an explanation. What happened next? Did he get away with it? But I could answer that one for myself: of course he did, for he was the Gurdyman I knew.

I realized that Luliwa had got to her feet and, calmly and

with swift, efficient hands, was packing away our equipment as if nothing of importance had happened.

I could ask away until I was hoarse, I reflected ruefully, standing up to help her, but she wasn't going to tell me any more until she was ready.

The awareness gradually grew in me that there was suppressed excitement in the settlement.

I hadn't been told the purpose of what Luliwa was teaching me but, for all that it was not spoken of, I was fairly sure I knew. The long period of intense instruction had, however, produced a side-effect: it had made me far more aware of, and open to, the subtle currents around me. Or perhaps – and I thought this described the phenomenon more accurately – it had made me listen to my own inner self. Now, almost without noticing, this interior aspect of myself was observing, assessing and silently absorbing what were, with increasing frequency, amazingly accurate summaries of what was going on beneath the surface. And that quiet drone that sounded like a thousand summertime insects, first heard outside Edild's house in my own village of Aelf Fen, was now with me all the time.

Although nobody spoke of anything but the usual everyday matters in and around the settlement, nevertheless there was a very strong sense of anticipation.

I decided to watch and wait.

I had grown very fond of the people who lived in this hidden valley on the north of the coastal mountain range, and the girls and young women with whom I shared the lodging house were becoming friends. The people's life was one of two contrasts, for although we were now in a warm, moist and temperate spring, the winter months, as I had seen for myself during the last of them, were hard. In the harsh times there was a great deal of snow, and the valley became even more isolated as the few passes and tracks down to the lowlands and the coastal plain were blocked.

With the thaw, everyone in the valley, from the oldest great-grandfather to the youngest child capable of independent movement, went outside to the fields. They used every available piece of land, cultivating narrow strips carved out of steep hillsides, ploughing and manuring so as to get the optimum yield, and they grew a wide variety of crops: wheat, root vegetables, cabbages and, on the more sheltered of the south and south-west facing slopes up against that great tongue of mountain, oranges, lemons, vines and peaches. They had livestock: goats, a few enclaves of pigs and even some cows, although grazing land was in short supply. It was an isolated community. Everyone knew everyone else and, perhaps as a consequence, they all seemed to live in harmony.

To a man, woman and child they were in awe of Luliwa. That had been clear from the start. They were also wary of Itzal, who was so close to her. He was her bodyguard, her lieutenant, her confidant. Taking the chance to watch them closely whenever they were together – which wasn't very often as Itzal's visits were short and infrequent – I was almost sure he was her son, or, at any rate, a close relation. He had her same skin tone, there was a similarity in their features – especially the mouth and the strong, straight nose – and, like her, he had those golden brilliants in his brown eyes, although his were not so noticeable and you had to catch him in the right light to see them.

When it had first struck me that they were probably mother and son, I wondered why I wasn't more surprised. And I answered myself: *You already knew.*

It seemed I had noticed, had absorbed the fact, had quietly stored it away until I was ready to think about it.

I was finding out rather a lot about myself and my thought processes.

So, as the warm spring days passed, I kept my eyes open and my senses vigilant.

On the evening when I knew for certain that whatever we were waiting for was now imminent, I had spent a long day underground and was emerging from the darkness weary and with a slight headache. I didn't mind, for it was a relief to be emerging at all. At the start, when Luliwa's instruction had been so intense and I had frequently been on my knees in a mixture of awe, wonder, disbelief and exhaustion, we had quite often stayed beneath the mountain for days – even on one occasion more than two weeks – at a time. But that phase had passed; she never explained why we'd had to drive ourselves so hard, but in my own mind I believed it was because the huge impact of what was being revealed to me was received more readily if it was not diluted with everyday life.

Even now after all this time, coming out of the dark world into the light was difficult; especially on evenings like this one, when I was so tired.

Luliwa had gone on ahead of me, murmuring something about a task she must do, or perhaps some place she needed to be; I hadn't really taken it in. She had left me in the cave with the horse images – the place where I felt whatever came to join me there from out of the darkness with the greatest clarity – and I had been sitting cross-legged on the rocky floor, the cloak that Jack had given me folded up beneath me (I don't believe anybody can sit on a cold rock floor for very long without something to act as a cushion, not if they're trying to dwell on anything but their own discomfort) and letting my mind turn into a silent, still, receptive blank.

Luliwa had been instructing me in ways to assist in the acquisition of this highly desirable state, one of which was the striking of one of the stalactites suspended from the cave roof so as to make sounds that ranged from a deep, reverberating, long-lasting boom to a sharp, sudden plink; I had recognized that variation the moment I first heard it, for it had rung through the summertime drone that had been inside my head for so long. Today I had been experimenting with these sounds. I'd discovered that, as I tuned my hearing to pick up the moment when the sound at last faded away to nothing (which took a surprisingly long time), my mind slipped very easily into the dream-like trance state.

I was looking forward to telling Luliwa of my success.

I took care, as always, on the steep path leading down from the concealed entrance, for it was perilous, there was an alarming drop to the left, and I was often far from my practical, daylight self as I emerged out of the darkness. Presently the going became easier and I came to the point from which the little settlement could first be seen. Smoke was rising up from several of the dwellings, and it appeared quite a lot of cooking was going on. My empty stomach growled and rumbled in anticipation of a good meal.

The visibility was good and the westering sun was illuminating the valley with golden light. I could see a long way, and as I came out onto a stretch of the path that was relatively flat and didn't require my full attention, I let my eyes follow the line of the river that wound its way from the place where it emerged, as an icy-cold flow of white water straight from the mountain's heart, to the increasingly wide series of loops and bends that took it down to meet the sea.

There was a track that ran beside the water. A figure was on it, walking briskly away from the village. As I looked further on, I saw a second figure, coming up from the coast. The two had seen each other and were hastening towards each other.

The one coming from the settlement was Luliwa. I recognized her long robe, but, even more, I recognized the way she walked: briskly, economically, her carriage straight and elegant.

The person hurrying towards her moved in the same way, and I said aloud, 'It's Itzal.'

But what was he doing, coming from that direction? As far as I knew, when he wasn't in the village he was invariably off away in the south; in all likelihood, back in the City of Pearl. He often brought news of the doings of people there and sometimes even a message for me from Gurdyman, although Gurdyman's words were always disappointingly mundane and bland. If he knew what was happening to me – and I couldn't think that he didn't – he was determined not to refer to it.

The distant figures of Luliwa and Itzal had joined up now, and they had their arms round each other in a hug. It was a rare show of emotion. Usually they were courteous but cool with each other, and it was possibly a symptom of my new insight that now I detected the profound love between them.

Whatever mission had taken Itzal off in this unexpected direction must have been a perilous one. Even from where I stood high above them, I could read anxiety in the way Luliwa was standing. She was leaning forward, her hand clutching his arm, looking into his face as if searching his features for the truth behind whatever account he had just given her, and I could clearly see her relief when he repeatedly nodded, as if to say, *Yes, yes, all went well, all is just as it should be!*

They were moving off now towards the village, and quite soon the path took them beneath an outcrop of the hillside and I could no longer see them.

Perhaps Itzal's return from whatever tricky mission he had been on had prompted all that cooking? A celebratory feast . . . oh, it was a cheering thought.

I increased my pace and strode on down into the settlement.

The room where I slept was deserted, as was the long trough in the little yard behind it where we washed. I went outside, washing my face and hands as thoroughly as the very cold water allowed. The trough was in shade, and the water we pumped into it came in a channel straight from the flow emerging from the heart of the mountain. Then, summoning my courage, I plunged my head under the water and gave my hair a wash. I'd brought some of the special liquid that Hanan had supplied, back at the City of Pearl, and had been using it from time to time. My vanity informed me that the pleasure of seeing my own bright, coppery hair was worth the intense brow-ache that ensued from the icy water.

Back inside, dry and clean, I put on a fresh undergown and laced myself back into my outer garments. I braided my still-damp hair, covered it with one of the white caps I always wear and arranged my shawl over the top. Then I went out to join the community and share the keen anticipation of a fine feast.

Many people greeted me as I entered the long room where we ate our meals. They knew me, they accepted me, they were polite and friendly, but I felt they kept their distance: no doubt because they all knew why I was here and with whom I spent the vast majority of my time.

Communities need their healers, and value those among them who are prepared to walk into the shadows and learn from the spirits. But they do not necessarily want them as their closest friends.

Fires glowed in the pits and iron pots were suspended over

them, bubbling promisingly and giving off savoury aromas. On a board against the far wall, women were piling small loaves of bread into baskets. There were big jugs of ale, and a few smaller ones of wine.

I passed slowly through the assembly, exchanging a greeting with the young woman whose bed in the dormitory was beside mine, pausing to speak to a woman whose sickly child I'd treated, responding with a grin to the flirtatious remark of a very old man who, despite being almost blind, claimed he could detect a pretty woman by the way she moved. He was about the only villager who treated me like any other human being, his name was Basajaun – it meant, he had informed me, Old Man of the Woods – and I had grown very fond of him.

I had spotted Luliwa over in the far corner. Itzal stood beside her, his back to me. He had the high collar of his cloak turned up, and I could only see the top of his head and his white-streaked brown hair. Slowly, steadily, I worked my way over to them.

'Lassair,' Luliwa said as I reached their corner. 'You look tired, child.'

'I am,' I admitted. 'I spent longer than I had thought up in the cavern of the horses.'

Itzal turned. 'It is often the way,' he said. 'Time is different, in the painted darkness.'

Now he was facing me, a faint smile on his face.

And I was utterly confused.

For it *was* Itzal; it had to be, although wasn't he smaller than I remembered? Surely it was him, for the features were so similar, the hair worn long and centrally parted, the eyes the same gold-lit brown, bright and shining in the firelight.

Nobody could look so like Itzal and yet not be him.

Could they?

They could.

I knew, with that newly discovered inner eye that I was learning did not let me down, that this was not the man I knew. This man was indeed smaller: shorter, less broad in the shoulder, less . . . solid, was the word that sprang to mind. The facial features did not have the hard edge that Itzal's had.

And, as if as a reward for my insight and my willingness to believe the unbelievable, suddenly Itzal was there too, standing on Luliwa's other side, smiling – laughing – at my puzzlement.

'Well done,' Luliwa said quietly, her words only for the three of us who stood so close to her. 'You believed what your inner self was telling you, not what your eyes were seeing. The pair of them are very alike, aren't they?' Then, with a hand to the newcomer's back, she pushed the slender young man forward a pace or two and said, 'Lassair, this is my other child. This is Errita.'

I looked into the strange eyes, prepared to smile, to be friendly, to . . .

But the thought trailed away, for something – something coming out of this Errita? – stopped me dead.

It was as if his mind spoke directly to mine, and the words were no polite greeting. Even as his mouth formed and expressed that courtesy, his eyes said something else.

They were sending out a warning.

I knew, even in that first instant, that he was dangerous.

Very, very dangerous.

EIGHTEEN

The feast was an abundant celebration of everything the settlement had to offer. I realized quite soon that it wasn't in honour of Errita's return. He had indeed been absent for a long time – months rather than weeks, I gathered from the whispered comments – and he'd been far away. He had been expected earlier, but it seemed he had mistimed his departure. The last sailing of the autumn from wherever he'd been that would have brought him back to the north coast of Spain had gone without him. He had been forced to overwinter and wait until the voyaging times began again with the onset of spring.

You'd have thought his eventual return would be cause for relief and happiness. But I picked up quickly and quite strongly that nobody was very pleased to see him, and that he was tolerated in this company only because he was Luliwa's son, and belonged to the place. It was his home, the general attitude seemed to be, and everyone, no matter how unpopular they were, had a right to live in their own home.

I slipped away from Luliwa and her sons and found a place on a bench in the middle of the room. The women on either side of me smiled politely, saw that I was provided with some of every dish on offer, then largely left me alone. It was my old friend Basajaun, seated opposite, who informed me that the feast was in honour of a saint's day. He mentioned the saint's name but it meant nothing to me, so I guessed it was a local one. The date coincided happily with the true arrival of spring, so that was cause enough to be cheerful and, apart from the corner where Errita sat with Itzal and Luliwa, cheerfulness certainly reigned. Most of us, myself included, went to bed merry with ale and wine, and I made sure before I slept that I had a good supply of the willow-bark preparation that is good for headaches, especially those brought about by an over-indulgence in alcohol.

*   *   *

As the next morning progressed, my sense of foreboding grew until it felt like a dark cloud over me.

Luliwa did not send for me. She was, I heard someone mutter, shut away in her own little dwelling on the upper edge of the settlement, tucked away underneath the mountain's shoulder, and alone, they said, but for her sons. But then I remembered having seen Itzal slip away from the feast late last night, his travelling pack on his shoulder.

On a day when I could have done with the distraction of her company and the demands of a particularly tricky session of instruction, I was left alone.

In the end, I set out up the path into the mountain. I went to the ledge I'd sat on with Luliwa the morning after I had first arrived. I made myself comfortable and waited.

I knew I was waiting, and I was almost sure what I was waiting for.

They came from the mountain, as I knew they would. Itzal must have set off under the mountains last night on some pre-arranged mission, for now there he was, in the lead, half-turning on the steep path to help the old man making a careful descent behind him. The old man was being guided from the rear by a tall, dark-faced figure in dazzling white robes.

Itzal had seen me.

He left his charge to the man in white, then ran lightly down the path and came up to me. He said, 'I have brought a friend to see you.'

I already knew.

I elbowed Itzal out of the way and leapt up the path towards the little group. The man in white robes stepped back and the old man stood there alone, gently smiling.

I was hesitant to throw myself against him, much as I wanted to, for I might unbalance him and the path was high and perilous.

But he beckoned me, his smile widening.

I ran forward and felt Gurdyman's arms go around me.

'You haven't walked all the way from the City of Pearl?' I exclaimed. The first rush of joy had subsided and I had managed to untangle myself from him. Now we were back on the ledge where I'd just been sitting.

'Of course not, child. I rode in luxury in that little cart, and your friendly pony is now eating his fill in the stable on the south side of the mountain.'

'But you can't have come beneath the mountain!' I vividly remembered how hard the passage had been, how tight the tunnels, how perilous and exhausting the ascents and the sudden, terrifying descents.

Gurdyman, smiling, shook his head. Itzal said, 'There are other routes, Lassair. The one by which I brought you here is reserved for people like you.'

I stared at him. For people like me . . . who had to demonstrate that they could endure danger, fear, the claustrophobic terror of the darkness? I didn't really want to think about that.

'What are you doing here?' I demanded, turning back to Gurdyman. We were sitting side by side on my rocky shelf, Salim on his other side, Itzal standing before us, and I think Gurdyman was glad of the rest.

He looked at me, his bright blue eyes intent on mine. 'You have changed already, child,' he murmured. He looked sad fleetingly. 'The Lassair I knew is not there now.'

'She is! I am!' I cried. For some reason I wanted to weep.

He took my hand, trying to smile. 'It is what happens,' he said, but so softly that I wasn't sure I'd heard right. Then, brightening, he went on, 'You asked what I am doing here. I believe you can answer the question yourself.'

I went inside myself, as Luliwa had been teaching me, and, just as he had said, the answer was there.

'You're on your way home,' I said.

And he nodded.

I knew something else, then. But I wasn't ready to think about it.

Itzal was looking down the mountain. 'Come,' he said. 'We should move on.'

We made our careful descent. Itzal went ahead, Salim supported Gurdyman from behind, and now I walked beside him wherever the path allowed, my arm held out to him and his hand gripping it tightly.

He had just observed that I had changed, but I could have said exactly the same thing about him.

Gurdyman was old.

There was no escaping it; he had lost an element of himself, and old age had finally rushed in to take up the space.

Even as I walked beside him, chattering brightly about the little settlement in the valley and describing my life there, part of my mind was detached and occupied with much more sombre thoughts.

What had gone out of him?

Was it the heart trouble that had robbed him of his essential vitality? Had his long convalescence come at too high a price, draining him of strength he could not really afford to expend?

No, said the inner voice.

It was trying to tell me something more. But I closed my ears.

We climbed down the last few paces of the track that led out of the mountains and walked on into the settlement. I'm not sure what I was expecting to happen next; I think I actually had some idea that there would be another feast like last night's, with Gurdyman the guest of honour. It made no sense, though, and perhaps I was only basing it on the fact that Itzal had been respectful, solicitous with Gurdyman as they made the descent, making sure he came to no harm.

But, of course, he knew the perils of those narrow paths and naturally he would look after an old man trying to traverse them. As we came level with the long refectory there were no signs that people were industriously preparing a celebratory meal.

The refectory was deserted. Its door was fastened, its small windows were tightly shuttered. The narrow path through the village was also deserted, and even as the four of us walked slowly along, I heard shutters closing quietly over other windows, and mothers hissing to their children through almost-closed doors, ordering them to come inside.

The people of the settlement seemed to know what was

about to happen and they were making it clear they wanted no part of it.

I began to feel very uneasy.

Where were we going? My alarm had made my pulse beat faster and, reminded abruptly of Gurdyman's ailing heart, I drew closer to him, trying to look into his face without it being too obvious, trying to check for signs of anxiety, for the pallor, the blueness about the lips, that might indicate he was under a dangerous amount of distress. He knew what I was doing, though, and turned briefly to give me a swift smile. 'I am all right, child,' he said softly.

We walked on.

We passed most of the dwellings of the settlement. We passed the stables, the small inn where infrequent travellers coming up from the coast sometimes put up.

We drew level with the last of the houses. We passed it.

Then Itzal, in the lead, took the narrow little track that led up into the lower slopes of the spur of mountain that sheltered the village. Out of consideration for Gurdyman, he slowed his pace. Salim came up beside Gurdyman and took his arm. We climbed, sometimes up the steeply sloping path, sometimes up short flights of steps cut into the rock and the hard-packed earth, until we came to the low-roofed, single-room dwelling where Luliwa lived.

And I knew, then, what was going to happen.

I knew I was about to have the answer to all the questions.

I also knew it would not be pleasant; that I would be forced to face things I would far rather not have known.

We stood on the platform in front of the house. It faced west, and I thought irrelevantly that it must be nice to sit out there and watch the sunset. Itzal stood before the door. Quaintly – for surely his mother's house was his home too – he raised his hand and knocked.

The door opened. Luliwa stood before us, her face expressionless, her eyes unreadable. She glanced at us; briefly, with an almost imperceptible nod at Itzal; at Salim; at me, with the merest hint of a smile; at Gurdyman. She held his eyes for a long time. Neither of them spoke. Neither of them moved.

Then she stood aside and, with a slight bow and a courteous, graceful movement of her arm, said, 'Please, come in.' She indicated a bench set against the wall. 'Let the travellers be seated,' she went on, 'for you have journeyed far.'

Salim and Gurdyman sat down, Gurdyman with a sigh as he leaned back and let his tired body relax. Itzal had gone to take up a position in front of the closed door, and I went to stand beside him. Only then did I notice a stool in the far corner of the room, where a figure I took to be Errita was sitting, muffled in his cloak.

Now was the moment when most people welcoming travellers would offer comforts: hot water for hand-washing; a warming, restorative drink; something to eat.

No such comforts were offered. I had not expected they would be, for I knew why we were there.

After what seemed a very long time, Gurdyman broke the silence.

Looking directly at Luliwa, standing straight and elegant before him, he said, 'I did you a grave wrong.' Something moved in her face, quickly suppressed. 'I am sorry.'

She seemed to be struggling with herself. Trying to tune myself to her, I sensed distress, pain, deep resentment and savage anger. It was a great deal for her slim frame to encompass, but she stood there perfectly still, barely a quiver of emotion on her face. Her eyes, however, were brilliant.

After a moment she nodded. 'You took what was mine,' she replied. 'In the City of Pearl, when we were all young' – she shot a quick glance at Salim – 'and under the tuition of Nabil. And of Makram.' Her voice faltered as she said his name, but quickly she recovered. 'I was the one. My very name told them all that.' A flash of fury in her eyes. 'But you pushed me out of the way and you set your feet on the path that ought to have been mine.'

Now the anger was blazing silently out of her, and the golden lights in her eyes were like flames that shot towards Gurdyman as if they would consume him. He held her gaze, his face calm, his blue eyes empty of any emotion except perhaps sorrow.

'I know,' he said.

I thought he might have spoken in his own defence; said, perhaps, *I was young and ambitious, heady with the power I had discovered in myself, and I could no more have acted differently than have given up my life.*

With my new-found, fledgling ability to read people, I was almost sure that's what he was thinking.

But he held his peace.

And I realized that he was waiting for Luliwa.

She gave a deep sigh and, when she spoke, her tone had changed. 'But then I too did a deed I have regretted ever since' – her face worked with some deep emotion – 'and the result was far, far worse.'

Gurdyman nodded. 'Yes,' he said quietly. 'You set the fire in the building behind my parents' inn. It was your blue flames that started the blaze, and the fire was so hot that nobody could survive.'

'I did not mean them to die,' Luliwa whispered, the words barely audible. 'I was . . . not in full control. All I could think of was hurting you. Being revenged on you.' Her eyes blazed at him again. 'I do not regret that impulse, for what you did was unforgivable.' She paused, and I guessed she was fighting for control. 'But I do regret casting the flames when I was not in the right state of mind.'

I realized what she meant. What should have been hers had been purloined by Gurdyman, and in her hurt and her fury she had drawn on her own wild, undisciplined power and gone after him. She wanted only to hurt him, to be revenged upon him, to alarm him, to terrify him, perhaps even to say to him, *You think you are so great and mighty, but see what I can do!*

And she had set the fire in his parents' inn.

But he wasn't there.

She should have known, of course. She *could* have known, a woman like her with her abilities, but she had been too full of fury, too set on harming the young man who was her enemy, to stop and prepare properly.

'I should not have done it,' she whispered.

And, something I thought was compassion in his eyes, he nodded.

'Believe me, Gudiyyema,' Luliwa said on a half-sob, 'I have

regretted the suffering of those people every day since the moment I came back to myself and knew what I had done. I have done such penance for their deaths that you would not believe.'

'But it did not bring them back,' Gurdyman said softly.

'No, I know, and I am so very sorry,' she whispered. 'I was so angry, and I wanted you to know I was there, and see the power I had, and I started the fire to show you.'

'Yes, I knew it was you when they told me.' He paused. 'I wasn't even there, Luliwa.'

'I *know*!' The word came out as a sob.

There was a long, painful silence. Salim sat like stone, eyes straight in front of him, giving no sign of what he was thinking. Beside me, Itzal too was still, and only the soft sound of his calm, steady breathing indicated that he was flesh and blood and not a statue. I looked quickly at his brother, but Errita's face was still hidden in the shadow of his high collar.

Then, as if he felt that Luliwa's confession demanded more of him in return, Gurdyman spoke. 'I underestimated how deeply my actions would affect you,' he said. 'I thought, if I even bestirred myself to think of you at all, that someone with your skill, your talent, your gifts, your power, would succeed, even if the inheritance you believed to be your right went to someone else.'

'It *was* my right, and it did,' she said neutrally. Her calm words carried more force than if she had screamed them at him.

'Yes,' he said, so quietly that I barely heard. Then: 'And you never forgot, did you? You made a life for yourself, you matured into what you were destined to be, your powers grew as the years passed. But it was not enough, for all the time I was out there somewhere in the world, I who had taken what was yours, who had sat at the feet of the master and steadily absorbed everything that he so generously gave me.'

'It should have been me,' she whispered.

'And in the end, you had to act,' Gurdyman went on, his tone distant, his eyes fixed, unfocussed, on the plain stone wall opposite. 'I do not know how you discovered my whereabouts – perhaps you sent someone to enquire at my parents' village, for once upon a time, so many years ago, I sent word to them to tell them where I was, and people have long memories.' He glanced at her, a quick, hard flash of sharp blue eyes. 'Or perhaps someone like you has other methods at her disposal.' He sighed. 'But it is of no matter. You found out that I had returned to my native land and settled down in a city in the east of the country; that I lived in a house set in a maze of little alleyways that is full of secrets and the perfect dwelling for a *brujo* such as I.' He smiled briefly. 'Oh, yes,' he murmured, 'I well remember the word.'

For the first time, I saw Luliwa smile in return.

'You sent someone to my home.' Was it my imagination, or did he really glance briefly at Errita? 'To Cambridge, with instructions to make sure I had no choice but to come back.'

'Yes,' she said simply.

Now Gurdyman in his turn was angry. I sensed the cold fury rise in him and it was as if a sudden draught was swirling round my face and neck. But his anger was different from hers: never, whatever the provocation, would it escape his control and inflict terrible damage that he did not intend.

'Did somebody else have to die?' he asked her. There was outrage in his powerful voice. 'More than one person, for there were two victims of the fire in the lower areas of the City of Pearl, when your other child' – now he looked straight at Itzal – 'used your trademark blue flames to attract my attention and remind me why I had been brought back.'

Now Itzal stirred, and I sensed a sort of chill flowing off him. 'Like my mother before me, I did not mean there to be victims,' he said, but despite the appeasing words I sensed a cold nonchalance in his tone, as if he didn't really care one way or the other. The feeling of cold intensified and I perceived that there were unknown depths to Itzal that I hadn't begun to fathom. 'I had checked earlier,' he went on, 'and the building was derelict and deserted.'

Gurdyman looked at him. After a moment, Itzal's eyes slid away.

Silence fell once more. The small space enclosed by the stout stone walls of Luliwa's house was vivid with the pain of memories and the emotions evoked by them. It seemed to me that I could see them, like strands of harsh colour weaving a jagged pattern in the air. What harm these two people had done to one another, and to the innocent victims who suffered such terrible deaths because they were the unwitting witnesses to their personal war.

'Between us we have made a breach in the natural order,' Luliwa said, and her voice had changed again. Now she was the one who held control; she who would determine the outcome of this extraordinary, surreal encounter.

She had spoken to me of this breach before, I thought suddenly. She had spoken of a wrinkle; a fracture in the plan that was set out for us; *the way that ought to be*. She had gone on to say – I could hear her words now – that *sometimes people discover they have the power to interrupt this plan and they ignore the inner voice that tells them it is forbidden; that having the power is one thing but using it quite another.*

'This must be put right,' she went on. Her voice was waxing stronger, far more powerful now. 'You and I did wrong, Gudiyyema. We did the damage. We caused the breach.'

He nodded, dropping his head, and I knew he was accepting his share of the blame. 'And so it is up to us to repair it,' he murmured.

For a second time, she managed a very small smile.

He must have sensed it, for when he looked up into her face his expression too had softened. I knew then that, once, before they had become such bitter enemies, Luliwa and Gurdyman had been friends. Good friends; affectionate, perhaps even loving friends.

And love, I thought, never truly dies.

But Gurdyman was speaking. I made myself listen.

'You have already begun this process of repair, I see.' Slowly he turned his head until he was looking straight at me.

'I have,' Luliwa replied. 'She is altered, you find?'

'I do.' He sighed.

'She has the makings,' Luliwa said. 'She was already on the path when she came to me, for she has been well taught by others.' She gave Gurdyman a small nod in acknowledgement.

'Not only I,' he said.

'Above all,' Luliwa went on, 'she has her own innate ability.'

They were both looking at me now, and I felt the force of their two pairs of eyes as they stared into my mind. With an effort – quite a strenuous effort – I shut them out. I heard Gurdyman chuckle.

'Indeed she has,' he agreed. He glanced back at Luliwa. 'She learned how to do that very early on.'

It was strange to be standing there hearing myself talked about. Even stranger that, now I had stopped them probing into my head, I didn't seem to mind.

I thought about what they had just said . . .

'She must fulfil her destiny,' someone – Gurdyman, Luliwa, I didn't know – said.

They were focusing on me again; I felt it immediately. But it was different this time, for I understood straight away that they were not trying to read my thoughts, or determine what I knew, or in any way examine me. This felt quite different. It was novel, unfamiliar, and yet I had the strongest conviction that I knew what they were doing.

The two of them were subsuming themselves and their power into me.

Then I understood.

In a flash of insight, I saw the pattern, the natural order, and I saw the damage that between them they had done to it. I saw how Luliwa had set about repairing it; how she had sent out the agency that had roused Gurdyman and made him understand that he had no choice but to return to his own past and put right what had gone wrong. Both he and Luliwa must acknowledge the harm that they had done. They must both put aside their pride, their sense of self-righteousness, of being the innocent party. Then they must both begin to give. They must yield something of what made them themselves.

And it seemed, if I understood aright, they must somehow transfer it into me.

And that was how this breach of which they both spoke, this rupture in what should have been the right, the natural order, would be healed.

I took a very shaky breath.

It was quite a daunting prospect.

NINETEEN

The *Malice-striker* lay a short distance off the north coast of Spain, close to where a mountain river joined the sea.

At the meeting point of river and sea there was a small fishing port, used only by local people and limited in its facilities. There was no quay, for the fishermen went out in small boats that were easy to carry up onto the shore, above the high-water mark. Those on board the long, graceful, alien craft wishing to land would have to ferry themselves across using the ship's boat.

Jack stood on *Malice-striker*'s deck, staring at the river winding its way from the foothills and surging out into the sea. Thorfinn had assured him repeatedly that the small settlement just visible that crouched beneath a spur of the mountain was the slim young man's destination, and where they would finally end the long pursuit and confront him.

Thorfinn had also assured him that Lassair was there.

Jack had been determined to hold on to his doubts and his scepticism in the face of Thorfinn's certainty which, far from wavering, had instead grown stronger as they sailed south. Every time Jack had raised an objection – 'We cannot know he is on that ship!' 'How can we be so sure he's going to this one port in the whole vastness of the northern coast of Spain?' 'How can you possibly be convinced that this river you once explored is somehow linked to Lassair?' – Thorfinn would smile and say, 'What alternative do you suggest? If you have a sound plan, tell me and we will consider adopting it.'

But Jack had no plan, sound or otherwise. And as the days passed and events appeared to confirm that Thorfinn's wild assumptions might be valid, Jack's protestations grew fewer.

They had pinned all their hopes on the slim young man being aboard the *St James* as she left Concarneau to begin her long journey south. So when she put in at Bordeaux, *Malice-striker* simply waited behind a small island in the estuary until she set sail again for Bilbao and then the more westerly ports of the north coast of Spain. Jack lost his temper and raged at Thorfinn – and Hrype, who seemed mysteriously to have changed position so that now he supported the old man with few, if any, protests – that they must find a way to make absolutely sure they were pursuing the right ship. And Thorfinn simply said, 'We are. Even if we were not, it is of no matter, since we—'

'We know where he is going,' Jack finished for him, the words uttered in a cruel parody of the old man's speech.

They had kept the *St James* in view, which was not difficult since *Malice-striker* was a much faster craft. They mirrored her movements as she hopped from port to port, always hanging back from a direct challenge but never far away.

And, eventually, when she put in at Bilbao, Thorfinn stirred himself from a very long silence during which he had done nothing but sit huddled in his cloak staring out at the *St James*.

Extracting a long arm, he pointed to the *St James*. 'Watch,' he said to Hrype and Jack. 'Watch very carefully.'

Jack stood elbow to elbow with Hrype and both strained their eyes across the short stretch of sea between *Malice-striker* and the quay where the *St James* had tied up.

Cargo was unloaded and barrels set in neat stacks along the quayside. One or two passengers disembarked: a fat man, an elderly woman with a girl.

And then a slender figure walked swiftly down the gang-plank, jumping the last few feet as if he couldn't wait to be on dry land and hurrying off in the direction of a low line of structures – an inn, a stall selling hot pies, a couple of ware-houses – at the far end of the quay.

Jack turned to look at Hrype. 'Was that him?' He could barely bring himself to believe it.

Hrype smiled. 'Yes.' Then, his smile broadening, he added softly, 'Infuriating, isn't it, when logic and sense have to give way to following what the heart says?'

But Jack wasn't quite ready to admit the truth. 'If it really is him, what's he doing here? I thought Thorfinn said something about a river coming out of the mountains, and I can see nothing like that.'

Thorfinn had left his perch and come to join them. He had heard Jack's question. 'Wait,' he said calmly. 'I do not believe this is our young man's final destination.'

He pointed across the busy harbour to where a track ran along behind it, between it and the main settlement of the port. There was quite a lot of traffic on the track. 'It is the east–west route,' he went on. 'If I am right, our young man will turn east.'

It was barely a surprise when, some time later, the young man's slim, cloaked figure slipped away from the harbour buildings and set off along the track.

Going eastwards.

Soon afterwards, when *Malice-striker*'s crew had set to the oars to take her along the coast after him, Jack felt Thorfinn's eyes on him. Without turning round, he muttered, 'We still cannot be certain he is our man.'

And Thorfinn just chuckled.

Now, Jack sensed his two companions come to stand either side of him.

'This is the place that I remember,' Thorfinn said, not for the first time. 'I am more sure of it with each detail that I spot. We sailed up there' – he indicated the river estuary – 'and I made us go on into the darkness, for all that my crew were unwilling, fearing the echoes, the silence, the sense that some alien consciousness within was aware of us, inspecting us and perhaps not welcoming us.' He sighed. 'Of all the hundreds, thousands of places I have been to, it is this one that has always haunted me.'

'Perhaps now you know why,' Hrype said softly.

Thorfinn grunted his agreement. Nodding in satisfaction, he stumped off up the deck to where Einar and the crew were preparing to lower the ship's boat.

But Jack was not satisfied. 'Explain,' he said curtly to Hrype.

There was a silence as Hrype appeared to collect his thoughts. Then he said, 'I will try, Jack, but you will have to set aside your ruthless insistence on not accepting anything that you cannot verify with your own senses.'

'That is the only way to the truth!' Jack protested. 'It—'

'Do you want to hear the answer to your question?' Hrype demanded.

'Yes.'

'Very well. Listen, then.' Hrype paused. 'When Thorfinn was here before, this place made a deeper impression upon him than he realized, and it was only afterwards that he understood this. It – the place refused to be forgotten, if you like.'

'Rot,' Jack muttered.

Hrype chose to ignore that. 'Have you never experienced something akin to this, Jack? Can you truly say that some places do not stand out in memory?'

'Yes, of course they do, but it's usually for a good reason, and—'

He heard what he had just said.

'A good reason,' Hrype echoed. 'Precisely.'

'So you're asking me to believe that this underground river made Thorfinn remember it with particular vividness because one day he'd have to find his way back here?'

'Can you not even accept it may be possible?'

'No.'

'And yet,' Hrype breathed, the words barely audible, 'here we are.'

'It's just a series of gambles. Coincidences. Lucky guesses,' Jack said.

Hrype shrugged. 'Have it your own way. Look, they are lowering the boat. It's time to go.'

The boat was in the water, and Thorfinn took the oars. From *Malice-striker*'s deck, Einar and the crew looked down on them.

'Good luck,' Einar said. 'We will be here ready for your return.'

Thorfinn muttered a reply. Hrype, eyes on Einar, said, 'Remember what I said.'

Einar nodded. 'Yes. One extra passenger for the voyage home.'

Hrype was, Jack reflected, very confident that they'd find and apprehend the young man.

But then a very different interpretation of what Hrype had said occurred to him. It filled him with such a boil of emotions that he pushed it to the back of his mind.

It was not far to the shore, and soon the keel was grinding into the gravelly sand. Jack leapt out, splashing through the shallows and dragging the boat ashore, and quickly Hrype and Thorfinn did the same. They drew it well up above the waterline and Thorfinn secured a long rope to one of the posts set in the ground, to which a small group of fishing boats were also fastened.

Thorfinn stood looking into the mouth of the river, some fifty paces to the east. 'She knew that I was once there,' he murmured. 'She has the stone, and I had it then, and the memory lies within its dark heart.' Then, as if belatedly recalling Jack's presence, his expression became guarded. 'That is to say, I—'

'It's all right, he already knows,' Hrype said.

'He . . . he *knows*?'

Hrype leaned closer to him and muttered something, and Thorfinn's deep frown eased a little. He stared at Jack, a new expression in his eyes.

'You begin to understand, then,' he murmured.

But Jack had had his fill of enigmatic remarks and weighted silences. 'Come on,' he said roughly. 'We're far from done here.'

They set out along the track by the river, and presently the settlement came into view as they completed the rounding of a long bend around the foot of the mountain's lower slopes. Jack saw rows of small dwellings either side of the path, for the most part well maintained. There was a larger structure, long and low, from which cooking smells sneaked out. There were enclosures for chickens, here and there a few tethered goats in narrow strips of rough ground, some plots under cultivation where the vigorous springtime growth pushed bright green shoots above the earth.

Jack caught movement from the corner of his eye. Looking up, he saw a narrow path looping its way to and fro down a steep slope, at the top of which there was a shelf of flat ground where a solitary house stood. It was small, and it had a platform along the front with a bench and a couple of stools set beside a water barrel.

A slender figure was stepping lightly down the path, so familiar with its twists and turns that he didn't bother to look where his feet fell. Instead his eyes under the deep hood were fixed on the trio of strangers on the track below.

He reached the end of the path and jumped down onto the track. Jack, slightly in advance of Hrype and Thorfinn, strode to meet him.

'You have been following me.' The voice was husky. 'Over the sea, for so many miles, you have pursued me.'

Thorfinn stepped up to stand beside Jack. 'I have come to believe that, far from continuing to evade us, in the end you brought us here.'

The lower part of the young man's face – the only area clearly visible – seemed to crease in a smile. He was clean-shaven, Jack noticed, his skin clear and smooth. He was very young, Jack thought suddenly.

'No,' the young man was saying, 'I did not want you to come. But in the end, when you would not give up and it seemed you were joined to my trail as if it had been decreed that I should not escape you, I gave in to the inevitable.'

'You tried to kill us at Concarneau,' Jack said.

The young man shrugged. 'You made me angry.'

Jack tried to order his whirling thoughts. 'I am a Cambridge lawman,' he stated, aware even as he spoke of the irrelevance of the statement, 'and I believe you spent the winter in my town, and that you committed crimes including breaking into a house, damaging an attic room and, very possibly, the murder of a vagrant.'

Again, the young man shrugged. 'The vagrant was very near to death. It is true that I helped him out of his pain, but I was merciful. And, you see, I had to make sure that he remained where he sat.'

'Outside Gurdyman's house,' Hrype said softly, 'so that

there was no chance that the token he had in his hand would be missed.'

'Indeed,' the young man said, a note of satisfaction in his voice making it clearer, higher. 'The pearl, you see? Gurdyman' – he pronounced the name differently – 'would instantly comprehend the significance.'

'He did,' Hrype said grimly. 'Finding it made him very sick.'

'Good,' the young man muttered.

'Why did you wish him harm?' Jack demanded. 'Why did you have to make him set out on his journey?'

The young man spun round to stare at him. 'He was an irrelevance,' he proclaimed, the harsh, dismissive tone even more telling than the abrupt gesture of his slim hand. 'It wasn't the old man who had to be summoned, it was—'

'Errita.'

The one word, uttered quietly but clearly, affected the young man like a slap across the face. His shoulders slumped, his head drooped, he drew his hood forward and seemed to grow smaller. The woman who had spoken had advanced down the path from the solitary house so soft-footedly that none of those on the track below had noticed her, and now she glided forward until she stood beside the young man. She was slim and not tall, but she held herself well and had an air of authority – of power – about her. She was dressed in a robe, a veil arranged elegantly over her head and hair.

'Enough,' she said to him. Then, peering under the folds of the heavy hood, she added, 'Enough, too, of hiding; of assuming the identity of someone you are not.'

She pushed back the hood – the young man made an instinctive gesture of protest but then, as if he knew it was hopeless, his hand dropped – and for the first time the three men who had followed him so far and so long saw him clearly.

The face was a smooth oval under a broad forehead and the light-brown eyes had golden lights. The hair was brown, long and luxuriant, twisted into a braid over one shoulder. A band of silver ran through it at the temple.

And it was the face of a woman.

The robed woman moved closer to her, one hand lightly on

her arm. 'I am called Luliwa,' she said, bowing, 'and this is my daughter Errita.' She glanced in turn at Jack, at Hrype and, lingeringly, at Thorfinn. 'You cannot know it, but our names both have a meaning; they say the same thing in two different tongues, and both translate as *pearl*.'

Jack understood from her tone and her expression that this utterance was of some great significance, but what that might be evaded him. 'You used the pearl as your token,' he said hesitantly. 'It was how your – how your daughter alerted Gurdyman.'

'How she awoke his long-dormant conscience; yes, indeed,' the woman agreed.

'But why was that?' Jack persisted.

She stared at him, the expression in the golden eyes calm; even friendly. 'Because everything that has happened has its roots in the City of Pearl,' she said.

She must have seen his lack of comprehension.

'Come,' she said, holding out her hands towards all three of them. 'Food is being prepared in our communal eating house, and once we have broken bread together, there will be time for questions and explanations. Come!' she repeated, and, hesitantly at first and then eagerly, Jack, Hrype and Thorfinn obeyed.

Jack hadn't known what to expect as Luliwa led them up to the long building, and he dreaded that they would have to endure some endless feast with far too many people present and a hubbub of loud, insistent voices. But as she opened the door and ushered them inside, Errita bringing up the rear, he saw that only one table had been set ready. An old man was sitting at it, flanked by a young man who looked very like Errita and a tall, dark-skinned, older man in a white robe.

And Lassair.

Beside him Thorfinn gave a gasp, and before Jack could move, he had shoved Jack out of the way and was hurrying towards her. He took her in his arms and enveloped her in such a hug that she disappeared between his brawny arms and among the folds of his cloak. 'I *knew* you were here!' he exclaimed. She said something in reply, but Jack couldn't make it out.

Hrype had hastened over to Gurdyman, and was now crouched by his side, his face creased in a frown of concern. Jack could hear the urgent questions: 'You have been unwell – was it your heart again? What has been done to help you, to make you better?' The tall man in white went to stand behind the old man, and it was he who answered Hrype, describing some sort of remedy in painstaking detail.

The woman – Luliwa – had moved across to speak to the young man who, from his resemblance to Errita, must be her brother. Errita trailed after her.

Jack stood alone.

Villagers appeared from a small area off the main room, bearing bowls of savoury-smelling stew, baskets of bread, platters of goat's cheese and jugs of ale. Places were found for everyone and Jack found himself sitting at the end of the table, Gurdyman on his left. Lassair sat further down the table, separated from Jack by both Gurdyman and Thorfinn.

So far, Jack had only managed a very brief exchange of glances with her.

As the food and ale circulated and they were invited to help themselves, Gurdyman leaned closer to him and said, 'Now, Jack, which of your many questions do you wish to ask first?'

'Not a question, an accusation,' Jack replied. 'You took her into danger. A shadow from your past sought you out and summoned you, and you knew you couldn't manage the journey without her.'

'I did,' Gurdyman sighed. 'Moreover, I let her believe it was for her sake that we were going away; that I was doing her a favour by removing her from the scene of her recent – ah, her recent distress.'

'Yes, very well, we all have our own guilt to bear,' Jack muttered. 'My own does not expiate yours.'

'No, of course it doesn't,' Gurdyman said. 'And you are right: I did take her into danger, and the perils were far greater than I envisaged. But, Jack, I did not know. I did not understand, when I saw that pearl in the dead man's hand and knew I had been summoned, what it was really about.'

'Are you going to enlighten me?' Jack asked.

'As much as I am able – as far as I now understand it – yes.' The blue eyes met Jack's. 'I feel that I must, for it closely concerns Lassair, and I judge by your presence here that what concerns her is of rather more than small interest to you.'

Jack said neutrally, 'You'd better go on.'

Gurdyman paused to take a mouthful of bread dipped in stew, chewed and swallowed, took a draught of ale. Then he said, 'I did someone a grave wrong when I was a young man. Here in this country, in a beautiful city south of the mountains and the plateau beyond, I took from that woman' – he indicated Luliwa, sitting opposite a couple of places down the table – 'the role of apprentice to the wisest of masters of our craft, when both she and I knew full well it should have been hers. I did not waste the opportunity I stole – oh, by no means! – but it does not excuse what I did. She, in her pain, her despair, her anger, took revenge on me. She let her fast-waxing powers get away from her and she did something that took the lives of many innocent people. She thought I was of their company, but her fury was so great that she did not listen to the warning that told her I was not.' He sighed, his face full of sorrow. 'My parents were among the dead and so, when I learned what had happened, I understood that their deaths were the direct result of what I had done.'

He stopped speaking. His story, it seemed to Jack, had taken away his appetite. He did, however, raise his mug and drink another deep draught.

'When I saw that pearl in the beggar's hand, I knew that my past had caught up with me. I knew I must go back to the City of Pearl – for that was where I became what I am, and where I stole what should have been Luliwa's – and, at long last, face up to the wrongs that between us we had brought about.' He turned to Jack, and in his eyes Jack saw a new urgency. 'But even when Lassair and I reached the city, still I did not understand. And then I became sick, I began to perceive that a vital part of me was slipping away and, in the end, I was brought here. To her.' Again he looked at Luliwa and this time, sensing his glance, she turned her head and gave him a smile.

'She appears to have forgiven you,' Jack observed.

'She has. I have forgiven her, too, and we have made our

peace and been reconciled to the past.' He paused. 'And, now that this has been achieved – and please forgive me, Jack, if I do not try to explain how crucially important this reconciliation is – at last I know why Lassair had to come with me.'

A chill was creeping through Jack's chest, and he felt his heartbeat falter.

'Why?'

'Because, as I have just implied, the reconciliation *had* to happen.' Briefly he thumped on the table, emphasizing the word. 'And it has been achieved via her.'

'She has nothing to do with your past misdeeds!' Jack wanted to shout it aloud, but managed to keep his voice low. 'Why must she be involved?'

Gurdyman sighed. 'I said just now that when I was unwell in the City of Pearl, I was aware of a part of me slipping away. I have spoken to Luliwa, and she has experienced the same thing.' He paused, and an expression of great sadness crossed his round face. 'The price that is demanded of us, of Luliwa and me, is that our power – oh, not all of it, for that is impossible, but a significant amount – will gradually be taken from us. And transferred to Lassair.'

Jack could barely draw breath. Amid the onslaught of emotions that this dreadful statement aroused in him, one question burned. Leaning close to Gurdyman, he said, 'And just how does *she* feel about this?'

'She has no choice.' Gurdyman's voice was hard. 'You cannot understand, Jack, so do not try, but her path was rolled out before her feet long ago. This is merely the next step.'

From long ago, back when life was different, Jack thought he could hear Hrype's voice, saying much the same thing. The words echoed again: *There was more in her than a village healer, and I began to understand that a very particular path had been decreed for her.*

'She'll accept this?' he demanded. 'She'll go along with you and that old woman passing on to her the dubious gift of your *power*?' He could not prevent the scathing emphasis he laid on the word.

'She will, Jack,' Gurdyman said, and there was sympathy and kindness in his voice. 'She has.'

With deep dismay, Jack experienced the sudden fear that he knew what this must surely mean. But he might be wrong . . .

'Will you remain here?' he demanded, the urgency in his voice making Gurdyman look at him in alarm. Almost immediately, however, he nodded in understanding.

'Eventually, yes, for I have come to believe that this is where I shall end my days. For now, though, I will return to Cambridge, for there are matters that I must attend to and it will take some time to – er, to prepare my house for what will happen there next.'

But Jack had taken in nothing but *I will return to Cambridge*.

And the small flame of hope that he had done his best to ignore since the moment when he'd learned that *Malice-striker* would carry an extra passenger on the way home flickered and went out.

TWENTY

I wished with all my heart that I was sitting next to Jack, but I had been shown very firmly to a place at the long table between Thorfinn and Itzal, and Jack was several seats down.

I couldn't eat. I managed to drink, but the ale was strong and soon my head felt muzzy.

I reckoned it was good to feel muzzy, though, for it seemed to be lessening the pain.

What was he doing here?

He's come to find you, answered the voice in my head.

But he doesn't want me. He turned me away. He said, *When I get back I'd like you not to be here.* The words were engraved inside my head.

He's come to find you, repeated the voice patiently.

And he'd come with Hrype! Almost as extraordinary as Jack appearing in the big eating room of the settlement was the fact that he seemed to have travelled all this way in the company of Hrype.

Who had just greeted me, I couldn't help remembering, with the sort of warmth I hadn't felt from him since I left childhood behind.

What a day it was turning out to be.

Jack.

Whenever my determination to distract myself slipped a little, there he was, right in the forefront of my thoughts.

Beside me, Itzal seemed to pick up my unease.

'Are you all right?' he asked. 'Not too great a shock, to see your grandfather and your two friends from home suddenly appear before you?'

'A shock, yes, but a good one,' I said evenly. Itzal was not going to be allowed a glimpse of what I was really feeling.

He was quiet for a few moments. Then I felt him moving as he put a hand inside his robe. Extracting it, he held out a small package. 'For you,' he said.

'Why are you giving me a present?' I might not have asked so bluntly had I not been working so hard to hide my distress. Then I thought, what does it matter?

Itzal paused before answering. Then he said, 'I sense there is unease between you and me. I saw your face and read your thoughts when we spoke of the two young people who died in the fire in the City of Pearl.'

'You were indifferent to their suffering and their deaths,' I said.

'No.' He was shaking his head. 'Lives were lost, and I can never be indifferent to that. But, Lassair, their deaths were not intended, and I had done what I thought necessary to ensure the old buildings were empty.'

'It wasn't enough.'

'It wasn't, no.' Once again he hesitated. Then he said, 'You are at the start of a hard road, Lassair. One of the many things you will have to learn how to deal with is that occasionally lives are lost, not by intention but as a by-product of something that is so important that it cannot be avoided.'

'I'm not sure knowing that would have made those two young people's pain any easier or done anything to lessen their relatives' grief.'

He went on looking at me, sympathy in his golden eyes.

Then he said, 'Open your present.'

It was a hard object, round, quite heavy, slightly smaller than my palm. He had wrapped it in a piece of woven fabric, brightly coloured in shades of red and orange, and tied with a piece of twine. I unfastened the twine and the fabric fell away.

In my hands I held a thick piece of glass, broadening in the middle until it was the thickness of my little finger nail. It was highly polished, smooth, delightful to the touch and very beautiful in its simplicity.

'It's lovely!' I exclaimed. 'What is it?'

He was smiling. 'Hold it up and look at your other hand.'

I did so. Immediately the hand I was looking at changed. It leapt out at me, every freckle and crease visible, and twice, three times, the normal size. I gasped. 'How does it do that?'

'It is a magnifying lens,' Itzal said. 'They make them in the

City of Pearl. They make all sorts of lenses in fact, some of which they put into metal frames for old men and women to wear over their eyes when their sight begins to fade.'

I was playing with my new possession, holding it this way and that, entranced by its possibilities. I held it up to Itzal's face, and a huge golden eye gazed back at me.

And then I remembered the night out on the plateau, when I thought I was about to die.

And the enormous single eye that looked down upon me.

'It was you,' I whispered.

'It was,' he agreed. 'I am sorry that I frightened you.'

I wasn't going to admit just how terrified I had been. Instead I said lightly, 'One more reason, then, why you owe me a present.'

The exchange had served to loosen the tight knot inside me, and now I reached for bread and cheese and managed to eat a mouthful or two. After a while, Itzal said, 'Those men who came from your home to find you are quite interesting.'

Interesting. Yes, I had to agree with him. 'In what way?' I asked.

'The man with the silver eyes has great power,' he replied, 'but without a doubt you are already aware of that.' I didn't answer. 'You have known him long?'

'All my life. He's married to my aunt,' I added.

'Is he indeed?' That seemed to surprise Itzal. I wondered if marriage was rare among people like him and Hrype. 'Your grandfather, too, is a man of great power, and he carries a long, eventful and frequently perilous life in his memory.'

'Indeed?' I said.

Itzal smiled, clearly aware that I was blocking him. 'He was once the guardian of the object now in your keeping,' he added very quietly, his mouth close to my ear.

'I wasn't aware you knew of it.'

'Of course I do,' he said with a short laugh. 'You surely could not have hoped to hide its existence from us?'

'Does everyone know?' I hissed, anxious suddenly.

'Oh, no! I apologize, Lassair, I did not mean to worry you. You have done very well, and despite my best efforts I have not caught so much as a glimpse of it. But its power cannot be concealed from people like us.' He nodded across the table to where Luliwa and Errita sat side by side. After a moment he said quietly, 'Perhaps, in time, when you come to know us better and to trust us, you will feel able to show us what it is you carry.'

And then I knew for certain what I had tried so hard to deny: that my immediate future lay with them, with Itzal, Luliwa, Errita; possibly also with the men and women down in the south in the City of Pearl, so generous with their time, so determined to pass on their knowledge to those who became their pupils.

I had tried to tell myself I was going home.

I wasn't.

Itzal seemed to have picked up that there was an emotional storm raging within me. He gave me enough time to bring it under control, and then he said, 'We have spoken of the man who is married to your aunt, and of your grandfather. But as yet we have not mentioned the big one with the strength of an ox, the anger that tends to burst out of him and the stance of a fighting man.'

'That's Jack,' I said quietly. 'He came here because—' I stopped, for in truth, despite my inner voice I still wasn't certain.

'You know why he is here,' Itzal said.

'*He's* not a man of power like Hrype and my grandfather,' I said sharply, 'so don't go saying he—'

But Itzal said softly, 'Oh yes, he is.'

'He can't be!' I breathed.

'You are blinded, perhaps by – er, by other emotions that you feel for him,' Itzal said. 'When you look with clear eyes, you will see it for yourself.' He leaned closer. 'You and your big fighting man, Lassair, are not quite as different as you have been assuming.'

And then, undoubtedly aware that he had already said quite enough to set my mind whirling, he reached out for the ale jug and topped up our mugs.

But I did not drink more than a few sips from my refilled mug. I forced down some more food, drank some water and fought the soft-edged, pleasant effects of the alcohol I had consumed so far. I needed to be fully in myself and in control of my emotions, for I had the clear impression that others in the room knew far, far more about what was happening, and what was about to happen, than I did.

Both Thorfinn and Itzal were talking to their neighbours on the opposite side from me, Thorfinn to Gurdyman and Itzal to his mother. I summoned my strength, focused my concentration and went inside myself.

Itzal had known Gurdyman and Salim were on their way here, for he had set out late at night to go along the passage beneath the mountains and escort them for the last and most difficult stretches. Well, there was no mystery about that, for Itzal went regularly to the City of Pearl and had presumably agreed the day of Gurdyman's and Salim's arrival when he was there on his last visit. Salim had undoubtedly travelled with his old friend to take care of him – for my beloved Gurdyman's health had clearly deteriorated in the weeks since I had seen him – and Gurdyman had come to the settlement because . . .

Because he's going home, the voice said in my head.

Yes.

The long tale of his life was at last starting to wind to a close, and there would be many matters for him to attend to back in Cambridge.

I did not allow myself to think any further than that. Already the tears were pricking at my eyes, and this was not the time to grieve. I glanced at him. He was laughing, enjoying the meal, engaging with Jack beside him and Salim sitting opposite, blooming in the company, and clearly he wasn't going to die soon; he had a good few years yet.

I sharpened my concentration and turned my thoughts to Thorfinn. He had sailed from my homeland, bringing Hrype and Jack with him, and they had turned up here just as Gurdyman had arrived requiring passage back to England. The conclusion that the two events were connected just couldn't be gainsaid.

'Of course they are,' my grandfather said softly, right in my ear. 'I cannot explain the timing, but as for our arriving precisely here, in just the right spot, we were following him.' He jerked his head in Errita's direction, 'Or, as we now know, her.'

'But she arrived on foot,' I said. I had seen her, making her way up from the little fishing port, Luliwa going to meet her.

'Yes,' Thorfinn said. 'We had been on her trail all the way, however, and by the time she left the ship at Bilbao, I was no longer in any doubt as to where she was going, because—'

'Because you've been here before,' I finished for him.

I turned to look at him, and his bright, light eyes held mine for a long moment. 'You make good use of the shining stone,' he murmured.

'Yes.'

'You—' He stopped. Then said, 'Do not let it—' Once again, he didn't go on. There was a longer pause, and when he broke it, he said, 'You are not like me, Lassair. I think you will be safe.'

And then he turned to answer some question from Salim, seated on the opposite side of the table, and I knew our moment of intimacy was over.

I returned to my thoughts.

And, presently, I understood what would happen next.

Thorfinn had been gradually becoming more restless, looking out through the wide-open doors at the angle of the sun, once going to stand outside, head tilted as he sensed the wind. When, presently, he got up from the table again and quietly said it was time to go, it was no great surprise.

I stood back, letting everyone else go about the business of giving thanks for the food and drink, for the kindly welcome, and for the first of the farewells. I watched Salim and Gurdyman embrace and I heard Salim mutter, 'I shall see you again, old friend.' And Gurdyman nodded.

Luliwa, Itzal and I walked with them down the path to the fishing port, Luliwa deep in conversation with Gurdyman, Itzal silently beside me just behind them. Jack and Thorfinn had gone on ahead, and as we rounded the great out-flung shoulder of mountain and could suddenly see the sea, there was *Malice-striker*, close in to shore, and I thought I could make out Einar in her stern, looking out for us.

When we were almost at the beach, Luliwa suddenly stopped, took Gurdyman in her arms and gave him a long, close embrace. Then she broke away and came striding, almost running, back towards Itzal and me. She did not stop; did not even acknowledge us. There were tears on her face.

'Let her go,' Itzal said softly; I must have made some small movement to follow her.

He and I stood together, watching her as she went on back up the path. Then, with a sigh, he said, 'I must go. She is not in the mood to deal with my sister just now.' His golden eyes stared into mine. 'Take your time, Lassair. I will see you later.'

I nodded. I stood there for a few moments more, thinking about Errita and trying not to let dismay overwhelm me; amid the tangle of emotions I was experiencing, worrying about how I was going to cope with her in the weeks and months ahead was occupying me to far too great an extent. *You will find a way*, the quiet voice in my head said.

Presently, as Itzal strode out of sight around the shoulder of the mountain, I turned and went on down to the shore.

Thorfinn and Hrype were dragging a small boat down the beach and onto the water. *Malice-striker*'s boat, of course; as I studied it more closely, I recognized it as the craft that had served as my grandfather's accommodation whenever he was at Aelf Fen.

My mind was flooded with images of home. Of the fens, where I had been born and bred; of my family; of my father. Once again, the tears began to prickle and this time I let them come, for in that moment I wished with all my heart I would be going with them when *Malice-striker*'s sail filled with the strong south-westerly breeze and her elegant shape rode away on the evening tide. I had travelled on her before, I knew her power and the joy of her.

But it was not to be.

As I stepped down onto the beach, Thorfinn caught sight of me, said something to Hrype and both of them walked up the gravelly sand towards me. Jack took Thorfinn's place beside the boat, holding it steady as it was washed gently to and fro in the shallows.

Thorfinn stood back so that it was Hrype who reached me first.

'Have you any word to send to your kin?' he asked. He was smiling at me, an expression of kindness and perhaps even love softening the hard lines of his handsome face. My new-found insight informed me that whatever strife there had been between us had gone, never to return.

Impulsively I stepped closer and embraced him. 'Give them my love,' I said. 'I'm not sure they will understand that I have to stay away.'

His smile widened. 'I won't tell them how long it'll be,' he said. 'That will not be difficult, since I do not know and neither do you.'

'No,' I agreed.

He said gently, 'But you are wrong when you suggest they won't understand. Your father knows you better than you think, and your mother, for all that you puzzle and sometimes frustrate her, understands that it is your right to follow your own path, and she will not complain.'

I waited until I could be sure of speaking without the emotion showing, then said, 'Make them know, if you can, that I *will* come home. In the end.'

'You have my word,' he replied. 'Good luck, Lassair.' Then he bent to kiss my cheek, turned and walked away.

Thorfinn now approached, wordlessly wrapping me in his habitual enfolding hug. After a moment he said, 'I shall miss you, my granddaughter. Life in the fens will be less interesting without your bright presence.'

I stood with my arms round him, trying not to weep. He is old, I was thinking, and I am going to be away for a long time. What if he dies before I return?

He released me and, holding me at arm's length, looked into my eyes. 'I know what you are thinking,' he said. I guessed it must be fairly obvious. 'I cannot say.' He grinned briefly. 'I shall do my best to stay alive. That's all I can do.'

I nodded. It was in the hands of the gods, as he might have

added, and all we could do was pray that they looked upon us favourably.

'Safe journey,' I whispered.

He grinned again. 'It will be. You forget who *Malice-striker*'s master is.'

Then he too kissed me and went to join Hrype by the water's edge.

And Jack walked towards me.

He came to within a pace of me and then stopped.

I stared at him, at last able to see him at close quarters. He looked well. His face and bare forearms were deeply tanned, his muscles firm and smooth. He had regained the weight he had lost after his near-fatal injury and once more looked like the fit, strong man I had first met on the quayside in Cambridge a year ago.

Except that his expression was unsmiling, there were hollows under his cheekbones and shadows beneath his eyes.

'You're not coming with us.' He hadn't needed to ask for he already knew.

I shook my head. 'I can't.' I lifted my chin, trying to sound calm and firmly in control. 'I have to stay here. It's where I am meant to be, and this is the place to which the long road I've been unknowingly following for so long – and others before me – has brought me. People have died, and I think that the reason they did was to bring me to – to the person who's going to show me the way.'

'The way.'

I didn't know how to explain. 'Jack, I've been put on a path. It began a long time ago, in my childhood, when I discovered I could find lost objects, and later when I realized I could see the hidden ways across the fens and the marshlands that were invisible to others.' I paused, looking away, for his hard expression was all but unbearable. 'Then I went to live with my aunt Edild, and she began to teach me the ways of the healer. Then I became Gurdyman's pupil, and—'

'Yes. I know what you were learning with him.'

He did. I'd forgotten, but now the memory came rushing back. We – Jack and I – had narrowly escaped a meeting with a killer, and I'd so wanted to give him some hint about the deep matters beyond the veil that I was just beginning to learn about. I'd told him that Gurdyman was passing on to me the learning he had acquired in his youth in Moorish Spain, and Jack said quietly, 'But that's not all he's teaching you.' Then, when I'd said, 'You know, don't you?' he'd replied, 'Of course I know.' And he'd added softly, 'You cannot know how I envy you, being his adept.'

'Well, then,' I said lamely. 'This is the next part of the instruction. Here there are such mysteries hidden away, and it's as if the veil is thinner and I sometimes get just a glimpse of what it is she's – of what it is I must discover. And then it seems to me that I know it already, and all I have to do is find a way to uncover it. Oh, it's not easy to explain!'

'Of course it isn't.' His voice was harsh. 'And how in God's name is someone like me meant to understand?'

'But you—' I began.

His angry words drowned my protestation. 'All these weeks since you left I've spent with people who seem to be aware of what is going on without even the semblance of a rational explanation! Can you imagine how *sick* of it all I am? How everything in me yearns for a few simple, straightforward words that I can understand?'

'You *could* understand,' I said quietly. 'You can.'

But I didn't think he was listening. His anger beginning to fade, he added, 'I tell you, Lassair, spending all this time with men like Hrype and your grandfather is going to make it hard to be with my own kind again.'

But he is like them, said the voice in my head.

I know, I replied. *But I don't think it's the time to tell him.*

He was silent now, standing tense before me looking away along the shoreline. I thought about what he had just said; about how he was aware of the true nature of my studies. Not that it was going to make this moment any easier.

But I had to try.

'Jack.' I spoke quietly, but instantly he turned back to face me.

'What?'

'It began with Gurdyman; with something he did. There was . . . a body of knowledge that became his, but that should have gone to somebody else. To Luliwa.' I spoke hurriedly, trying to find the right words, all too aware that I was making a poor job of making him understand. 'It became her life's work to wrest it back, and in a way she did, only I believe she went even further and delved deeper. But for a while she was outside her own control, and people died because of it. It wasn't intentional' – I couldn't have him believing Luliwa was a killer, although I suppose that's exactly what she was, as were her son and her daughter – 'the deaths happened because of a – a misunderstanding.'

'A misunderstanding,' he repeated tonelessly.

'She was mad with fury and grief! She—'

But, cool and quiet, I heard the firm voice inside my head: *No.*

I met Jack's eyes.

'There are things she needs to learn from me,' I said instead, 'things that I have absorbed from Gurdyman, but in return, there is very, very much more that she will impart to me.' I had a sudden vision of the deep cave, of the light on the figures, of the power that thrummed in the air when the chanting began. And, despite everything – despite Gurdyman, his heart beginning to fail and heading home for the last time; despite my grandfather's strong presence and the deep sadness of knowing I had just said goodbye to him; above all, despite Jack whom I loved standing right in front of me – despite it all, I felt a stab of joy so pure and bright that it made me want to sing.

This is where you must be, I heard my inner voice say. *This is where the path of your life has brought you.*

The voice, as always, was right.

And all at once I knew without having to be told that being taught by Luliwa was only a part of it, for I had been drawn to the City of Pearl and I had only just begun to absorb all that its generous people were willing to share with me when I had been dragged – summoned – away.

But also there was Jack.

I looked straight into his eyes. I understood exactly what he was feeling, for I felt it too.

'You sent me away,' I reminded him softly.

His mouth twisted in a grimace. 'I know.'

'You went out, and you said, "When I get back, I'd like you not to be here."'

'I *know*,' he said again.

'And here you are,' I said softly, 'and you have come all this way because—'

Because you feared I was in peril, I nearly said. But was that right? Was I assuming a sentiment he did not really have?

'I came to save you,' he said roughly. 'I sensed that – that *thing* that came to Cambridge. Oh, yes, I've seen it – him – *her*, now, and I can see that she is flesh and blood. Or I think she is,' he added in a mutter. 'I felt the malign power that had been in Gurdyman's house, that tore and broke and destroyed the place where you sleep' – my little attic room! Oh, no – 'and all I could think of was that it meant you harm, and that I had to find you to protect you.'

To protect me.

I wished so very much that he was going to be there with me when the true battle with the malign spirit that was within Errita truly began.

But he would be far away, and I would face it – her – alone.

I reached out and took his big, strong, warm hand.

It was a mistake, for the touch of him nearly undid all my resolution. We stood like that for some moments, then slowly he leaned forward, bending down so that our foreheads touched. It was probably my imagination, but I thought I felt a flow of profound love between us.

Perhaps he did, too, for when he straightened up again he no longer looked so devastated; in fact, I thought he might just have been smiling.

'I will come back,' I whispered. 'Eventually.' I held his hand up to my lips and gently kissed it. 'I promise.'

He stared into my eyes for a long moment. Then he nodded, let go of my hand and turned. I watched as he strode swiftly away down the shore; as he vaulted into the ship's boat; as he went to sit beside Thorfinn and take up the second oar. Then, far too soon, they were alongside *Malice-striker*, and Einar and his crew were reaching down to help them aboard and to stow the boat.

The sail started to climb the mast.

As the wind began to fill it, the outgoing tide found and picked up the beautiful ship. Slowly at first and then with swiftly accelerating speed, the wind and the water began to take her away. I stood and watched, for I could not have moved, and aboard *Malice-striker*, a lone figure in her stern looked back at me. He was quite still. But then, finally, he raised his hand in farewell.

My tears were blinding me by then and mercifully his face and the subtleties of his expression were lost to me.

I waited until *Malice-striker* was a dot on the navy sea, her sail filled and bulging with the wind that would speed her home.

Then I turned my face to the foothills rising up behind the cove, to the great spur that curved out from the mountain range to guard and protect the little settlement, to the peaks soaring up high beyond them. It was a long, hard path back to Luliwa, to the painted darkness, to all that she had to impart to me; then, some unguessable time later, to the City of Pearl that lay beyond the mountains, waiting patiently until I should return.

I stood there for some time, finding my strength, shoring up my resolution.

This was where I had to be; everything that had happened to me so far in my life had been leading me here. I did not need my inner voice to confirm it.

I looked up the winding track that rose gently towards the settlement. Luliwa would be there, and Itzal; the thought gave me comfort. I would call in to say that our visitors had gone, and then I would go on to the lodging house and seek out my friends there.

This was my life now. It was up to me to embrace it.

I took a step towards the path, then another, and all at once I was striding swiftly, eagerly.

For I couldn't wait to start.